THERE COMES A MIDNIGHT HOUR

STORIES BY GARY A. BRAUNBECK

RAW DOG
SCREAMING
PRESS

There Comes a Midnight Hour © 2021
by Gary A. Braunbeck

Published by Raw Dog Screaming Press
Bowie, MD

First Edition

Cover Image: Lynne Hansen
www.LynneHansenArt.com

Book Design: Jennifer Barnes

Printed in the United States of America

ISBN: 978-1-947879-24-9

Library of Congress Control Number:
2020948716

RawDogScreaming.com

Previously Published

"We Now Pause For Station Identification" originally published as a chapbook
    by Endeavor Press
"Paper Cuts" originally appeared in *Seize The Night*
"Consumers" originally appeared in *Borderlands 6*
"The Music of Bleak Entrainment" originally appeared in *Weirdbook*
"Onlookers" originally appeared in *Midnight Premiere*
"Brother Hollis Gives His Final Sermon…" originally appeared in
    Appalachian Undead
"Tales the Ashes Tell" originally appeared in *Library of The Dead*
"Old Schick" originally appeared in *Lords of the Razor*
"AND STILL YOU WONDER WHY OUR FIRST IMPULSE …"
    originally appeared in *Monster's Corner*
"One Night Only" originally published as a chapbook for MONROVILLE
    ZOMBIE FEST
"Shoe Fly Pie and Apple Pan Dowdy" originally appeared in *Shadows Over
    Main Street, Vol. 2*
"Smiling Faces Sometimes" originally published as a chapbook by White
    Noise Press
"Glorietta" originally appeared in *The World is Dead*
"Down in Darkest Dixie Where the Dead Don't Dance" originally appeared
    in *Mardi Gras Madness*

"Light on Broken Glass" appears here for the first time

Acknowledgements

I'd like to thank Jennifer Barnes and John Edward Lawson for taking a chance with this collection; I also want to thank Janet Harriett, Laird Barron, Lisa Morton, Christopher Golden, Michael Bailey, all of my Patreon sponsors, Jerry Gordon, Brian Shoopman, The Horror Writers Association, and Lucy (always) Snyder: in various ways, all of you have kept me from visiting the garage again.

In Memory of Ed Gorman, Harlan Ellison, and William Goldman

"Do you not know that there comes a midnight hour when every one has to throw off his mask? Do you believe that life will always let itself be mocked? Do you think you can slip away a little before midnight in order to avoid this?"

— Søren Kierkegaard

Contents

We Now Pause For Station Identification

"…three-fourteen a.m. here at WGAB—we gab, folks, that's why it's called *talk* radio. So if there's anyone listening at this god-awful hour, tonight's topic is the same one as this morning, this afternoon, and earlier this evening… in fact, it's the same topic the whole world's had for the last thirteen days, if anyone's been counting: Our Loved Ones; Why Have They Come Back From The Dead and What The Fuck Do They Want?

"Interesting to say 'fuck' on the air without having to worry that the station manager, the FCC, and however many hundreds of outraged local citizens are going to come banging on the door, torches in hand, screaming for my balls on a platter. And to tell you the truth, after being holed-up in this booth for five straight days, it feels good, so for your listening enjoyment, I'm going to say it again. Fuck! And while we're at it, here's an earful of golden oldies for you—shit, piss, fuck, cunt, cocksuscker, motherfucker, and tits. Thank you George Carlin…assuming you're still alive out there… assuming anyone's still alive out there.

"Look at that, the seven biggies and not one light on the phone is blinking. So much for my loyal listeners. Jesus, c'mon people, there's got to be somebody left out there—a goddamn *plane* flew over here not an hour ago! I know the things don't fly themselves—okay, okay, there's that whole 'automatic pilot' feature but the thing is, you've got to have a pilot to get the thing in the air, so I know there's at least one airplane pilot still alive out there and if there's an airplane pilot then maybe there's somebody else who's stuck here on the ground like I am! This is the cellular age, people! Somebody out there has got to have a fucking *cell phone*!

"…sorry, about that, folks. Lost my head a little for a moment. Look, if you're local, and if you can get to a phone, then please call the station so that I know I'm reaching somebody. I haven't left this booth in five days and that plane earlier…well, it shook me up. You would have laughed if you'd been in here to see me. I jumped up and ran to the window and stood there pounding on the glass, screaming at the top of my lungs like there was a chance they'd hear me thirty thousand feet above. Now I know how Gilligan and the Skipper and everyone else felt every time they saw a plane that didn't…Jesus. Listen to me. It's TV Trivia night here at your radio station at the end of the world.

"The thing that shocked me about all of this was that…it wasn't a thing like we've come to expect from all those horror movies. I mean, yeah, sure, the guy who did all the makeup for those George Romero films—what was his name? Savini, right? Yeah, Tom Savini—anyway, you have to give a tip of the old hat to him, because he sure as hell nailed the way they *look*. It's just all the rest of it…they don't want to eat us, they don't want to eat *anything*. All-right-y, then: show of hands—how many of you thought the first time you saw them that they were going to stagger over and chew a chunk out of your shoulder? Mine's raised, anybody else? That's what I thought.

"Oh, hell…you know, in a way, it would be easier to take if they *did* want to eat us—or rip us apart, or…*something*! At least then we'd have some kind of…I don't know…*reason* for it, I guess. Something tangible to be afraid of, an explanation for their behavior…and did you notice how quickly all the smarmy experts and talking heads on television gave up trying to offer rational explanations for how it is they're able to reanimate? Have you ever…when one's been close enough…have you ever looked at their fingers? Most of them are shredded down to the bone. People forget that it's not just the coffin down there in the ground—there's a concrete vault that the coffin goes *in to*, as well. So once they manage to claw their way through the lid of the coffin, they have to get through four inches or so of concrete. At least, that's what all you good folks who've buried your loved ones have paid for.

"Think about it, folks. I don't give a Hammer-horror-film *shit* how strong the walking dead are supposed to be, *no way* could they break through concrete like that, not with the levels of decomposition I've seen on some of the bodies. So, then, how do you explain so many disturbed and empty graves in all those cemeteries all around the world? Easy—*you've been getting screwed*. Those vaults that you see setting off to the side during the grave-side service? Have any of you ever stuck around to watch the rest of it be lowered over the concrete base? Shit—it wouldn't cost anything to pour a base underneath the coffin. A lot of us have been getting scammed, people, and I think it's high time we got together and did something about it! Funeral homes and cemeteries have been charging all of us for a *single* concrete vault that never actually gets put in the ground!

"Anybody out there got a *better* explanation for how a moldy, rotting, worm-filled bag of bones can dig its way out of a grave so quickly? If you do, you know the number, give me a call and let's talk about it, let's raise hell, organize a march on all funeral homes and cemetery offices...

"But the ones who came out of the graveyards, they're only a part of it, aren't they? Remember the news footage of that Greenpeace boat that went after what they *thought* was a wounded whale, only once they got close enough to see that it was dead and had just come back to life, it was too late? One of them had already touched it by then. Christ, how many kids did we lose when they went outside to see that Fluffy or Sprat or Fido or Rover was back from doggy heaven? I smashed a silverfish under my shoe a few days ago, and what was left of it started crawling again. I've got towels rolled up and stuffed under the doors in case there're any ants or cockroaches your friendly neighborhood Orkin man might have missed the last time he was here.

"Were television stations still broadcasting when Sarah Grant came home? Wait a second...some of them had to've been or else I wouldn't remember seeing it. Okay, right. Anyway, locals will remember Sarah. She was a four-year-old girl who disappeared about five years ago, during the Land of Legend Festival. Ten thousand people and nobody saw a thing. The search for her went on for I-don't-know how long before they just had to give up. Well, about two weeks ago, the night all of this first began, what was left of Sarah Grant dug its way out of the grave in its pre-school teacher's back yard and walked home. She tried to tell them what had happened but her vocal cords were long gone...so when the police showed up and saw her, they just followed her back to her teacher's house where she showed them the grave. The police found the teacher hanging from a tree in the back yard; he'd evidently witnessed Sarah waking up from her dirt nap and knew what was coming.

"By then the police had seen more than a few dead bodies get up and start walking around, so little Sarah didn't come as much of a surprise to them. A lot of missing children started showing up at their old homes. Sometimes their families were still living there, sometimes they'd moved away and the kids didn't recognize the person who answered the door—this is when people still *did* answer their doors, in the beginning, when we thought it wasn't something that would happen here, no—it was just going on in China, or what used to be Russia, or Ireland, or…wherever. Everywhere but here. Not here, not in the good ole US of A. Downright un-American to think that. Christ, there were idiots who stood up in front of Congress and declared that all of this was just propaganda from Iraq, or Hong Kong, or Korea. Can you believe that? And *of course* it was all a plot against America, because the whole world revolves around us. *Fuck* that noise. Nations as we knew them don't exist anymore, folks—and this is assuming that the entire concept of 'nations' was *ever* real and not just some incredible, well-orchestrated illusions dreamed up by the shadows who've *really* been running the show all along. It doesn't matter. It's all just real-estate now, up for grabs at rock-bottom prices.

"Remember how happy a lot of us were at first? All that news footage of people in tears running up to embrace their loved ones fresh from their graves? Mangled bodies pulling themselves from automobile accidents or industrial explosions or recently bombed buildings… all those terrified relatives standing around crash-, accident-, or other disaster sites, hoping to find their husbands or wives or kids or friends still alive? Reunions were going on left and right. It would have moved you to tears if it hadn't been for a lot of them missing limbs or heads or dragging their guts behind them like a bride's wedding-dress train. That didn't matter to the grieving; all they saw was their loved ones returned to them. They had been spared. They had been saved from a long dark night of the soul or whatever. They didn't have to give in to that black weight in their hearts, they didn't have to cry themselves to sleep that night, they didn't have to get up the next morning knowing that someone who was important to them, someone they loved and cared about and depended on, wasn't going to be there anymore, ever again. No. They were spared that.

"It didn't take long before we figured out that the dead were drawn back to the places or people they loved most, that meant everything to them while they were alive—at least Romero got *that* much right in his movies. At first I thought it was just a sad-ass way of reconciling everything, of forcing it into a familiar framework so we could deal with the reality of these fucking *upright corpses* shambling back into our lives—hell, maybe it was just a…I don't know…a knee-jerk reaction on the dead's part, like a sleepwalker. Maybe their bodies were just repeating something they'd done so many times over the course of their lives that it became automatic, something instinctual. I mean, how many times have you been walking home from someplace and haven't even been thinking about *how* to get from there to here? Your body knows the way so your brain doesn't even piss away any cells on that one. Home is important. The people there are important. The body knows this, even if you forget.

"But then the Coldness started. I…huh…I remember the initial reports when people started showing up in emergency rooms. At first everyone thought it was some kind of new flesh-eating virus, but that idea bit it in a hurry, because all of a sudden you had otherwise perfectly healthy, alive human beings walking into emergency rooms with completely dead limbs— some of them already starting to decompose. And in every single case, remember, it started in whichever hand they'd first touched their dead loved one with. The hand went numb, then turned cold, and the coldness then spread up through the arm and into the shoulder. The limbs were completely dead. The only thing the doctors could do was amputate the things. If the person in question had *kissed* their loved one when they first saw them… God Almighty…the Coldness spread down their tongues and into their throats. But mostly it was hands and arms, and for a while it looked like the amputations were doing the trick.

"Then the doctors and nurses who'd performed the surgeries started losing the feeling in their hands and arms and shoulders. Whatever it was, the Coldness was contagious. So they closed down the emergency rooms and locked up the hospitals and posted the National Guard at the entrances because doctors were refusing to treat anyone who'd touched one of the dead…those doctors who still had arms and hands, that is.

"The one thing I have to give us credit for as a species is that the looting wasn't nearly as bad as I thought it would be. Seems it didn't take very long for us to realize that material possessions and money didn't mean a whole helluva lot anymore. That surprised me. I didn't think we had any grace-notes left. Bravo for our side, huh?

"Look, I've got to…I've got to try and make it to the bathroom. I can at least cut through the production booth, but once out in the hall, I'm wide open for about five yards. The thing is, I've been in this booth for five days now, and while the food's almost held out—thank God for vending machines and baseball bats—I've been too scared to leave, so I've been using my waste basket for a toilet and...well, folks, it's getting pretty ripe in here, especially since the air-conditioning conked out two days ago. I gotta empty this thing and wash the stink off myself. If you're out there, please don't go away. I'm gonna cue up the CD and play a couple of Beatles songs, 'In My Life' and 'Let It Be'. I'm feeling heavy-handed and ironic today, so sue me. If I'm not back by the time they're over, odds are I ain't gonna be. Light a penny candle for me, folks, and stay tuned...."

"...Jesus H. Christ on a crutch, I made it! It was kind of touch and go there for a minute...or, rather, *not* touch, if you get me...but here I am, with a gladder bladder and clean hands and face, so we're not finished yet, folks. There's still some fight left, after all.

"I need to tell you a little bit about our receptionist here at We-Gab Radio. Her name's Laura McCoy. She's one of the sweetest people I've ever met, and if it weren't for her, most days at this station would be bedlam without the sharp choreography. Laura has always been a tad on the large side—she once smiled at me and said she didn't mind the word 'fat,' but I do mind it...anyway, Laura has always been on the large side but, dammit, she's *pretty*. She's tried a couple of times to go on diets and lose weight but they've never worked, and I for one am glad they didn't. I don't think she'd be half as pretty if she lost the weight.

"Laura's husband, this prince of all ass-wipes named Gerry, left her about ten months ago after fifteen years of marriage. Seems he'd been having an affair with a much younger co-worker for going on three years. Laura never suspected a thing, that's how true and trusting a soul she was. The divorce devastated her, we all knew it, but she was never less than professional and pleasant here at the station. Still, whenever there was any down-time—no calls coming in, no papers to be filed, no tour groups coming through, no DJs having nervous breakdowns—a lot of us began to notice this...this *stillness* about her; it was like if she wasn't busy, then some memory had its chance to sneak up and break her heart all over again. So we here at the station were worried. I asked her out for coffee one night after my shift. I made sure she knew it wasn't a date, it was just two friends having coffee and maybe some dessert.

"Laura was always incredibly shy when dealing with anyone outside of her job. The whole time we were having coffee she spent more time looking at her hands folded in her lap than she did at me. When she spoke, her voice was always…always so soft and sad. Even when she and Gerry were together, her voice had that sad quality to it—except at work, of course. At work, she spoke clearly and confidently. Sometimes I thought she was only alive when on the job.

"I said that to her the night we went for coffee. This was, oh…about eight months after the divorce, right? For the first time that night, she looked right at me and said, 'David, you're absolutely right. I *love* working at the station. That job and the people there are the only things I've ever been able to depend on. That's very important to me now.'

"After that, things were a lot better for a while. Laura took her two-week vacation just before everything started. In all the panic and confusion and Martial Law—which didn't exactly take very well, as you might recall—no one thought to call and check on her. She'd said she was going up to Maine to visit with her sister, so I guess most of us just figured or hoped that she'd made it to her sister's place before all hell broke loose.

"Two days ago, Laura came back to work. I can look over the console and through the window of the broadcast booth and see her sitting there at her desk. She's wearing one of her favorite dresses, and she's gotten a manicure. Maybe the manicure came before the great awakening, but it looks to me like the nail polish was freshly applied before she came in—and, I might add, she drove her car to work. I remember how excited I was to see that car driving up the road. It meant there was someone else still alive, and they'd thought to come here and check on me.

"I can see her very clearly, sitting there at her desk. About one-third of her head is missing. My guess is she used either a shotgun or a pistol with a hollow-point bullet. My guess is that this sweet, pretty woman who was always so shy around other people was a helluva lot more heartbroken than any of us suspected or wanted to imagine. My guess is she came back here because this station, this job, her place at that desk…these things were all she had left to look forward to. I wish I had been kinder to her. I wish I hadn't been so quick to think that our little chat helped, so I didn't have to give her or her pain a second thought. I wish…ohgod…I wish that I'd told her that she wouldn't be as pretty if she lost weight. I wish…shit, sorry…gimme a minute….

"Okay. Sorry about that. Forty-fucking-three years old and crying like a goddamn baby for its bottle. I'm losing ground here, folks. Losing ground. Because when I look out at Laura, there at her desk, and I remember Sarah Grant walking up to her family's home, and realize how many of the dead have been able to come back, have been able to walk or drive or in some cases take the goddamn bus back home…when I think of how they recognize us, how they *remember* us…you see, the thing is, Laura used to always bring in home-made chocolate chip cookies once a week. No one made cookies like Laura, I mean *nobody*! She'd always wrap them individually in wax paper, lay them out on a tray, cover the tray with tin-foil, and put a little Christmas-type bow on top.

"There's a tray of home-made cookies setting out there on her desk, all wrapped and covered and sporting its bow. Half her fucking brain is gone, splattered over a wall in her house…and she still *remembered.* Is this getting through to you, folks? The dead remember! Everything. It doesn't matter if they've been in the ground ten years or crawled out of a drawer in the morgue before anyone could identify them—*they all remember! All of them!*

"Is this sinking in? And doesn't it scare the piss out of you? Look; if they can crawl out of a grave after ten years of being worm-food and volleyball courts for maggots and *still remember* where they lived and who they loved and…and all of it…then it means those memories, those intangible bits and pieces of consciousness and ether that we're told are part and parcel of this mythical, mystical thing called a soul…it means it never *went anywhere* after they died. It didn't return to humus or dissipate into the air or take possession of bright-eyed little girls like in the movies…it just hung around like a vagrant outside a bus station on a Friday night. Which means there's *nothing* after we die. Which means there is no God. Which means this life is *it*—and ain't that a pisser? Karma is just the punch-line to a bad stand-up routine, and every spiritual teaching ever drilled into our brain is bullshit. Ha! Mark Twain was right, after all—remember the ending of *The Mysterious Stranger?*—there is no purpose, no reason, no God, no devil, no angels or ghosts or ultimate meaning; existence is a lie; prayer is an obscene joke. There is just…nothing; life and love are only baubles and trinkets and ornaments and costumes we use to hide this fact from ourselves. The universe was a mistake, and we, dear friends...we were a fucking *accident*. That's what it means...and that makes me so...sick. Because I...I was kind of *hoping*, y'know? But I guess hope is as cruel a joke as prayer, now.

"Still, it's funny, don't you think...that in the midst of all this rot and death there's still a kind-of life. You see it taking root all around us. I suppose that's why so many of us have found ceiling beams that will take our weight, or loaded up the pump-action shotguns and killed our families before turning the gun on ourselves...or jumped from tall buildings, or driven our cars head-on into walls at ninety miles an hour...or-or-Or-*OR*!

"There's a window behind me that has this great view of the hillside. In the middle of the field behind the station there's this huge old oak tree that's probably been there for a couple of thousand years. Yesterday, a dead guy walked into the field and up to that tree and just stood there looking at it, admiring. I wondered if maybe he'd proposed to his wife under this tree, or had something else really meaningful—pardon my language—happen beneath that oak. Whatever it was, this was the place he'd come back to. He sat down under the oak and leaned back against its trunk. He's still there, as far as I can make out.

"Because we found out, didn't we, that as soon as the dead come home, as soon as they reach their destination, as soon as they stop moving...they take root. And they *sprout*. Like fucking kudzu, they sprout. The stuff grows out of them like slimy vines, whatever it is, and starts spreading. I can't see the tree any longer for all the...the vines that are covering it. Oh, there are a couple of places near the top where they haven't quite reached yet, but those branches are bleach-white now, the life sucked out of them. The vines, when they spread, they grow thicker and wider...in places they blossom patches of stuff that looks like luminescent pond-scum. But the vines, they're pink and moist, and they have these things that look like thorns, only these thorns, they wriggle. And once all of it has taken root—once the vines have engulfed everything around them and the patches of pond-scum have spread as far as they can without tearing—once all that happens, if you watch for a while, you can see that all of it is...is *breathing*. It expands and contracts like lungs pulling in, and then releasing air...and in between the breaths... if that's what they are...everything pulses steadily, as if it's all hooked into some giant, invisible heart...and the dead, they just sit there, or stand there, or lie there, and bit by bit they dissolve into the mass...becoming something even more organic than they were before…something new…something… hell, I don't know. I just calls 'em as I sees 'em, folks.

"Laura's sprouted, you see. The breathing kudzu has curled out of her and crawled up the walls, across the ceiling, over the floor…about half the broadcast booth's window is covered with it, and I can see that those wriggling thorns have mouths, because they keep sucking at the glass. I went up to the glass for a closer look right after I got back from the bathroom, and I wish I hadn't…because you know what I saw, folks? Those little mouths on the thorns…they have teeth…so maybe…I don't know…maybe in way we *are* going to be eaten…or at least ingested…but whatever it is that's controlling all of this, I get the feeling that it's some kind of massive organism that's in the process of pulling all of its parts back together, and it won't stop until it's whole again…because maybe once it's whole…that's *its* way of coming home. Maybe it knows the secret of what lies beyond death…or maybe it *is* what lies beyond death, what's always been there waiting for us, without form…and maybe it finally decided that it was lonely for itself, and so jump-started our loved ones so it could hitch a ride to the best place to get started.

"I'm so tired. There's no unspoiled food left from the vending machines— did I mention that I took a baseball bat to those things five—almost *six* days ago now? I guess the delivery guy never got here to re-stock them. Candy bars, potato chips, and shrink-wrapped tuna salad sandwiches will only get you so far. I'm so…so *tired*. The kudzu is scrabbling at the base of the door…I don't think it can actually break through or it would have by now… but I'm thinking, what's the point, y'know? Outside, the field and hillside are shimmering with the stuff—from here it almost looks as if the vines are dancing—and in a little while it will have reached the top of the broadcast tower…and then I really *will* be talking to myself.

"If anyone out there has any requests…now's the time to phone them in. I'll even play the seventeen-minute version of 'In A Gadda-Da-Vida' if you ask me. I always dug that drum solo. I lost my virginity to that song…the *long* version, not the three-minute single, thanks for that vote of confidence in my virility. I wish I could tell you that I remembered her name…her first name was Debbie, but her last name…*pffft*! It's gone, lost to me forever. So…so many things are lost to me forever now…lost to all of us forever… still waiting on those requests…please, *please, PLEASE* will somebody out there call me? Because in a few minutes, the vines and thorns will have covered the window and those little mouths with their little teeth are all I'll be able to see and I'm…I'm hanging on by a fucking thread here, folks…so….

"…three minutes and forty seconds. I am going to play 'The Long and Winding Road', which is three minutes and forty seconds long, and if by the end of the song you have not called me, I am going to walk over to the door of the broadcast booth, say a quick and meaningless prayer to a God that was never there to hear it in the first place, and I am going to open that door and step into those waiting, breathing, pulsing vines.

"So I'm gonna play the song here in a moment. But first, let's do our sworn FCC duty like good little drones who are stupid enough to think anyone cares anymore, and we'll just let these six pathetic words serve as my possible epitaph:

"We now pause for station identification…."

Paper Cuts

Mutato nomine de te
Fabula narratur.

Change the name and it's about you, that story.
                              —Horace 65-8 b.c.

They came for us, as they always did, when the sun shone high in the safe daytime
sky. They pulled us from our coffins, from our beds, from our corners and alleys
and pits, and they hurt us; oh, how they hurt us. Driving stakes through our chests
as their legends told them they should, and then cutting off our heads—ah, but
not before tearing our limbs from our bodies one by one; not before burning out
our eyes with acid; not before tearing our intestines out in their dripping fists, not
before wrenching out our tongues with their fingers, or pliers, or cutting them
out with dull scissors; not before shredding our members from between our legs,
or burning them closed with hot irons, laughing in God-fearing righteousness as
the stink of our ruined flesh filled the air.

We did not scream, even though the pain of our dying was great.

Even when, once they were done, they built the massive fires upon
which our physical remains were tossed. No indignity, no torture, no final
humiliation was too terrible for the likes of us, not in their eyes.

Nowhere in the world did they show us mercy; at no time in the history
of their laughable, pathetic talking-monkey race did they ever attempt to show
understanding. It was always their fury, and then the pain, the degradation, the
torture, agony and dismemberment, and always, always, the flames to be fed after.

Annette Klein would be the first person to admit that she wasn't the most
graceful or coordinated person, even on her best days—she'd once twisted

her ankle attempting to just *stand up* in a pair of high-heeled shoes that one of her friends had goaded her into trying on in a trendy shop—but even she wouldn't have thought it possible for her to cause herself to shed blood in, of all places, a second-hand bookstore, yet bleed there she did. To make matters worse, it wasn't just a little—no, that would have been a blessing; she had to get a series of not one, not two, but *a trio* of paper cuts on the tips of the center fingers of her left hand, as well as a decent gash across the palm of that hand. Until that moment in the bookstore, she'd forgotten just how much blood flowed through the hand and its fingers, but as soon as she felt the sharp slices and saw the drops of blood spattering down on the pages of the book she'd been skimming, it came back to her. She'd always been something of a bleeder, even as a child, and for a few years her parents worried that her difficulty in clotting might be due to hemophilia, but luckily that turned out not to be the case. Her veins were just a slight bit closer to the surface than in most people, and as a result her bleeding was quick and her clotting slow but it was never a genuine danger to her well-being.

That evening in the second-hand bookstore, however, she wondered just for a minute if things were about to—as many mystery and suspense writers might phrase it in the pulp novels she so loved to read—take a turn for the worse. Flash of lightning, roll of thunder, cue ominous background music.

A few minutes before wandering into the bookstore she left her office, much later than usual, at the downtown branch of the community college where she worked as the school's website designer. She was heading to the parking garage when she got the sudden urge for a cruller from Riley's Bakery, so, despite the lateness of the hour, she turned abruptly and headed toward the fulfillment of her bliss. Riley's was unfortunately out of crullers by this hour (*Well, duh!* she thought to herself; *it's after 7,* of course *they're out*), so she decided to mend her broken heart with a box of chocolate-coated sugar-dusted doughnut holes. Walking out the door, popping the first one whole into her mouth, she bit down and closed her eyes as the rich, heavy flavors and textures spread out over her tongue. Then she nearly tripped over her own feet because she was walking and eating with her eyes closed. Despite her skill and dexterity at the computer, multi-tasking in the real world was not her forte—well, okay, she wasn't quite *that* bad, she could walk and eat at the same time, even talk on her cell simultaneously without leaving a path of destruction in her wake, but that required that she not, well, have her eyes closed. It's the little things that keep us aboveground and breathing, so this one was on her. She caught her balance just in time by shoving out her arm and catching her weight on the brick doorway of the bookstore. Her doughnuts, however, failed to survive the mishap, because the hand she used to brace herself against the doorway also happened to be the one that was holding the box of treats.

Cursing under her breath, she fished a small bottle of hand sanitizer out of her purse and applied it to her hands and then—because she didn't have any tissues—surreptitiously dried them on the sides of her jacket. She might very well have walked out of this story right there and then but she caught a glimpse of something in the bookstore's display window that caused her to remain: what appeared to be a near-pristine first edition of Carson McCullers' *Reflections in a Golden Eye,* one of her all-time favorite novels. She had two other editions—a trade paperback and a cheap discarded hardback found at a library book sale—and while each was in at-least *readable* condition, she'd always wanted to have a really nice copy of the novel—and here it was, it seemed. She looked up at the streetlights that were just beginning to buzz and sputter to life and reminded herself that, despite the quaint appearance of the building fronts in this area, there was still enough serious crime taking place after dark that she really ought to be heading back to the garage—but just as quickly as these thoughts presented themselves, the book junkie in her laughed it off, its metaphorical gaze fixed unblinkingly on the McCullers novel.

Smiling to herself and feeling a bit like Helene Hanff finally walking into 84 Charing Cross Road, Annette opened the door and entered, wondering for a moment if she were about to meet the man who would play Frank P. Doel to her Helene. She couldn't quite figure out if the small hanging sign was supposed to be turned to **OPEN** or **CLOSED** because one part of it had come loose from the string, leaving the rest hanging there like a desperate spelunker who'd lost his grip on the way down and now dangled there, waiting for someone above to give the rope a tug and pull him to safety. Oh, well—if the place were closed, the proprietor would say so soon enough.

Those fires that consumed the degraded remains of our physical bodies burned well into the nights throughout history and the world over; a few flames could still be seen licking upward from the embers in the days following our deaths, when the men of the villages set about the final stage of their so-called holy tasks.

The pits were dug, our agonized ashes poured in, soil and dung spread atop the smoldering remains, and in the following mornings, saplings were planted in the spots. And there they thought it would end.

But eternal life means eternal*; it mattered not that we no longer had our meat puppets to transport us from place to place. Even in the core of a single agonized ash, eternal life remains eternal, as does the consciousness amassed during that life; and as such, we slowly felt ourselves absorbed into the young roots of the infant saplings, and then, slowly, into the rest of the trees that grew from the pits where our remains were buried.*

The Earth spun. The moon waxed and waned. Vegetation began to grow around the trees, snaking up through the ashes. The scarred spots where we had met our degrading deaths gave way to blankets of green. The trees grew straight and tall, branches reaching toward the sunlight.

A season passed, and then a year, and then ten more.

Many came to these trees to admire their beauty and to enjoy their shade. Many a young man proposed to his true love beneath these canopies. Weddings were performed beneath them. Children were christened there.

A decade passed, and then another, and then forty more. The stars shifted their courses. Constellations appeared and then vanished. The sky changed. The villagers who had watched our deaths, who participated in our brutalization, themselves died, as did their children, and their children's children, and the next three generations who followed.

But the trees remained, tall and imposing. Within their cores, we waited patiently, spreading our eternal strength throughout the trees until every leaf, every twig, every branch and piece of bark became one with us.

The Earth spun, the moon waxed and waned, townships replaced villages, and engineers and architects covered the land with roads and bridges and train tracks.

We waited, growing stronger in our new forms, our new homes. Through the vibrations above, below, and within the planet itself we found one another, and we shared our stories, and our memories, and sang our bloodsongs to the night.

The Earth spun. The seasons changed. Telegraph wires were replaced by telephone poles.

The Earth spun. Townships were sacrificed in favor of cities; Community was traded for Commerce, cobblestone for asphalt and concrete, horse-drawn wagons for automobiles and airplanes. Telephones gave way to cellular communications.

And we waited.

People moved on. Families grew larger. Cities sprang up, demanding the death of trees to make room for them.

And we waited, knowing that it would begin again soon.

The first thing that threatened to seduce Annette's senses once she was fully inside was the so-very-right *smell* of the place, something only a true lover of books could understand; the comforting, intoxicating, friendly scent of bindings and old paper was almost joyous; decades' worth of floor wax and the almost pungent aroma of real wooden in-wall bookcases was nectar.

The walls were lined from floor to ceiling with sagging shelves full of books, and she could see at a glance that, though the stock in this section immediately inside the entrance contained everything from academic texts to the usual classics, its primary focus was on matters philosophical and occult; everywhere she turned there were books such as Agrippa's *De Occulta Philosophia*, the ancient notes of Anaxagoras of Clazomenae detailing his conclusions that the Earth was spherical, *The Gospel of Sri Ramakrishna*, the Hindu *Ris Veda*, the poems of Ovid, the plays of Aeschylus, Lucan's *De Bello Civilia*; there were numerous sections that contained long out-of-print works by Robert Nathan, Booth Tarkington, even Jessamyn West and Katherine Anne Porter ... her heart beat with surprising excitement. Aside from the rare edition of the McCullers novel in the display window, who knew what other treasures she might find in here? She'd driven past this store dozens—*hundreds*—of times, but had never given it so much as a second thought. The majority of the shops in this area of downtown were geared toward an older, more seasoned customer—that is to say, people whose families had lived here since the turn of the last century. Every city has its section of town where the merchants catered to an exclusive selection of patrons, and Annette had always assumed that this store was one of them; judging from the oak-framed cover from the first issue of *Playboy* magazine that was displayed on the wall behind the counter, she was wrong about that, as well.

Approaching the counter, she saw that the proprietor didn't use anything electronic when tallying up sales, no; he or she had an antique, National cash register 2 deep drawer, 3 keybank machine in polished cherry wood with flawless persimmon inlay, the kind of register that hadn't been in use for at least a hundred years, and this machine was in superb condition.

She was admiring a copy of *The Complete Short Stories of F. Scott Fitzgerald* that sat by itself on a wooden display square in a delicate, exquisite bell jar. The jar was on a small table by the counter; this book, too, seemed to be a first edition. Touching her fingertips against her thumbs to be certain no detritus from the late and much-lamented doughnut holes remained there, she looked around the store for any sign of the proprietor. *Okay*, she said to herself, *you know damned well that this thing has to be set apart like this for a reason, right? They've put it inside a bell jar, for pity's sake. You shouldn't even be* thinking *about this.*

But even at thirty-six—just as she'd been at six, and twelve, and twenty-six—Annette Klein was never one to let common sense override curiosity, especially when it came to old books. She reached out, hesitated for only a moment, and then carefully, even delicately (for her) lifted the glass covering and set it to the side, making sure that it was balanced and in no danger of falling.

She picked up the book and began flipping through the pages until she came across "Bernice Bobs Her Hair," always her favorite of Fitzgerald's stories, and had just turned the page when she felt the unmistakable, fiery-sharp slice of paper cuts on her fingertips. Pulling back her hand, she watched in disgust as blood from her index, middle, and fourth finger spattered onto the page she'd been reading. *Shit*, she thought. *Oh, well—you bleed on it, you bought it.* She absent-mindedly stuck the tips of the three fingers into her mouth and sucked at them, tasting the faint coppery flavor and almost gagging. She fumbled the book, still opened to the pages she'd bled on, down onto the counter and was searching her jacket pockets for some tissues, or a handkerchief, or anything at all she cold use to wrap around her bleeding digits when she saw why she'd managed to get paper cuts on all three of her fingers; each upper and lower corner of the two opened pages facing her had for some incomprehensible reason been dog-eared so that four surprisingly sharp-tipped triangles jutted up, and the paper stock itself was of a sufficiently strong quality that these dog-eared corners felt almost solid. Why on earth would anyone do that to a rare edition of a book, let alone a Fitzgerald? Squeezing the fingers of her left hand tightly in her right fist, she leaned forward and stared at the book.

Was she imagining things, or did it look somehow thicker than before she'd picked it up? She squinted, feeling the blood running down her wrist. What else was it about this that seemed…off? She reached out to close the book and felt the edges of the page almost snap out. She knew she felt the sliver of fierce, quick pain slice across her palm. This time she cursed out loud at the pain, and turned away from the book before she soaked it with any more of her blood.

There was another book on the wooden display block where the Fitzgerald had been a minute before. How the hell had it gotten there?

"Oh, dear me," someone said. "Oh, dammit, dammit, dammit. My fault, my fault, so very sorry."

A short, stocky man dressed in clothes easily twenty years out of date came up to her and took her bleeding hand in his. "Oh, Jesus Christ in a second-hand Chrysler," he said in a voice that sounded as if it gargled with Wild Turkey four times a day, "you really hurt yourself, didn't you?"

"They're just paper cuts."

The man shook his head, in obvious pain. "No cut is *just* anything. Not to me, anyway. Come back here with me, I'll fix you up. Lots of doctors in my family. I'm not one of them but I've picked up a few tricks here and there." He started to say something else, but then noticed the Fitzgerald lying on the counter and the new book that had taken its place on the display block. "Excuse me one moment," he said. He grabbed the bell jar and covered the new book, and then glanced for a moment at the Fitzgerald. His face blanched, but he quickly gathered himself and smiled at Annette. "Sorry. I'm a bit fussy about certain things. People say it makes me colorful. That's what happens when you get to be as old as me. You become colorful. A local character, even." He led her back to an area near the back of the store that was separated from the sales floor by a large wall of frosted glass.

"I was trying to close early. I guess I didn't check the sign." He wore a pressed white shirt open slightly at the collar so that the thin gray-and-black-striped tie wasn't completely strangling him. He sported not one but two pairs of glasses; a regular black-rimmed pair with a second, wire-framed pair just an inch farther down his nose; judging from the thickness of the lenses, this second set were either bi- or more likely tri-focal lenses. His vest, like his tailored cuffed pants, was pinstriped. A chain led from one vest pocket to another, where Annette could see the outline of a gold pocket-watch.

Definitely old-school, she thought. She liked that.

He pulled out a old wooden rolling stool and helped her to sit, and then opened the main area of a roll-top desk and removed what appeared to be a well-stocked medical kit from beneath stacks of receipts and order forms. The entire room was stuffed with books, stacked from floor to almost shoulder height, and in some places the stacks were three deep. Annette couldn't help but marvel.

"I'll bet you know where every last book in this store is, even if it's buried in a stack like one of these and in the basement or something."

"You'd win that bet," said the bookseller, as he opened the lid of the medical kit and began assembling everything he needed to tend to Annette's cuts. As he reached over to take hold of her hand his sleeve rode up slightly, and Annette saw the row of fading-but-not-faded numerals tattooed near his wrist. The bookseller caught sight of what she was looking at, and so pulled his sleeve a bit father up, turning his wrist to give her a better look.

"I'm sorry," said Annette. "I didn't mean to stare. It's just that I…I've never met anyone who was…was…."

"I was in a concentration camp," said the bookseller. "I was taken there as a child. My family and I were marched from our home in Hungary, along with thousands of others, to a camp in the Austria forest called Gunskirchen Larger. Most of my family died on the way. My sister lasted until two days after we arrived. She'd hurt her feet on the march and gangrene set in. Her death was slow and agonizing and I still cry when I think about it too much. I haven't been one for long walks since. If it hadn't been for a boy named Uri who befriended me in those early days, I think I would have just willed myself to die."

His tone was so matter-of-fact that Annette felt momentarily anxious. Was this man a little on the crazy side? Who could talk about something so horrible in such an almost-nonchalant manner?

"I don't mean to sound unfeeling," said the bookseller as he set about cleaning her cuts with some kind of ointment that immediately killed the pain, "but I find that if I talk about it any other way, I just…implode. Please,

27

don't be offended. Sometimes I talk too much and go into stories by rote. I don't get a lot of company these days."

A dozen questions that she wanted to ask him flooded across Annette's mind: was he a widower? Didn't he have any children? Was he always alone here? But the question that won out was: "What happened out there with the books?"

He hesitated a moment, a fresh cotton ball hovering over the cut on her palm, and then released the breath he'd been holding and continued ministering to her. "That, I'm afraid, will take a bit of explaining, and I'd rather that you not think I'm looney-tunes and go screaming off the premises. Also it would be nice if you didn't sue me because of these cuts."

"Like I said, they're just paper cuts."

"And like I said, no cut is *just* anything, not to me." He finished cleaning the cuts, and began rummaging around in the kit for a small tube of—all things—Super Glue. "Cyanoacrylate," he said, showing her the tube. "Believe it or not, it wasn't invented so guys could suspend themselves with their hardhats from steel beams, it was developed for medics to use in the field during Vietnam. Best way in the world to quickly and safely close a bleeding wound."

"Believe it or not," said Annette, "I already knew that."

"Of course you did. Anyone curious enough to take a Fitzgerald out from under glass *would* know something like that."

Annette cleared her throat. The bookseller paused and looked up at her.

"Speaking of the Fitzgerald…" she said.

"You'll think I'm crazy."

"Will I? Let's review: I took a book out from under a bell jar. That book had pages with dog-eared corners that I swear bit my fingers. The pages absorbed my blood and the book grew thicker. And when I turned around, another book had taken the Fitzgerald's place even though you were back here and I was alone in the store. Does that about cover it?"

"A worthy highlight reel if ever there was one."

"Do you think *I'm* crazy?"

"You don't strike me as unbalanced, no."

Annette smiled. "So tell me what happened out there. It wasn't normal."

The bookseller shrugged. "That depends on your definition of the word."

"Please?"

He sat back and stared at her for a moment, and then rubbed the back of his neck. "You want a drink? I'm going to have one. Pick your poison, I got a little bit of everything stashed around here."

"Got any wine?"

"White or red?"

"Red?"

He went behind the roll-top desk and emerged a few moments later with a bottle of red wine and a pair of tulip-shaped wine glasses. After pouring each of them a glass, the bookseller held up his wine and said, *"Doamne apara-me rău."*

"What's that mean?"

"It's a kind-of Rumanian blessing. It's a good thing, trust me."

"Okee-day," she replied, and took a drink of the wine. It was incredible. "This is the best red wine I've ever tasted."

"Really? I made it myself. I have another bottle in the back if you'd like one to take home."

"Oh, I'd *love* that."

The bookseller smiled widely; this genuinely pleased him. What do you know? Someone thinks something I made with my own hands is the best they've ever encountered. And here I thought there wasn't going to be anything special happening today.

He put his glass aside and returned to Annette's hand. "Have you ever heard those rumors about Hitler seeking occult or supernatural assistance during the war?"

Annette shrugged. "I just thought it was the stuff of legend, or pulp fiction."

The bookseller snorted a laugh and shook his head. "Not all of it was as far-fetched as you might think. The Longinus spear, for instance, the spear that supposedly pierced Christ's side while he was on the cross? It was purported to possess great power. It was said that whomever possessed the spear would have the power to conquer the world. Hitler very much believed that, and until the moment he blew his brains out down in the bunker, he had hundreds of people searching for it.

"One of the things that made Gunskirchen an oddball among the concentration camps is that the majority of people sent there were professionals—physicians, lawyers, professors, artists, musicians. During the first weeks there, Uri and I could almost get *drunk* on the conversations that were whispered at night in the barracks. Philosophy, music, law, mathematics and myth…it seemed early on that maybe it wasn't going to be as horrible as we'd been told. That notion was quickly buried.

"The conditions were sub-human. There was a series of twenty toilet pits that had been dug out at the far edge of the camp, and if you went to the bathroom anywhere but in one of those pits the Germans shot you dead on the spot. These pits were never covered and so the stench of it was always in the air. But the thing is, disease spread quickly, and many people became afflicted with diarrhea. It didn't matter if a person was standing in line for one of the pits, if they lost control of their bowels—and many did—and soiled themselves in line, they were dragged out of line, made to kneel down, and shot in the head. We weren't allowed to move their bodies. The Germans liked to laugh at the dead Jews lying in a puddle of their own liquid filth. Of all the images I can't rid myself of, it's the image of all those people, those *skeletons*, standing in the pit lines, shuddering with all the strength they had, to not shit themselves." He blinked his eyes, and gave a small shudder. "Yeah, I'm a cheerful guy with many happy stories.

"I know—the bell jar and books. Hang on, I need a refill."

"I think I do, too," said Annette, holding out her glass. The bookseller refilled both, and they drank in an awkward, sad, sudden silence.

They came for us, as they always did, when the sun shone high in the safe daytime sky.

We waited in our majestic trees as the bulldozers and other heavy equipment came toward us. We listened as they broke through the heavy woods and overpowered the shale beneath the hillsides. We readied ourselves as they neared us. We heard the grinding of their gears, the snarl of their gas-powered saws. We stood tall and proud so we could see them clearly as they arrived. The stench of their smoke and diesel fuel reached us before they and their machines did.

Workmen walked up to us wherever we stood across the surface of the planet, craning their necks to see our glory.

"Damn shame this has to come down," said one.

"Don't matter what we think," replied the second. "We got our orders."

The first one picked up his axe. "Trees're supposed to feel things just like a person does, y'know? My grandma told me that. Let's try to make it quick and clean, huh?"

"I've heard enough of that griping from you," said the second workman, powering up his chain saw. "Bad enough we got to cut down all these trees without you bellyachin' over every one of 'em. Least they'll be put to good use. That's something, anyway."

They set to work.

Our waiting was over.

Within half an hour, we came crashing down.

This was not death; it was the first stage of our rebirth.

And this time we did scream, but in ecstasy; sweet, all-consuming ecstasy.

The sound of re-birth.

"There was a group of occultists," said the bookseller, "called the *Studiengruppe für germanisches Altertum*—'Study Group for Germanic Antiquity,' but most people know them by the name The Thule Society. The Thules had members like Hans Frank, Rudolph Hess, Heinrich Himmler, it was even rumored that Eichmann and Mengele were members. One of the commandants at Gunskirchen Lager, Gruppenfuehrer Joseph Karl Steiner, was a member. I remember as a child huddling down at night in the mud and filth and cold—God, I hope you *never* experience that kind of cold, it almost made you wish for the warmth of a grave. At least then there would have been something above you to hold in the heat and gasses as your body disintegrated and purified.

"Anyway, there were those nights when Steiner would have other Thule members in his expansive quarters, and the lights would burn, the glow mocking us, and I remember the sounds of their cackling laughter, their murmuring voices, sometimes they would sing drunken, obscene songs... there was so much...*haughtiness* in their tones. But always—*always*—there came a time during the night when they would send two SS officers out into the camp to select one of the healthier prisoners, a worker, to bring back into the building. I remember that I used to feel envious of those selected to be taken inside. Rumor had it that these men—mostly it was men, sometimes a stronger woman or a younger boy, I never saw them take a young girl…but the rumors persisted that those who were selected were fed meat and cheese, given wine, a warm, clean blanket, and treated well. But we never saw them again. They would enter that building, there would be more celebratory noise for a while, and then things would quiet down. There was never silence, only an ebbing of sound. I swear to you I could hear the sounds of someone… not exactly groaning, there wasn't enough strength for it to be a groan, but a noise somewhere between a whimper and a grunt. And it would continue for a minute or two at a constant but low level, just low enough that I was never certain if I was actually hearing it or if it was just the cold and sores and hunger making me imagine some unseen depravity going on there. I was six years old, and the images those sounds created in my mind should never have existed in the mind of any truly decent human being.

"Uri would hold me close to him on these nights and hum soft songs in my ear. One of his favorites was 'The Yanks are Coming.' He always hummed it off-key. It made me laugh. He was taken away one morning for a burial detail, and he never came back. I prayed that he had gotten away somehow.

"The last time our dear Gruppenfuehrer held a Thule gathering in his quarters, the SS officers came out and took nearly a dozen men, women, and young boys into the Gruppenfuehrer's quarters. That night, there was no mistaking the screams; children begging for their lives, women pleading that *they* be tortured instead of the children, men weeping and wailing. We saw blood spatter on the inside of the windows. We saw shadows jerking back and forth, some of them flipping, fluttering, but always there was the blood, and wailing, and the screaming…and then the not-quite-silence, the muffled noise of many throats releasing something between a whimper and a grunt.

"The date that night was April 27, 1945. The Germans had received word that the Americans were coming. You have to understand, rumors that the war was ending soon—was perhaps even over—had been whispered for weeks, but that night was the first time that I allowed myself to think that maybe, just maybe, the end was finally here. If that end meant my death, then so be it. I was so hungry and sick by then that I almost didn't care.

"The next morning all of the Germans left the camp. They gave what they called a 'generous' amount of food—one cube of sugar to each person, and one loaf of molded bread for every seven people. There were nearly as many dead as there were still alive, if you can call it alive. Men, women, children so drawn and weak and starving they could barely walk, but that didn't stop them from trying when the Americans arrived. The 71st Infantry Division entered Gunskirchen on the morning of May 1, 1945. By then what little rancid food we'd been left was gone, and we had been without water for several days even before that. I can still hear the cries from the throats of those who could still speak, calling out "*…wasser!*" and "*…ich habe hunger!*" One child whose legs had been broken and were now blackened with infection used her elbows to pull herself through the mud toward anAmerican soldier. I saw her die in his arms as he gave her a drink from his canteen. All around me skeletons crawled or shuffled through stinking, ankle-deep mud and human excrement. I started crying, staring out through the fence, as I saw the decayed bodies of horses and dogs that lined the road, carcasses that had been torn into by the teeth of the starving as they wandered from the camp days before, after the Germans had abandoned it; physicians, lawyers, people of education, men of letters, rabbis, women and children reduced to chewing on rotting animal intestines like beasts.

"It was then I felt a hand on my shoulder and looked up to see my friend, Uri, still alive and standing. I hadn't seen him in months and had assumed that he was dead. He smiled at me—his teeth were rotted, many of them missing, but it was still one of the most beautiful smiles I had ever seen. I hugged him and wept. As the Americans moved into the camp, many of the prisoners lined the way, hands outstretched to touch the sleeves of our saviors. Uri took my hand and led me through the throng toward the Gruppenfuehrer's quarters. I did not want to see whatever it was that waited in there, but I was too weak to resist and, I hate admitting this, a part of me wanted to know if there had been any truth to the hideous, perverted images that the sounds had helped put into my head. If there were horrors waiting in there that were worse than those I imagined, then perhaps my soul wasn't forever tainted. Perhaps God had given me a glimpse of something horrible to prepare me for something even worse. In such ways is spiritual strength tested and achieved."

He fell silent after this for a few moments as he finished up ministering to Annette's wounds. He completed what could only be called an expert job of bandaging her hand, turning it first to the left, then to the right. "Does it still hurt?"

"Not in the least. Thank you for being so kind."

The bookseller gave a tight smile that contained no joy in it whatsoever and nodded his head. "I am truly sorry this happened."

Annette shook her head. "I shouldn't have taken the book from under the bell jar."

The bookseller held up a hand in protest. "No, that was my fault. I should have taken the book as soon as it appeared. At the very least I should have made sure the **CLOSED** sign was in place and the door locked." He looked once again toward the two books at the end of the counter; the new one under the bell jar, and the volume of Fitzgerald whose pages had so cut Annette's fingers and hand.

She leaned forward and touched the bookseller's arm. "What was in there? What did Uri and you see?"

The bookseller nodded toward the bell jar. "That. It was sitting on a lovely oak table in the corner of Steiner's office. There was a book inside, in Arabic. The paper was old, thick, and stiff. Neither Uri nor I ever knew what the book was. It was filled with symbols and writings in verse that Uri thought might be incantations. It *felt* like something evil that was being imprisoned under glass. And it was the only book in the building.

"The floors of the Gruppenfuehrer's quarters were littered with the bodies of those dozen prisoners who had been taken four nights before the Americans came. They were not only decomposed, they were...deflated. Their flesh was gray, drained of any moisture. I remember how Uri knelt down next to several of the bodies and shook, pointing to their wounds. Hundreds, *thousands* of cuts—paper cuts. And not a single drop of blood anywhere. I think Uri knew then what unholy rites the Gruppenfuehrer and his Thule had been practicing on those nights of singing and soft glowing lights. I couldn't grasp it. I felt sick and dizzy and more afraid at that moment than I had been during the years I'd been in the camp. I tried to turn and run out, to find an American to give me a drink or a taste of his K-rations, but as soon as I turned around the world went black.

"I awoke in a makeshift hospital, in a massive tent. The Americans had established a camp just outside Lambach, not that far from Gunskirchen itself. I opened my eyes and saw glass bottles hanging next to me, saw clear tubes running into my arms. I turned my head and saw Uri sitting on the floor next to my bed. He was sleeping, his head resting on his bended knees. I reached out and touched the top of his head. He shuddered, made a terrible wet sound, but then lifted his head and blinked his eyes. I could see that he had been in the midst of a nightmare, and the phantom images of it still reflected in his eyes told me how horrible it must have been. I never asked him to recount any part of it.

"He gave me a sad and tired smile—his teeth were now gone, having been removed by an American dentist, what an old man he looked like! But I loved seeing that old-man smile. Did I mention that Uri was only nineteen? He looked fifty, and looked that way until the day he died.

"He took hold of my hand and kissed the palm, then held it against his cheek. 'I have secured the evil vessel,' he whispered to me. 'It can harm no one ever again.'

"I asked him how he'd done this, how did he know it was evil, and several other questions that seemed to confuse him as much as they did me. He told me that an American soldier had helped him to remove the bodies of the prisoners and give them a decent burial, and that this 'Yank'—that's what Uri called the Americans—had helped him to find a crate and blankets and secure the bell jar and its contents. 'The Yank will help me send it to what family remains to me in the States,' he said. 'In my letter I will ask them to not open the crate, and I know they will honor my wishes.' He then squeezed my arm. 'When we get to the States, my friend, you will be with me. I have told them that we are brothers, and we are—if not by blood, then by choice, by loyalty, by our having survived this madness, by our love and friendship.'

"'Brother' I said to him. 'My brother. Thank you.'

"He never left my side after that day. I remember that the day I awoke, it was V-E Day. The war was at last over. I felt almost reborn." The bookseller looked up at the clock on the wall. "My goodness, I've been talking your ears off for a while, haven't I?"

"I don't mind," said Annette.

"If your friends didn't mention it, this is not the type of neighborhood where one wants to be caught on the streets after the streetlights come on—*if* the streetlights come on. It's always something of a crapshoot."

"Please," she said, "tell me the rest. I have to know. I'm the one who bled on the thing. It's because of me that another book's appeared. I saw the expression on your face! You were terrified...and a little sickened, I think."

The bookseller gently took her un-bandaged hand in both of his and said: "Do you believe in such a thing as evil? Wait, before you answer, I'm not talking about evils like starvation, or genocide, rape, torture—as sickening, as horrific as those things are; I'm talking about a power that transcends what we know as 'nature' to dwell in a space that we can not only *not* comprehend, but that our five senses are powerless to recognize in its purest form."

"Are you asking me if I believe in supernatural evil?"

"I guess I am, yes."

"I don't know," she replied. "I mean, I guess I've wondered like everyone else if there's something more than just this life, a force that guides everything, holds all matter together, but I never…I never tried to imagine much beyond that. It scares me. Most of the time I have a hard enough time just getting through the *day*, you know?"

"Don't you have friends?"

"Not any close ones, not really. I've always been a bit solitary. That's why I love books so much. I can lose myself in another world, another time, another person's adventure. I always liked pretending when I was a child, and I guess that hasn't changed much over the decades. I read a book and it's like it actually comes alive, the story's a living thing and the pages are…I don't know…like the thing that gives the story its voice. Does that make sense? Probably not. I just love reading."

"Don't you find it lonely?"

Annette considered the question for a moment. "I try not to think about it in terms like that. I figure as long as the same old sun rises to greet me, and the same old moon is there at night, then things are okay. It helps."

The bookseller nodded his head and patted her hand. "I really like you. You're quite sweet and kind."

"I think you're a pretty nice person yourself. *Colorful*, but nice."

The bookseller laughed. "Oh, you're a quick study, you are. Hey—why did you come in here in the first place?"

"I want that copy of *Reflections in a Golden Eye* in your display window."

"Ah, McCullers! Exquisite writer. Died far too young." He rose from his chair. "Come on, then. Let's get your book while I finish my story. You know, it's interesting that you talked about books like they're living things. What would you say if I told you some of them are?"

36

We savored the sensations of every moment as we were cut into dozens of large, heavy sections and loaded onto gigantic flatbed trailers; we admired the world our human bodies had not lived to see as our pieces were driven to mills where they were cut into logs; we drank in the cool goodness as the logs were treated in a flow of water made steady and constant by grindstones; we tingled with wild, unbound excitement as the logs were turned into wood chips, and then treated under pressure with a solution of sulphurous acid and acid calcium sulfite, followed by caustic soda, carbon, and sodium sulphide; we centered our collective consciousness and began to focus our thoughts as the lignin contained in the chips decomposed, allowing f-dextrose to form as our cellulose was purified; we briefly flashed on the smug expressions our executioners wore as they staked us, dismembered us, blinded us with bodkins or acid, but those images vanished and were replaced by exhilaration as the wood chips were pulped and then immersed in water; the water molded the pulp into fibers; the fibers were felted together as the water was purposefully agitated; then, at last, after centuries of patient waiting, the felted fibers became sheets as they were lifted from the water by a wire screen.

And we lived again as the mammoth rolls of virgin paper were loaded onto trailers and hauled away to the waiting presses and binderies. We were given our new forms. Words were imprinted on us, emblazoned on the covers used to hold us together. We lived the stories on our new flesh, every word, every feeling, every dream and pain and agony and glory and triumph and defeat and tragedy. They made it easier to wait a little longer.

Because eternal life means eternal, whether you live inside a puppet of meat or the materials used to produce the pages of a book. Eternal life means eternal.

And our eternal life means the hunger never goes away. And we have been very, very hungry. And we've waited. And some of those meat puppets have helped to find more of our brothers and sisters of the night. And we wait. And wait. And wait.

But something about this night, this night, *vibrates deep within our yearnings and whispers "Soon...."*

Annette stared at the volume of Fitzgerald on the counter, now back to its original size and thickness, and then glanced at the book now inside the bell jar: *Heraclites' Theory and Modern Social Thought.*

"You seem…stunned," said the bookseller.

"It's just…you're right, if you had told me this earlier, I would have thought you were crazy."

"Imagine my reaction when Uri first showed it to me. We come back here to live with his aunt and uncle who owned this bookstore, and after a decade-and-a-half, when his uncle grew too sick to continue working, the bookstore is passed to us, *then* he finally opens the crate and removes the bell jar and the book inside. 'Living demons,' he told me. 'Something evil was scattered into the earth, and became part of the trees and plants that were used to create certain books. These books are demons. They live. They hunger. They demand a blood sacrifice.' Yeah, I nearly ran screaming from the premises myself. And then he proved it to me.

"He lifted the bell jar, opened the book, and I *saw* its pages bend, I *saw* the corners turn into teeth, and I *saw* them bite into his flesh and drink his blood. I don't know what kind of monsters these things were when they walked the Earth, but just because their bodies were burned and buried and became part of the trees that were used in the making of these books…good God, I sound crazy to myself right now. But that's the truth. I don't know how—Uri and I were never able to agree on a theory, we argued about it until the day he died and left this store to me—but when one of these books feeds, it somehow…it somehow *communicates* with others of its kind, acts as a kind-of beacon, and another of them follows its…its *signal*, and appears on the display block. That is why anyone taken into the Gruppenfuehrer's quarters was never seen again. Steiner and other members of the Thule Society were sacrificing them to these demons—or whatever they are—in order to ensure victory for their Supreme Fuehrer. When I trick one of those books into appearing here, it remains beneath that bell jar until it feeds and another one of its kind arrives to take its place."

"H-how…how do they feed?"

The bookseller held up his hands. For the first time, Annette noticed the dozens of healing paper cuts on the old man's fingers.

"I feed them my own blood," said the bookseller. "It doesn't take that much to slake one of them, but I've never given one more than a few drops. About the same amount the Fitzgerald took from you."

Annette took a step back from the book. "What do you do with them? How do you protect yourself—protect *others*—from them?"

"When Uri and I realized what we were dealing with, we had a vault installed in the back of the store. There are *banks* in this city that don't have vaults this impenetrable. When you came in I was back there, saying a protection prayer as I unlocked it. I was going to put the Fitzgerald in there as soon as it fed and then close and seal it again. You beat me to the first part."

Annette stared at the small man with the Wild Turkey voice and wondered if, like her, he was alone and isolated in his own skin. She felt a sudden, surprising rush of affection for the bookseller that she could not find the words to express.

"Why?" was all she could manage. "Why do this?"

The bookseller's eyes seemed to be looking at something a thousand feet away, something filled with misery and desperation and hopelessness and, perhaps, near its edge, a hint of redemption, a dim, nebulous promise of salvation. "When I was a child I watched men in crisp black uniforms and shiny dark boots stomp the faces of people I loved into the mud. I watched them bury sick children in deep graves of feces and gore. I watched as these men laughed and drank and goosestepped their way across continents in a zealous effort to turn this planet into a graveyard filled with the bodies of those they deemed less pure, less worthy, less deserving of life and dignity than their own blond-haired blue-eyed Aryan ideal. I watched this evil and was powerless to do anything to stop it. All I cold do was watch, and weep, and pray to a God I wasn't certain was even *there* any longer. 'Make it stop,' I would pray. 'Please, make it stop. Make them see the evil they do.'" He shook his head and wiped at his eyes. "Never again. I promised myself that I would never again watch as evil took the blood of the innocent. I promised myself that I would never allow that kind of suffering to continue, not as long as I have strength in these hands and breath in this body." He looked at Annette, his gaze nailing her to the spot. "So I do this. I don't know what it is I help to prevent by these actions, but I know—I *pray*—that I am, in some small way, in some small way that only one small, old, weak man can, preventing another evil from being set loose upon the world.

"I can sleep at night, and the nightmares aren't as frequent or as terrible as they once were. So I think maybe I'm doing the right thing."

Annette nodded her head. "May I...may I come with you and watch you put this book away?"

"Of course. It would be an honor for me. Since Uri's death, I have had no one to share this secret with. Sometimes it weighs on me. It will be nice to have a friend with whom I can share this, if just for one evening. I thank you for it." He removed a large, pristine white handkerchief from his pocket. The material was heavy, thick, and when he snapped it open the smell of starch was almost overpowering. He placed the handkerchief over the cover of the Fitzgerald book and quickly folded it around until the entire volume was enshrouded in cloth.

"Blessed by a rabbi," he said, picking it up. "Here, take this, please." He offered her a thin gold necklace from which dangled a lovely but oddly-shaped charm of some sort. "It's called a 'Hamsa.' It protects against darkness."

Annette smiled her thanks and put the Hamsa around her neck.

The bookseller nodded. "Now we are safe. Come, you really must see the vault. It's quite impressive."

"I'll bet it's fuckin' impressive," said a voice behind them.

Annette and the bookseller turned to see a tall, thin, and pale young bald man pointing a gun at them. Annette didn't know much about guns, but she'd read enough detective novels and seen enough movies and television shows to recognize that the gun—whatever its make—was equipped with a silencer.

"Just give me the money, old man, and I won't hurt either one of you."

The bookseller calmly walked over to the register, hit a few of the keys, and the cash drawers popped out with a loud *ding!* He stepped back from the register and pointed at them. "There's about three hundred dollars there, maybe another twenty in change. Please take it and leave."

The gunman moved toward the register and began yanking out the bills, stuffing them into the pockets of his black leather jacket, never moving his gaze from the bookseller. When he finished emptying the drawers of the bills he slammed them closed and pointed the gun directly at the bookseller's chest; it was only then that Annette noticed all of the tattoos that covered the gunman's neck, but the one that stood out among the images of blood and violence depicted on his flesh was the large, dark swastika.

Oh, shit. A skinhead.

"Now," said the gunman, "how about we all go back and take...take a look at that vault of yours?" He was shaking, and seemed to be in pain.

"Are you all right, son?" said the bookseller, taking a step toward him.

"I ain't your son, you fuckin' kike!"

The bookseller stopped moving. If he was afraid, it didn't show on his face or in his eyes.

"'Kike'?" he said to the gunman. "Seriously, 'kike'? That's the best you can do? Oh, I admit, it has the tinge of nostalgia to it, but, really? 'Kike?' Is that all you've got?"

"Don't," said Annette. The gunman momentarily spun in her direction, pointing the gun at her shoulder, but then turned back to the bookseller.

"You r-really don't want to mess with me, heeb!"

The bookseller clapped his hands together. "*Heeb!* Now we're getting someplace. What's next—oh, wait, don't tell me, let me guess—um…what are some of the popular terms your brain-dead brethren like to bandy about? Oooh, how about 'himey' or 'Jewbacca' or 'matza-gobbler'—oh, no, I've got it! 'Easy-bake yid'! I haven't heard *that* one in a while, son."

The gunman clenched his teeth; whatever he was hurting for, it was getting bad. "I t-told you, don't call me son."

"Take the money and get out of here, please."

The gunman moved closer. "Not until you sh-show me what you've got stashed in that vault."

Annette was so scared she could barely breathe. What the hell did the old man think he was accomplishing, provoking the gunman like this?

The bookseller stood silent for a moment, and then said, "That's it? 'Not until you sh-show me what you've got stashed in that vault'? No racial slur at the end?" He made a *tsk*-ing sound and shook his head. "Losing your edge, son. What would your Aryan brothers say at the next meeting if they knew you dropped the ball like this?"

"*Shut up, motherfucker!*"

"Oh, *that's* original."

The gunman moved closer but the bookseller didn't budge from his spot. "Last chance, half-dick. Let's go back to the vault."

The bookseller shook his head. "I'm afraid I can't do that. Trust me, son, there's nothing back there that'll be of any value to you."

The gunman started laughing. A thin patina of perspiration covered his head and face, making him almost glow under the lights. "Ain't that just like a Jew? They'd rather die than part with any of their wealth." A sudden spasm ripped through his body and he started to double over; the gun went off and shot the bookseller. The round blew through the old man's shoulder with such ferocity that his blood spattered onto the gunman's face and hands. For a moment the bookseller remained standing, looking at the wound as it bled out, and then he looked at Annette with an unreadable expression and slowly sank to his knees.

Her fear suddenly gone, Annette rushed over and knelt beside the bookseller, holding him in her arms.

"Oh, Lord," croaked the old man. "I'd forgotten how much that *hurts.*"

"Don't move," she said, grabbing the edge of the handkerchief the old man used to wrap the Fitzgerald volume and pulling it. The book spun out and away, freed from its wrapping. Annette crumpled the handkerchief into a tight wad and used it to staunch the flow of blood from the bookseller's shoulder. "You'll be all right, you will."

The bookseller smiled his thanks to her, and then looked up toward the gunman. "*Please*," he said. "You *need to leave now.*"

"Not until you open that vault!"

The bookseller closed his eyes and sighed in resignation, and then looked at the gunman, pity in his gaze. "You poor, stupid, misguided son-of-a-bitch. It's already open."

The floor began to vibrate; it was just a low rumble at first—more of a thrum than an actual physical manifestation—but it quickly grew in strength and intensity.

The gunman looked around in panic. "What the—? Is this a goddamn *earthquake?*"

"Not exactly," said the bookseller. His eyes were filled with tears as he looked once more at the gunman and said, "I tried to get you to leave, son. I am truly sorry."

"For what?"

All around the store shelves began to tremble as their books shuddered, pushing against each other until there was no more room and they began falling, scattering over the floor as the glass-fronted cases began to shake and rattle, a few of the panes making loud crunching noises as spider-web cracks spread out from their centers. The cash register was shaking, its bells sounding softly but continuously, and as more shelves began to collapse Annette felt the floor beneath her shudder as if something large and fast like a subway train was roaring underneath them.

The vault, she thought. *They can communicate with each other. Oh, dear god.*

The roar of a freight train thundered up from the floor and became a deafening snarl as somewhere farther back in the store a door was splintered into a thousand pieces and its glass shattered, blowing outward with such force Annette could feel a few slivers of it hit the back of her neck.

"I'm so sorry," whispered the bookseller in her ear.

"I know," she whispered back, kissing the old man's forehead.

There was nothing they could do.

...our eternal life means the hunger never goes away. And we have been very, very hungry. And we have waited, here in this cramped, dark place. And we have found more of our brothers and sisters of the night. And they have waited with us.

But now...the scent. Brief and sweet, but enough to make our hunger all-consuming.

Our waiting ends again.

Now we feed.

A sea of books hurtled themselves through the air from the back of the store, pages snapping, dog-eared teeth chewing, filling the small bookstore with the sound of a thousand-thousand paper wings flapping in rage, flying around like panicked birds released from their cages for the first time in their lives, the prolonged *hsssssssss!* of a hundred thousand turning pages becoming almost deafening. The only sound louder was coming from the young man with the gun; he was screaming.

But the sounds of the books' snapping, gnawing pages quickly drowned out even that hideous noise as each dog-eared page found purchase in his flesh and slashed down, slicing, cutting, biting down, tearing through skin, shredding the material of his coat and the clothing beneath, each set of teeth puncturing deeper to make room for the next page's teeth to find fresh meat, fresh blood, fresh sustenance after so long imprisoned in dusty shadows where never a hand caressed their covers, never an eye read their words, never a warm fingertip stroked their sharp, waiting, numbered corners.

For one brief moment, the pile of raw hamburger that was once a young man with a gun staggered around, eyes not yet dropping from ruined sockets, and looked straight at Annette. There was pleading in its gaze, confusion, maybe even remorse.

Annette could only mange to say, "… so sorry…" before her throat hitched and she couldn't speak.

The meat-pile opened what might have been a mouth to issue something that might have been a scream, but nothing came out; no sound, no meat, no blood.

It took only a few more minutes, but soon there was nothing left of the young man with the gun except his weapon and the shredded rags that had once been the clothes he'd worn. Even his bones had been consumed.

The books, still scattered over the floor, shuddered as their pages drank in the blood, absorbed every bit of essence contained there, pages so bloated it looked as if the books would never be able to close again, stories so engorged it was hard to believe they would ever return to legibility, but soon enough the pages began to contract, to smooth out, return to normal; slowly, the pages fell back into place, neat as you please, as the covers came to close once again, one by one, book by book, tome by tome, until, at last, had anyone come in or looked through the display window, they would have seen (very neat) stacks and stacks of books and empty shelves along the walls, and they would have thought to themselves, *Oh, they must be cleaning up in there*, and gone about their business.

After a few moments, the bookseller reached up and took hold of Annette's hand. "We need to…to clean up."

Shaking the tears from her eyes, Annette shook her head. "Screw that— we need to get you to a hospital."

"How do you propose we explain this? There's no body."

Annette stood up and gently pulled the bookseller up with her. "Put your weight against me."

"It's not *that* bad."

"Tell that to my coat and blouse." Both were soaked in the bookseller's blood.

They made their way over to the counter and the bookseller sat down on a small stool. "Thank you for being so kind," he said.

Annette touched the Hamsa around her neck. "Thank *you* for protecting me."

The bookseller reached under his tie and behind his shirt collar, pulling out a similar Hamsa. "Don't leave home without it. Hey...will you...will you come back tomorrow and help me? The books have gorged themselves. They'll be sleeping for a good while. You won't be in any danger. Will you come back?"

"Come back? What the hell makes you think I'm going to leave your side anytime soon?"

The bookseller smiled. "Uri once said the same thing to me."

"Yeah, well...just don't ever call me that. My name is Annette."

"Mine is Saul."

"Nice to meet you."

"The pleasure is mine, dear lady. The pleasure is most definitely mine."

Annette found the telephone—a rotary-dial, it figured—and dialed 911. They'd get their stories straight before the police and EMTs arrived.

The bookseller looked down at the gunman's clothing and weapon and sadly shook his head. "And to think," he whispered, as much to himself as to his new friend, "Hitler wanted to conquer the world."

Consumers

At the New and Shiny Big-Box Store there's an old fellow who greets you when you come through the doors. His uniform is blue and well-pressed, his shoes shiny, his white hair glowing under the overhead lights, his voice tattered at the edges (he is, after all, an old fellow, and perhaps he drank or smoked too much in his younger days), and he smiles at you as if someone has just stuck a gun in his back and told him to act natural.

"Welcome," he says. "Thank you for shopping with us. If you need any help, please don't be afraid to ask." It doesn't matter a damn that you have just entered the store and have yet to buy anything, this is the way he greets everyone, with those memorized words and his gun-in-the-back smile. Were you to stop long enough and look in his eyes, you might see behind them something that is nailed down and in torment, even fear and horror, like a drowning victim too far from the shore who can do nothing more than wave their arms and cry out in futile hope that someone will hear them and they will be rescued.

"Don't forget to grab one of our fliers and check out today's sales," he says, his voice an offshore echo as the customers walk away.

At the New and Shiny Big-Box Store there is always a sale going on, always a blue-green-orange special in one aisle or another. Perhaps it's one of these brightly lit sales that the woman is hurrying to, carrying her toddler. She barely glances at the greeter as she makes her way to the shopping cart rack and, after a brief struggle, frees one from the corral. Her toddler—and a cute little one he is, perhaps eleven months at most—giggles and grabs at her with his tiny arms as she places him in the upper seat, as if it's some kind of game they've played a thousand times but to him never gets old. After that, it's on to the back of the store, near the Hardware and Home Repair area where no customers are elbowing their way past others to get to a sales item. The woman parks the cart next to the motor oil section, glancing around to make certain no one can see her. After a few moment she opens her purse and pulls out a small but well-used stuffed toy, an elephant missing one of its tusks, and gives it to the toddler, who excitedly snatches it from her hand and hugs it to his chest, squeezing it within an inch of its life. The mother leans down and gives her son a kiss on his forehead, brushes a hand through his hair so less of it is hanging in his eyes. Without a word or another glance she turns around and walks away. The toddler covers his eyes as if counting to ten while playing Hide and Seek. When he pulls them away his mother does not reappear. For a moment he is frightened, but then squeezes his toy elephant once more as if to say, *It's all right, Mommy will be back in a second.* And there in the cart he waits.

At the New and Shiny Big-Box Store it's not unusual to see an employee or department manager peeking out from behind the windows of swinging metal doors that lead back into the storage area, and today is no exception: a middle-aged gentleman watches from behind the swinging doors as the mother kisses the toddler on the forehead and turns and walks away. The manager waits a few moments to make certain no one is around, and then exits the storage area and approaches the cart. The toddler looks up at him and smiles. The manager smiles back, and then slowly pushes the cart down a few aisles, to the back of the Home Lighting department. The manager grabs a lamp from one of the displays, removes the shade, and places it to the side of the cart. He then reaches into the pocket of his manager's smock and removes the head of a toy doll, which he jams into place atop the bell that protects the bulb. Without looking at the toddler—who seems somehow larger than before—he walks over to a wall phone, lifts the receiver, presses a button, and says for the entire store to hear, "Shoppers, we've got a special over in our Toy Department. All the latest *Star Wars* toys are thirty percent off for the next fifteen minutes. A Toy Department employee will be happy to put one of our green-light stickers on the item of your choice." He hangs up and walks away. By now the little boy in the cart is crying—not a lot, not enough to draw the attention of any shopper who's all but running to the toy department, but enough that even a hug from the elephant can't stop the quiet tears.

At the New and Shiny Big-Box Store, you can always find a child who is crying.

At the New and Shiny Big-Box Store a line is forming at the Customer Service desk, and the woman who abandoned her toddler in the Hardware and Home Repair aisle is right at the front. She removes an envelope from her purse and hands it to the young man working the desk. He opens it, reads what is written on the piece of paper inside, nods to himself, and then begins pulling several thick books of coupons from a shelf below. He continues to stack the coupon books until there are twenty-five of them. The woman pulls a plastic bag from her purse, sweeps the coupons into it until the bag threatens to burst, smiles at the young man, and then leaves the store, still smiling.

At the New and Shiny Big-Box Store many people leave smiling.

At the New and Shiny Big-Box Store the little boy in the cart is trying to wiggle his way out of the cart but his legs have gotten a bit too long and a bit too chubby. By now he's all cried out and has nothing to hug because he's dropped his elephant. He's been moved several times, and each time someone jams a doll's head onto a lamp and places it near the cart. The boy watches as customers whiz by, on their way to a special sale that seems to be in a department on the opposite end of the store. And so the little boy waits, but he doesn't have to wait long.

At the New and Shiny Big-Box Store no one ever has to wait very long.

Soon the little boy becomes a larger boy who has split through most of his toddler clothing; soon the young boy is nearly naked, his privates covered only by the remnants of the clothes he was wearing when his mother brought him here; soon the young boy is a grown man whose weight the cart can no longer hold upright. The cart flips foreword, knocking over many of the impaled dolls' heads that scatter like marbles. The force of the falling cart is enough to free the young man's legs—a light shade of purple they seem to have become—and then falls over him as if it were a cage being lowered from above. The young man huddles beneath the cart, still crying, and tries to reach for his elephant, but it's on the other side of the cart. They young man tries to reach it but cannot get the cart to budge. Eventually he gives up, huddles in a fetal position, and wishes that someone walking toward the next sale would notice him. But no one does, even when he calls out to them in a voice that sounds frayed around the edges. He stays like that until he can no longer call out or even muster the tears to cry. He stays like that until his skin begins to wrinkle and his hair turns gray. He stays like that until the first manager to move the toddler's cart emerges from the storage area and lifts the cart off the old man. The manager helps the old man to his feet and begins to dress him in the new, bright, shiny, perfectly pressed uniform of a store employee. "Keeping this clean is your responsibility," says the manager. "It has to be dry cleaned, not washed." Helping the old man to put on his New and Shiny shoes, the manager walks the old man to the front of the store, explaining more of the store's employee policies.

"The most important thing," says the manager as he positions the old man by the entryway, "is to smile when you greet the customers. Remember that." He walks away, leaving the old man standing there, alone and confused. But then the old man sees a young woman come into the store holding a toddler, and a cute little thing he is. "Welcome," he says. "Thank you for shopping with us. If you need any help, please don't be afraid to ask." He watches as the mother puts her little stinker in a cart, hands him a small stuffed elephant missing a tusk, and makes her way back toward Hardware and Home Repair. "Thank you," the old man whispers, but it sounds more like a question.

At the New and Shiny Big-Box Store there's an old fellow who greets you when you come through the doors....

The Music of Bleak Entrainment

You should see the expression on your face right now—all the trouble you've been through in order to get the clearance to interview me, and I start off by talking about household appliances and math instead of those twelve people I killed. Not that anyone gives more of damn about them now than they did ten years ago—after all, what'd the world lose? A dozen mental patients who were a drain on society's pocketbook. None of them were ever going to be released, they were lifers, and as far as I ever knew none of them had any living family.

Huh? Do I feel *bad* about it? What the fuck kind of Journalism 101 question is that? No, I don't feel bad—I feel *horrible* about it. You weren't there, you didn't see those faces, those eyes…Christ. Those lonely, isolated, frightened eyes.

You want to know something that the news reports back then never mentioned? *Not a one of them tried to run away*, to get to safety. It was like shooting tin ducks at a carnival booth. Hell, some of them seemed to *welcome* it.

I tried to explain everything to the authorities at the time but I was pretty…out of control. No, wait, scratch that—I was so fucking *scared* it was like I wasn't even *me* any longer, I was trapped somewhere inside myself just watching it all happen and…ah, never mind. But I'll tell you the same thing I told my lawyer and the court—I was *not* insane. Not for one second.

As you can tell from our posh surroundings and this lovely canvas jacket with the wraparound arms that I'm sporting, they didn't believe me.

Look, it all started because Steve and I got this idea about using entrainment to visually illustrate how the human body can—

—excuse me? Oh, sorry.

It's been proven that externally imposed sound vibrations can have a profound influence on our physiology. We've all experienced this phenomenon—it's called entrainment. Say you're sitting in your kitchen trying to balance your checkbook and you begin to notice that your shoulders are hunched up and your back is tighter than normal. Suddenly the refrigerator snaps off and you heave a sigh of relief. Your shoulders drop, your back loosens up, and your whole breathing pattern changes. What do you think just happened? Certain biological rhythms have unconsciously "entrained" themselves to the 60 cycle hum of the refrigerator's motor.

Right—*sound* caused your body to temporarily alter itself from within.

Think you can bear with me for a minute or two while I bore you with some specifics?

No, *Steve* was the Music major. I was the Physics dude.

I was doing some research into the work of Hans Jenny. He was a Swiss doctor, artist, and researcher who helped pioneer the field of Cymatics—which is basically a very specified and intensely focused form of entrainment, geared toward using sound and vibrational waves to heal the human body. He followed the work of a German physicist and acoustician named Ernst Chladni who, toward the end of the 18th century, created intricate sand patterns by vibrating a steel plate with a violin bow. Jenny employed the modern technology of the day to carry out more precisely replicable experiments. He used a sine wave generator and a speaker to vibrate various powders, pastes, and liquids, and succeeded in making visible the subtle power through which sound *physically structures* matter.

Now, imagine hearing a tone, and watching as sound waves involute an inert blob of kaolin paste, animating it through various phases in a nearly perfect replica of cellular division—or watching as a pile of sand is transformed into life-like flowing patterns, mirroring fractals—the symmetrical geometric forms found in nature—simply by *audible vibration*.

Jenny described our bodies as being "nested hierarchies of vibrational frequencies" which appear as discrete systems functioning within larger, more complicated systems, which themselves are contained within even larger and more complex vibrational structures, right? *All physical existence* is determined by vibrational frequencies and their formative effects on matter.

You can view the whole universe in this way, from sub-atomic particles to the most intricate life forms, to the nebulae and galaxies themselves—all are resonating fields of pulsating energy in constant interaction with one another. The science of it all aside, I find it profoundly moving to think that sound in all its forms might very well be the glue that holds our consensual reality together.

I was really excited about this when I was explaining it to Steve, and I didn't want to bore him, so I started putting it in musical terms. The universe exists—beneath all or most other layers of perception—as essentially a vibrating-string note among a wild symphony of equally vibrating harmonic or non-harmonic quantum notes being played on similar strings—

—*yes*, like an orchestra. Exactly like an orchestra.

Steve asked me if it were possible to show him how this process worked, so he and I repeated one of Jenny's early experiments. We placed a small wooden ring containing about 20 cc. of kaolin paste on top of a magnifying lens, then attached a crystal to the lens and applied a small sound current, creating a specific vibration...which can vary, depending upon the frequency or the current if you apply electricity directly. Just as a speaker vibrates, displacing air and creating specific sound waves according to the frequencies it's subjected to, the vibrating crystal transmitted its oscillations from the sound current frequencies, through the lens, and directly into the paste sample. Light was projected up from beneath the lens, through the paste, and into a camera lens looking down from above. I was able to photograph the disturbances—the standing wave patterns—created in the paste as it vibrated in response to the sine waves—the music—to which it was subjected. Steve played some of his recent composition on the cello, which was attached to the lens by a string of piano wire. A bit on the primitive side, I admit, but effective nonetheless. The moment was captured, then it was just a simple matter of instantly freezing the shape the paste assumed and encasing it in amber.

No, we *didn't* freeze sound, we froze a specific instance of sound physically altering matter.

The next thing we did was even simpler. We ran the music through a basic computer visualizing program—you know, one of those extras that come bundled in with music-playing software? Right. We decided to use the Fractal Pattern option, and I gotta tell you, the flow of images that accompanied the music was quite lovely. So now we had both the music and the fractal visualization for sensory input.

This really got us both going.

Steve had just finished a new composition—he hadn't given it a title yet, he always sucked at titles, anyway—but he was stressing over it because something was missing. He kept lamenting how it was impossible to gauge a person's emotional reaction to music, aside from what they themselves would tell you after hearing it.

I thought of Jenny and Chladni.

I thought of all the Cymatic equipment gathering dust in the Bioacoustics Department.

And I thought about how both Steve and I were in danger of losing our scholarships if we didn't come up with a term-end project that would floor everyone.

Have you heard the piece of music that Steve composed for the initial phase of the experiment? No? Too bad—it's a beautiful piece of work.

It begins with an acoustic guitar rhythmically picking out four simple notes, the sound of raindrops pinging against a cold autumn window, four austere notes that remain constant and never change, then builds in musical and emotional intensity, culminating in a three-minute finale where the guitar is joined and then *replaced* by an orchestra whose individual instruments complement the underlying four-note foundation in the same way that wind, thunder, and lightning accompany a sudden spring downpour. The music is both glorious and sad, tinged at the edges with a certain disquieting darkness, an unnamable fear that we all experience during strong storms; as this section nears its end the four-note foundation suddenly stops, leaving only the melancholy musings of the other instruments, which mix into one another like the stray thoughts of one for whom the rhythm of the rain brings a sense of peace, but when robbed of that rhythm, when finding there is no longer the hypnotic pinging of those raindrops against the cold autumn window, is left to their own devices, slowly succumbing to the sadness and disquieting fear that the sound of the rain had helped them avoid facing. In these final moments one could close one's eyes and easily picture the drab gray sky and the cheerless, soaked, bleak world.

Initially, we decided to use individuals, people we knew. They'd come into one of the acoustically-tiled rehearsal rooms and sit in a chair, I'd hook them up to the EKG and EEG machines, and then Steve would play a recording of the piece for them while the fractal program was projected through an LCD screen. The EKG and EEG machines would measure their physiological reactions during the music while watching the LCD, and that was the extent of their participation.

After three or four people had done this, both Steve and I realized that, well, most of our friends had high blood pressure, for one thing, but more than that, there was no way to holistically quantify the results—at least, not the way we were doing it. All we had was a series of readouts to show how these people's bodies reacted to the music, nothing to prove that Cymatic theory was even applicable.

Then Steve got this bright idea about incorporating synthesizers into the experiment. I had to do a lot of begging and fast talking to the Bioacoustics Department heads, and I have *no* idea what Steve said to the bigwigs of the Music Department, but we were both given access to the equipment we needed.

I got the use of an EEG- and EKG-measurement/interpreter that served as a conduit between the EEG and EKG machines and the synthesizer bank. The M/I had once been used for Cymatic experimentation—specifically the direct estimations of the main parameters of neurons—time constant of integration, level of internal noise, etc.—received by the cells, or for our purposes, the auditory reactions located on different levels—or in this case, the subjects—hooked up to the system.

I'm sorry, I'm getting off on a technical tangent. I'll try to put it in simpler terms, but I make no promises. After all, I'm crazy, aren't I?

The basic experiment remained unchanged. A subject would come into one of the rooms and we'd hook them up to the EEG and EKG machines and then have them listen to the music and watch the fractal program, only instead of just getting a simple readout of their physiological reactions during the music, those reactions were filtered through the M/I into the synthesizer's computer where they were interpreted as an actual auditory event.

The computer then took all of this catalogued information and fed it into the output ports of the synthesizer banks, which—employing the information received from the M/I—assigned each set of recorded physiological reactions a specific musical scale, as well as a virtual instrument to play the individual notes within that scale.

This took all of maybe forty minutes—the piece was short, otherwise we'd've been looking at days, even weeks, of data processing. Anyway, the person was asked to come back in an hour, and when they did, they got to listen to a musical interpretation of their physiological reaction to the original piece of music, as well as watch a visual representation *of* those physiological reactions.

Steve and I were both stunned that it worked.

So we took it a step further. After we'd done this with half a dozen test subjects, we decided, just for shits and giggles, to play all six reaction pieces simultaneously. Now, all of them were in the same key—the computer had been programmed to make certain of that—but that's where any similarities in the pieces should have ended. But that wasn't the case.

Incredible as it sounds, when all six of those reaction recordings were played back simultaneously, they *fit together*. It was as if someone had taken a pre-existing piece of music and broken it up into six isolated parts. Individually, these six reaction recordings were pleasant enough, okay? No real melody to speak of, but not discordant, either. Each one was like a musical tone poem.

But when we combined them, they created an almost *complete* piece of music.

Are you getting this, Miss Reporter? Think about everything I've told you up to this point and apply it to those results.

All consciousness is connected as a primary wavefront phenomenon that allows us not only to resonate to such notes, but to play a few of our own back here where we sit among the other quantum woodwinds!

Which means, like it or not, that there exists some *base* wavefront to which all others are connected. I wouldn't go so far as to call it God, but…it gave me pause, that's for certain.

But it didn't stop there. We noticed there were sounds on the periphery of the music, soft chattering noises, so Steve made a master recording and started to isolate the sounds. It never occurred to us to play it with the visualization program—we were too excited about the music and the sounds. Maybe if it *had* occurred to us to run it with the fractal program, things would've…never mind. Shoulda-woulda-coulda. You could make yourself crazy cataloguing all the what-ifs.

So we started concentrating on the Cymatic side of the experiment. If these wavefronts, these vibrational frequencies, could also be employed to heal the body, then why not go for it? We'd proven—at least to ourselves— that there was a definite *structure* underneath all of this, so the question became, how do we *apply* it?

We didn't have to wait too long for our answer. Of the six people who participated in the original phase of the experiment, *four* of them reported that they'd been feeling better since doing so. One girl who suffered from migraine headaches—she told us she got at least one every two weeks, on average—told us that she hadn't gotten a headache in almost a month. Another guy, a halfback on the university football team, had been having severe problems with his back and was on the verge of being cut. *He* came back to tell us that whatever was wrong with his back, it had cleared up since he'd helped us out. Another person who'd been having problems with insomnia started sleeping like a baby, and the fourth person, who'd been on antidepressants for years, suddenly started feeling *fine*. She stopped taking her medication, and hadn't suffered any setbacks.

Word of this got to the head of the Psychology Department, and he requested to see all our data. We were more than happy to show him—hell, we'd documented everything from the first minute we began—and he was impressed, so much so that he suggested we take the experiment to the next level.

One of the things Jenny had attempted was to use Cymatics as a way to treat mental illness—entraining misfired synapses in the brain to fall into a steady, predictable pattern. So what effect might genuine madness have on the structure of things, and vice-versa?

The Psychology Director made arrangements for us to conduct the experiment on a handful of schizophrenics at the state mental hospital. I was amazed he was able to arrange all of this so quickly, but he pointed out that there was nothing about the experiment that put anyone in danger; it was a simple measurement of physiological reactions to auditory and visual data.

The only difference was that, this time, we'd be doing it with a dozen people simultaneously. The hospital had more than enough EKG and EEG machines to supply us.

So everything was arranged, and off we went.

The first part of the experiment went beautifully. The patients sat there and watched the screen and listened to the music—Steve's original composition, not the reaction recording—and then we made arrangements to come back in two days and play the results.

There was no deviation. Each of the twelve reaction pieces were the same kinds of tone poems that we'd gotten before, and just like the original batch of recordings, these twelve pieces, when played simultaneously, created a single melody. And just like the first series, there was that *chattering* on the periphery.

Steve had isolated the original chattering, but it was gibberish—a bunch of monosyllabic noises, like grunts or hums. This new series of noises was just more of the same, but then we overlapped the two sets of noises…and I suppose that was the moment we damned ourselves, because when combined, the two sets of noises formed a *chant*, some sort of…I don't know…incantation—Steve was the one who called that one. He said something about the rhythms and tonal phrasings matching those of Gregorian religious music led him to believe it was a chant of some kind. Neither one of us recognized the language—assuming it *was* an actual language. We thought about taking it to the Language Department, but that would have delayed the second part of the experiment at the state hospital, so we just added that to our To Do list for afterward.

By this time, the two of us were the talk of the university. Even though the term wasn't over, we received notification that not only would we remain on scholarship, but would be receiving a small stipend to help continue our work—hell, the Bioacoustics Department even decided to resurrect the Cymatics program for the next term. We were stars.

A week later we went back to the state hospital to perform the second half of the experiment. Besides the original twelve patients, the state hospital director was present, as were two armed security guards and the head of the university's Psychology Department.

The patients' chairs were arranged in a half-circle in front of the large LCD screen. The hospital director and Psychology Department head sat in chairs a few feet off to the left of the group, and one security guard stood at each end of the half-circle of chairs. Steve and I were hunched over the equipment in a far corner of the room, a good ten feet away from everyone.

The lights were lowered, and we began the playback. Steve had made two master recordings; one of the patients' reactions, and one wherein their reactions were combined with those of the original test subjects. We'd programmed the system to play these back to back.

During the playback of the patients' reaction recording, Steve and I began to notice that the Fractal Visualization program wasn't behaving normally; instead of showing a cascading series of images, it was showing bits and pieces of the same image over and over, sometimes combining pieces, but more often just displaying a flash here, a section there. The patients themselves seemed utterly transfixed by it all, so we made a note and sat back to watch what would happen during the next playback.

The patients' reaction recording segued seamlessly into the combined recording, but this time, even though Steve had done nothing to amplify the chanting, the words could be clearly heard: *Iä-R'lyeh! Cthullhu fhtagn! Iä! Iä!*

We looked at one another. The chanting was the same volume as the music itself, and we had done nothing to alter the recording.

Iä-R'lyeh! Cthullhu fhtagn! Iä! Iä!

It didn't take long to figure out why. Many of the patients were moving in their chairs, rocking back and forth, and repeating the chant over and over.

Iä-R'lyeh! Cthullhu fhtagn! Iä! Iä!

I was watching the reactions of the hospital director and the head of the Psychology Department when I felt Steve's hand grip my forearm and squeeze. I looked at him, and he pointed toward the screen.

I don't know if I can find the words to describe the image I saw displayed there. It looked at first like some kind of huge squid with its writhing feelers whipping and curling all over the screen, but the more the music played and the louder the patients' chanting became, the more the image began to solidify.

It wasn't a squid, not exactly—whatever this thing was, it had the *head* of a squid. Its shoulders were dark and massive, and it was *reacting* to the chant and music. Saw something like a clawed hand press against the screen and almost laughed, it seemed so absurd.

But then the screen itself began to…and I know how this is going to sound…the screen began to bend and expand, almost as if it were melting outward.

Iä-R'lyeh! Cthullhu fhtagn! Iä! Iä!

And then it happened: a tentacle moved forward from the screen and out toward the patients. The air was suddenly filled with the stench of dampness and rot. Both Steve and I started choking as soon as the stink hit us, and I saw, for one brief moment, the tip of another tentacle push outward as the screen continued to expand.

Both security guards unholstered their weapons and began firing at the tentacle, but by then the second one was fully free and they…Christ, they never had a chance. Each of them was grabbed by a tentacle that wound around their torsos, lifted them from the ground, and began crushing them. They dropped their weapons as blood began fountaining from their mouths and by this time the hospital director was running for the alarm and the head of the Psychology Department was screaming for us to turn everything off, turn it off now, and we did, we yanked the cords and hit the switches *but the music continued*, it grew in volume and intensity as the screen kept expanding and more tentacles began slithering through, only now I could see the first few clawed fingers tearing through the scrim, and I realized that whatever this *thing* was, it was the size of a small mountain on its side of the screen, but when it emerged into our world, it easily tripled in mass and if it somehow managed to get all the way through....

I started to move—where I was going or what I was going to do, I had no idea, it just seemed to me that it was important that I *do something, anything* to ground myself, to get a hold on matters, to somehow come to grips with this... this *nightmare* that was unfolding before my eyes, so I began to move and my foot kicked against something solid and when I looked down I saw one of the security guard's guns and I grabbed it up and fired into the nearest tentacle, but it slammed me aside and grabbed the Psychology Department head while another took care of the hospital director, and within seconds there were four crushed, thrashing, bleeding bodies bouncing around in the air above our heads like marionettes and I couldn't move without having blood rained down on my face and in my eyes, and that's when I realized that the music and the chanting were coming from the patients themselves, many of whom had risen from their chairs and fallen to their knees, arms reaching upward, imploring, giving me my answer, telling me that, yes, all consciousness is connected as a primary wavefront phenomenon that allows us not only to resonate to such notes, but to play a few of our own back here and that there *was* a base wavefront to which all of them are connected, and I would have been wrong calling that base God but not *a* god, because right here, right now, that god was pushing through the boundaries of perception to reclaim some part of the world over which it once must have ruled and, ohGod, God, *God*, there was no way to stop it, no way to send it back because the nested hierarchies of vibrational frequencies that had opened this doorway were no longer under the control of our machines, they were in the control of those kneeling before this god and howling *Iä-R'lyeh! Cthullhu fhtagn! Iä! Iä!*, and for a moment I was paralyzed with this knowledge, and then I saw Steve's broken, bleeding body dance across the air over my head and I did the only thing I *could* do, I scrambled on hands and knees to find the gun that I had dropped, and I found not only it but the other guard's gun, as well, and I ran to the front of the room and I began firing at each end every one of their heads. Some of them looked at me before I killed them, and their eyes...ohgod, their confused, frightened eyes...there were in the grips of some form of rapture that was both euphoric and terrifying and they couldn't choose, they couldn't fight against it—maybe they didn't *want* to fight against it, I'll never know—but I killed them, I killed all of them, and with the death of each one some part of this thing, this god, this monster, this creature of rot and death and putrescence, recoiled back into the screen until it was done, until they all lay dead at my feet, and I faced the screen and I saw it *looking* at me, sitting very still, and I *felt* as much as heard its voice vibrate through my body.

You have shown me the way back, and here I will wait, for I will not have to wait long. Thank you for this music of bleak entrainment, this song that will very soon call me home.

I was in the process of removing the discs when the authorities arrived.

And that, as the saying goes, is that.

What? Yes, I know I was charged in all seventeen deaths, but I'm telling you for the record—for all the good it will do—that I only *purposefully* killed twelve people. Though I suppose, in a way, I did kill them all.

Now let me ask you something—*why* are you here? I mean, I've been locked up in here for one-third of my life and you're the first reporter to show up here since the initial circus right after it happened. What's going on that's made me the focus of interest all of a sudden?

They *what?*

Oh, dear God...who's got them? When were they found? Have they been played yet?

Listen to me—*they must never be played again*, do you understand? *Never.* Because that's what it's waiting for, what it's been listening for ever since that night. Please, *please*, tell whoever has them that those discs must *not* be—

—why are you calling for the doctors? There's no need to—

—hello, folks, look, yes, I got a little excited, but she's got to be made to understand that—oh, Christ, not with the needle again, wait, wait one second, *just give me ten fucking seconds and I'll—*

—ohgod—

—please tell them, *please*, I beg you...don't play the discs...never play them...because...if you do...he'll come home...

...feeling so tired now...so tired...

...he's still listening...he'll always be listening...

...sing him no songs, or the world will never sing again....

Onlookers

"...all those bodies which compose the mighty frame of the world have not any subsistence without a mind—that their being is to be perceived or known."
—George Berkeley (1685-1753)

"It is a simple equation: take me, subtract film, and the solution is zero."
—Akira Kurosawa

They are filming something on the street, in front of our house, very close to the front door.

Even though he can't see them when he pulls up his blinds or pushes aside one of the curtains, my six-year-old son Brian senses that someone is watching. After dismissing his claims as "an overactive imagination," Dianne, my wife, finally admitted to feeling the same way, though with the nervous, slightly embarrassed, maybe-I'm-just-full-of-shit-today laugh she always uses whenever she can't put her finger on what's bothering her. So far neither of them have directly asked me what I think, how I feel, do I believe them or not.

I think this is exactly what the Onlookers want, for you to convince yourself that it's just your imagination playing tricks on you; it'll make the work easier for them, and perhaps less terrifying and painful for the rest of us, if and when we cumulatively figure out what's happening; after all, isn't perception both perceiving *and being* perceived? If the Onlookers are edging us toward a state of non-being without our knowing it, then what can we do to stop it, to re-balance the equation, to perceive while being perceived?

My wife and son are fading before my eyes, you see; and more than once in the last few days, both have asked me if I've been losing weight, which means I am lessening in their perception, as well.

All around, the colors of our life become paler. There is a dogwood tree in our back yard, and the red spots on all the leaves have turned to the same foggy gray as an old black-and-white film; as have many of the leaves on the other trees; as has much of the grass.

Dianne and Brian say I'm too pale lately. (Dianne called it "looking a bit gray around the gills.")

I can't bring myself to tell them they look the same to me.

They are filming something on the street, in front of our house, very close to the front door.

Something tells me they're going to want their interior shots soon, before they lose the light.

I don't think there's any way I can stop them.

I first saw the Onlookers when I was a child, but had no idea what they were, what they wanted, or of what they were capable.

In the summer of 1964, when I was five, my father—who sold medical supplies—took my mother and me along on a business trip to New York. Spending nearly a third of every year on the road, Dad always felt bad because we'd never had a "proper" family vacation; rightly thinking that Mom and I got sick of spending every summer stuck in Cedar Hill, he hoped this "madcap excursion in the wilds" (as he called it, like it was going to be some Great Adventure worthy of Jules Verne) would suffice.

We had a wonderful time, as I recall (being only five, my memories are divided into two categories: the bus, taxi, or subway ride *to* someplace in the city, and the *cool* stuff I got to do once we arrived).

Dad was meeting with some doctors whose offices were on the Upper West Side in the 140s, near the Hudson River, and for a few hours Mom and I were left to our own devices—which meant sightseeing and shopping.

We'd just left a restaurant where I'd had the best ice cream sundae in the history of ice cream sundaes (that I ate way too quickly; it would later come back to haunt me with a stomach ache) and were heading for some boring old antique store when we rounded the corner and walked right into a movie—or, rather, the movie walked into us, in the form of a hunched, roundish man in a dark coat that was far too heavy for the summer weather. His head was down so that his face was buried behind the high upturned collar of the coat; all I could see of him was that coat and the gray, flattened hat he wore (which Dad later told me was called a "pork pie" hat).

The man bumped into Mom, almost knocking her over (he was walking *very* fast and seemed to be trying to get away from something), then veered left and plowed straight into me.

I spun around, arms pinwheeling, trying to catch my balance, tripped over my own feet, fell backward against one of the sawhorses, went over, tried to twist around so I didn't crack my skull on the pavement, and landed on the other side on my butt. I immediately began crying; everything hurts more when you're five years old, and it *especially* hurts more when it happens in a big, strange, scary city that seems like it could eat visitors from Ohio for breakfast and still want a second helping.

I looked up, hoping to see Mom's face lowering toward me; instead she stood frozen, having just seen the face of the man in the coat and porkpie hat.

And that's when I saw my first Onlooker.

My head and vision were still swimming from the tumble—everyone and everything around me seemed to be spiraling—so it took a moment for me to realize that one of the people in the crowd had a camera for a head; to my momentarily skewed five-year-old's perception, that's what it looked like: instead of a human head, one of those old-fashioned oversized box cameras sat atop their shoulders, and on either side of the box, like the eyes of a horse, a half-sphere of metal blinked opened and closed with a soft metallic *shnick!* (no, I couldn't actually hear them, but I imagined that to be the sound these "eyes" made when they blinked). For a moment all I could do was stare at this weird but wonderful thing in the back of the crowd, then the pain from my fall fully registered and the world was lost under a heavy wash of tears that blurred everything into one shimmering mass; I pulled in a deep breath, wiped my eyes on my shirt sleeve, and looked up to see that the scary man in the dark coat was now on one knee and reaching for me.

"Hey there, little fellah," he said in a deep, croaky voice that sounded like it belonged to some old monster frog. "Took a little tumble there, did you? I'm sorry—didn't see you. But if you don't mind me saying, you can take a fall with the best of them!"

Mom laughed when he said that, and I cried all the harder because here she was, laughing at something this scary man in the dark coat said when she ought to be down here giving me hugs and telling me it was all right and promising me another ice cream sundae if I was brave. I looked around to see if Camera-Head was still nearby—the memory of it made me want to laugh and I figured if I saw it again I'd laugh and everything would be all right—then I saw the kneeling man's face and screamed.

I'd never actually seen someone with an eye patch in person; sure, there had been all those pirate movies, people *always* wore eye patches in those, but that was just pretend; the scary man in the porkpie hat had one for real and it was *so* scary. I tried backing away from him like a crab but then hit the curb behind me and almost did a somersault into the street.

Mom and the scary, one-eyed man applauded.

I stopped crying; my butt and back still hurt, but now I was just pissed, so I scowled at both of them.

"That's quite the little tumbler you got there," said One-Eye Porkpie, turning toward my mother, who introduced herself and shook his hand like she was meeting President Johnson or Elvis.

One-Eye Porkpie removed his hat and waved to a bunch of people with cameras and microphones and lights who were behind him (Camera-Head wasn't among them, either, and I wondered: had he been trying to run away from these people?), and that's when I realized that I'd landed on something that looked like a train track, and that one of the cameras that had been following One-Eye Porkpie was setting in a wagon of some sort that was attached to the tracks. I was suddenly terrified that the camera wagon was going to roll right over and cut me in half, but it stopped moving when One-Eye Porkpie waved. I thought it was weird that he'd been running *away* from the camera, because it seemed to me it hadn't been going all *that* fast.

Mom looked down at me and smiled. "It's all right, hon, he's not going to hurt you."

"Wouldn't hurt a fly," said One-Eye Porkpie in his froggy voice, helping me up.

Mom dug into her massive shoulder bag and removed the Cine-Kodak 8 Model 90 home movie camera that Dad had insisted she carry, "in case you see any movie or TV stars." She'd never been able to operate it properly, and as she chatted with One-Eye Porkpie she fumbled around with it until he took it from her and got it going.

"Wanna be in a movie with me, little fellah?" he asked me.

"My name's Patrick," I said, trying to sound grown-up.

"Is it now? Well, mine's Joseph," he replied, offering his hand. "Pleased to meet you."

Mom spent the next ten minutes filming him clowning around with me; at one point he made a big show of shaking out his hands and reaching behind my left ear to remove a shiny silver dollar, then did the same with my right ear. (He let me keep them, and that made him less scary, though it didn't help my butt from being any less sore).

As we were getting ready to leave (a man Mom said was "the director" told everyone they needed to get moving because they had a schedule to keep), Porkpie called over a sweet-faced woman he introduced as "my wife and official handler, Eleanor," and asked her to take some pictures of him and me. At one point, he removed his hat and put it on my head.

"Say there, little fell—'scuse me, *Patrick*—that hat looks right at home on your noggin." He looked at his wife. "Don't you think it looks right at home?'

She and Mom both agreed that it did. I thought it felt like it was going to drop down and eat my face, it was so big.

"You okay there, Patrick?" One-Eye Porkpie asked.

To which I responded, with all the tact of a child: "What happened to your eye?"

He laughed, then flipped up the patch to show me his other eye was still there. "Nothing. They just wanted me to wear it in this movie."

"How come?"

He leaned forward, whispering: "Heck, I have *no idea*. I guess they think it makes me look creepy or tragic or something. But it's want they wanted, and they're paying me to act, not think or ask questions, so I go along with it."

"Just pretend, huh?"

He nodded. "Just pretend, that's right."

Porkpie knelt down beside me for a few more pictures. He smelled like cigarettes and medicine. "I think you ought to keep that hat, is what I think, Patrick."

"But it's your only one."

Everyone around us laughed.

"I bet maybe I got a couple more around here someplace," he said, winking at me. "Besides, it ought to belong to a little buster like yourself."

"What's a buster?"

Another laugh. "That's a nickname Harry Houdini gave me when I was born. It means some little fellah like you that can take a tumble with the best of them." Then he winked, like he was letting me in on some Big Secret. "That hat's got a lot of miles on it. A *lot* of miles. You keep it safe for me, and if I ever lose the other ones, well…you'd let me borrow it back wouldn't you?"

"I sure would."

"That's all a fellah can ask for, then."

He called over someone else—a tall, skinny, hawk-nosed man with round wire-framed glasses and a shock of spiky white hair on his head—and said, "Sam, I want you to meet Patrick. Patrick here is a first-class tumbler."

"It's a honor to meet you, little sir," said Hawk-Nose. He had a rich, musical accent that reminded me of Father Fitzgibbon from that Bing Crosby movie *Going My Way* that Mom always watched whenever it was on TV. Porkpie insisted that Hawk-Nose be in a picture with us, and even though it seemed like the guy felt awkward about it, he knelt down on the other side of me so Eleanor could get us all in. Mom kept filming with the Kodak.

"*Esse est percipi*," said Hawk-Nose.

"Huh?" I said.

Porkpie shook his head. "It don't mean nothing, little fellah." He leaned forward so as to look past me at the other man. "Sam, I'm warnin' you, don't go starting in with all that malarkey about perception and non-being and the flight from extraneous perception breaking down in the inescapability of self-perception and…whatever in the hell else it is that this picture's supposed to be about. Brother—I just gave myself a headache *talking* about it."

Hawk-Nose smiled; I got the feeling the two of them argued like this all the time, and that both of them enjoyed it. "A thousand pardons, Joseph."

"I still say what this picture needs is a couple of good sight-gags."

"Anything more would distress your director," Hawk-Nose replied.

Porkpie shook his head. "And you wanted *me* to be in *Godot*. Half the time this Existentialist stuff makes me want to jump out a window."

I laughed at the way he said it— "win-duh", his froggy voice cracking— and he gave me a hug while his wife took some more pictures.

"You take good care of that this," he said, placing a hand on top of the hat on my head as Mom and I were leaving. "This's one of my magic ones, and I might need it back some day."

"I will, sir, I promise."

Hawk-Nose smiled at me, then touched his index finger between my eyes and said, *"Esse est percipi."*

"Thank you very much for the pictures, sir." Still having no idea what he'd said.

It wasn't until fifteen years later—when we were studying Absurdist Cinema in my college film class—that I figured out Porkpie had been Buster Keaton and that Hawk-Nose had been Samuel Beckett.

The course instructor had managed to track down a copy of *Film*, a 22-minute short black-and-white movie written by Beckett and starring Keaton. It was a little past the mid-way point of the movie that I began recognizing some of buildings from the Upper West Side, and was so stunned by the realization that I missed most of what happened for the rest of the movie.

Afterward the instructor was bemoaning how no filmed record of the production itself existed, and how "invaluable to film history" such a record might have been; I was about to raise my hand and say, "You're not going to believe this, but..." when it occurred to me that I had never seen the home movie Mom had shot that day. Until that moment, I'd all but forgotten about it.

By then both Keaton and my dad were a over a decade in their graves (Dad from a heart attack, Keaton from lung cancer), and while the college-me thought it was kind of cool in a for-shits-and-giggles way, it would be another ten years before I genuinely understood just what an honor it had been to meet the Great Stone Face in person—not only that, but have myself on film with him.

Somewhere, at any rate.

Still, actually having that film in my possession might do wonders for my final grade in Film class, so I went back to my dorm room that night and called Mom in Florida (where she'd been living for the past six years).

As soon as she was on the phone, Mom said, "I did it. I went wild and bought myself a Betamax. A Sony SLC9. I even bought a couple of movies, too. I got you *Apocalypse Now*—you liked that one, right?"

I admitted that, yes, I might have liked it, considering I saw it nine times in the theater.

"Does this mean you'll come down here and visit me on Spring Break?"

"I'll skip out a week early."

"You'll do no such thing. I already bought your plane ticket. You'll skip out *two days* early. Yes, I know, I'm the greatest mom in the history of moms."

"You sure are."

"Flattery will get you everywhere. Now—what's going on?"

"Why does anything have to be going on? Why can't I just call my mom to see how she's doing and chat?"

Mom sighed. "Because, *hon*, you're not a phone-chatter. If you call someone, me included, it's because you've got a specific reason. You're just like your dad in that way. So what is it?"

I told her about what happened in Film class, and asked her if she still had the home movie she'd taken that day.

"Not only do I still have it," she said, "but I just had *all* our home movies transferred onto videotape so we can watch them on my spiffy new Betamax—did I mention that I bought myself one?"

"Rub it in." At the time, the C9 was *the* state-of-the-art machine. I was so envious I could have bitten the receiver in half.

"You can play with it all you want while you're visiting."

And you bet I did just that.

Three days before Spring Break ended, Mom and I were watching the transferred home movies in her condo (part of a retirement community in South Florida, a really nice place, actually) when she popped in the videotape of that day in New York. I'd forgotten that the Cine-Kodak had sound recording capabilities, and it was amazing to both see and hear the five-year-old me, as well Keaton and Beckett.

"I tried reading some of that Beckett's plays," said Mom. "Either I'm dumber than a mud fence or he doesn't know how to write."

She started going on about *Waiting For Godot*, how all that happened during the entire play was that two bums sat by the side of the road waiting for some guy who never showed up.

I was only half-listening, having just spotted something in the background that was there only long enough to attract my attention and then vanish. I picked up the remote control, re-wound the tape, let it play, then pushed the "Pause" button.

Mom leaned forward. "What is it, hon?"

"Do you see that, to the left?"

"See what?"

"*On the left*. Look at Beckett's right shoulder, then look past it."

"I don't see any—oh, wait a second. Do you mean that guy with the big camera?"

I nodded, saying nothing, because it was most definitely there: half-sphere metal horse-eyes on each side of its square head, and a jutting lens from the front that from this angle looked like some kind of beak.

I leaned closer for a better look, slowly advancing the tape frame by frame.

"You're not supposed to do that," said Mom. "The instructions said you could break the tape, doing that too much."

I pushed "Play" and let it run. I'd seen what I was looking for; the camera was exactly in the place where a head should have been; I distinctly saw a human neck connecting the camera-thing to the body.

Of course it made sense *now*; *Film* was a piece of Absurdist Cinema, so it wasn't any great suspension of disbelief that in an Absurdist film written by Samuel Beckett, there'd be some extra in the background wearing a camera for a head—albeit one that was deliberately constructed to resemble that of a living thing, a horse or maybe bird.

"Can I take this tape back with me?" I asked.

"You sure can. After your call, I figured you'd ask me, so I had an extra copy made."

I looked at her and smiled. "You really are the best mom in the history of moms."

"Nice of you to notice, *finally*."

I watched Buster Keaton put his porkpie hat on my head, then turned to Mom and said: "Whatever happened to that hat?"

"I put it in plastic wrap and stored it in one of my old hat boxes."

"Can I take that back with me, too? My Film professor would get a big kick out of seeing it."

"The man gave it to *you*, it's yours. But you'd better take good care of it. That's a real piece of movie history."

"I promised him I would."

"Then how come I was the one who found it on the floor in your bedroom when you were seven?"

"Because I was *seven*."

"Good point."

I turned back to the television and watched as Keaton and Beckett, dwindling into the background as Mom and I walked away, stood waving goodbye. "I thought the Kodak took color film."

She nodded. "It did." She nodded toward the screen. "Colors look fine to me."

The movie was in black-and-white…except for the extra wearing the camera-head costume; admittedly, it was far into the background by now, but I could have sworn that its half-sphere eyes were bright gold and its lens-beak a shiny silver. I dismissed this as the result of an old 8mm home movie having faded over the years.

Around 10 p.m., after Mom had gone to bed, I popped open a bottle of Coke and went outside to the lounge under the stars. I thought about how much I missed Dad, and how lucky both Mom and I were that he'd had such great insurance, and how grateful I was that she'd gotten such a good price on the house. She was a thoughtful woman, Mom was; half of the insurance settlement and the house-sale money was in a trust fund that I had barely touched since turning twenty-one. One more year and I'd be out of school, my Journalism degree qualifying me to flip burgers somewhere until (or if) I decided to enter a graduate program. I considered it money that both Mom and Dad had spent their lives working for, and I was damned if I was going to spend it frivolously. I figured—

—*shnick!*

I sat up, looking around, trying to see what—

—shnick!

I knew that sound…or thought I did, anyway.

I stood up and scanned the nearby trees and bushes, and once thought I caught a glitter of moonlight reflected off of something old, then—

—shnick! Shnick! Shnick-nick-nick-nick-nick!

I figured one of the neighbors must be taking pictures of the moon; despite how bright it was outside, the trees and bushes surrounding the condo building created deep, elongated shadows all around the back area of the condo, so if they were behind me, I wouldn't have been able to spot them.

"I hope they turn out," I said, gesturing toward the moon. "It is a helluva sight to see, isn't it?"

As if to answer me in the affirmative, a last shnick! echoed from the shadows. I toasted the moonlight, then went back inside.

Film is a strange and difficult movie. Shot in black-and-white, it has no sound (with the sole exception of one character delivering a sibilant "Shhh!" early on). In it, Keaton plays a character called "O" (as in Object) whose face is never seen until the final moments of the movie. "O" is moving through the streets, sometimes walking very fast, other times running, always hunched down so that all we see of him is the back of his coat and the top of his porkpie hat (and for much of the 22-minute running time, that hat is the only indication that it's Buster Keaton we're watching.) It's obvious that he's being pursued, but by what or whom we don't know.

"O" passes several people during his flight; sometimes these people look at his face, sometimes they look past him, but in every encounter, these people end up shrinking away in horror. The more this happens, the more the viewer comes to understand that what "O" is running from—and the thing that elicits such horror from passersby—is the second main character, named "E" (as in Eye, as in Camera-Eye): "O" is running away from the camera; he does not want to be seen.

Upon entering his cramped apartment, "O" immediately shoos his cat and dog out into the hallway, closes the door, and begins ripping apart every family photograph in the room—he doesn't even wish to be seen by the faces in the pictures.

Once this is done, once he has isolated himself from all things that could perceive him or be perceived by him, only then does "O" turn around to reveal his face.

He has only one eye, the other covered by a heavy black patch.

"O" sees that all of his efforts have been for nothing, because "E" is right there in the room with him, and the movie ends with "O" releasing a silent scream of anguish and horror. The expression on Keaton's face when he turns to face the camera is right out of a nightmare: the look of unparalleled horror will sear itself into your memory.

Beckett's explanation (according to his published journals) is that he has sundered his main character in two: the character "O" who is pursued by the subject "E". As long as "E" stays behind "O", "O" will avoid being perceived. The camera is designated, in Beckett's phrase, an "angle of immunity" of 45 degrees which it must not exceed at the risk of causing "O"' to experience the "anguish of perceivedness."

My Film professor argued that the reason "O" has only one eye is because "E" is the other one, thus keeping the equation of perception continually split—"Because in order for 'O' to have full perception, he must also possess *depth-perception*; since he does not, full perception cannot be achieved." It is *the film's audience* that causes the final coalescing of the separate perceptions into one; it's not the presence of "E" that causes "O" to scream in horror, it's the presence of the audience (whom "O" can theoretically see when he turns around); by watching both "O" and "E", they force full perception to occur: the cinematic equivalent of the Observer Effect.

When asked during an interview what he thought *Film* was about, Keaton answered: "What I think it means is that a man can keep away from everybody, but he can't get away from himself."

The day after I returned from Florida, I arranged to meet my Film professor in the Media Center, where I showed her the porkpie hat, told her about my encounter with Keaton and Beckett, then showed her the home movie. While she was watching the tape, I asked her if I could screen *Film* because I wanted to see if I could figure out where in the story they'd been when Mom and I collided with Keaton.

I set up the projector, checked out the movie, threaded everything into place, and watched it.

Nowhere in the movie is there an extra wearing a camera-head costume. I knew from class that nothing had been cut from *Film*—the director, Alan Schneider (who came from the Theatre, specializing in Absurdist plays), was working in film for the first time, and had planned out every shot in almost fanatical detail so that everything would be used (his arguably humorless approach leading to numerous on-set disagreements with Keaton).

I watched *Film*, all the time thinking: *What the hell was that guy doing hanging around with that thing on his head?*

I answered the question almost at once: *Easy; he was a street crazy, or maybe someone who'd hoped to get into the movie by standing out.*

Only he hadn't stood out. As I remembered it, he seemed to be trying to stay in the background the whole time, trying to hide as much as "O" was trying to run away.

I decided to write it off as one of those passing oddities that sometimes make interesting conversational tidbits.

My Film professor was suitably impressed, as were my classmates, and for one day I was a Hot Topic; then the videotape and Keaton's hat went back into storage boxes, I graduated college, flipping burgers for only three months before I landed a job as a Feature writer at The Cedar Hill Ally, eventually meeting a young doctor named Dianne who lost her mind and agreed to marry me and, a year later, gave birth to our son.

Every so often I would hear a faint shnick! somewhere nearby, but never thought much about it (working at a newspaper, you get used to hearing the sound of a shutter-click); every once in a while the sound would be accompanied by a glint of gold or silver in my peripheral vision, but I never gave it much thought: Camera-Head was only a dim, distant, dusty memory, emerging every few years just long enough for me to decide it was too silly to bother with before retreating into the shadows where we keep all those things that no longer belong in our lives.

Then came the afternoon that Brian attended a matinee at the Auditorium Theatre with one of his friends and his friend's parents, and came home to tell me all about the "funny old man who did magic tricks when no one else was around."

"What do you mean, honey?" Dianne asked him, giving me a quick but seriously concerned look.

"Well," said Brian, "Jimmy had to go pee, so his dad took him, and Jimmy's mom, she asked me if I wanted some more popcorn—Jimmy and me ate all of it before the movie even started, and they got real good popcorn there—and I said yeah, that would be great, so she told me to stay right there in my seat and I did, I was good, I never moved, and then when I was all alone, this old man behind me reached around and pulled something from my ear." Brian reached into his pocket and removed a shiny silver dollar.

I took it from him and looked at the date: 1964.

"Did he tell you his name?"

"Nope."

"So it wasn't any of Daddy's friends that you've already met?"

"Nope."

"Brian, buddy," I said, "what exactly did this old guy say to you?"

My son became as bright and animated as I'd ever seen him. "He told me about the card tricks he knew, and then he told a couple of jokes, and then he pulled two more silver dollars out from my ears. He had real weird breath. It wasn't stinky. It kinda smelled like that cough medicine Mom makes me take when I'm sick. Oh, yeah—he told me to tell you that he needed his hat back, please."

The silver dollar slipped from my fingers and clattered to the floor.

"Did Jimmy's mom and dad see him?" asked Dianne.

"Nope. He was all gone before they got back."

Dianne saw something in my expression. "What is it? What's going on?"

I shook my head, telling her it was nothing, then—after telling Brian it was not a good idea to talk to strangers (something we re-emphasized from time to time, Brian being a particularly open, trusting, and friendly child)—went upstairs to my office and pulled Mom's hat-box from its place in the back of the closet. Unwrapping Keaton's hat, I heard the echo of his voice saying, *You take good care of this, this's one of my magic ones, and I might need it back some day.*

Silently, I added: *And you promised.*

I realized there was probably a rational explanation for it, that one of my friends who knew the story had spotted Brian at the movies and decided to play a joke on me, but as soon as I'd seen the date on the silver dollar, I knew something wasn't quite right: my friends *might* have gone to those lengths to play a joke on me, but I doubted it; and none of them would have approached Brian without first telling them who they were, especially if they'd not met him before.

I slipped the hat into my briefcase, told Dianne there was some background material for an article I'd forgotten at *The Ally*, and drove downtown.

Parking on the square, I walked past the soon-to-be renovated Midland Theatre and crossed the street to the soon-to-be-closed Auditorium Theatre. Paying no attention to what movie was showing, I bought a ticket for the showing that was already twenty minutes in and headed for the balcony (Brian and Jimmy always sit in the balcony).

The only other person up there was a small, roundish man sitting in the middle of the third row of the loge. Even from behind, I recognized him.

Making my way down toward him, I opened the briefcase and removed the hat.

"I thought for sure you'd have lost that thing years ago," he said in the same croaky voice I'd always remembered.

"I keep my promises," I said.

And took my seat next to Buster Keaton—not the fit, trim, athletic Keaton of his triumphant silent film days, but the pot-bellied, slightly droopy, cancer-ridden Keaton of *Film, A Funny Thing Happened On The Way To The Forum*, and *War, Italian Style*.

"What's going on?" I asked, handing over the porkpie.

"I'll be—you sure took good care of it." He straightened the brim, flattened down the top a little more, and set it on his head. Had I not been so frightened, I would have been in absolute awe. "Still fits. Thank you."

"You're welcome," I replied. "What the hell is happening?'

"It's the Onlookers," he answered, then turned to face me. "Them camera-head fellahs you spotted way back when?"

I nodded.

"Well, turns out there was something to Sam's malarkey, after all. That old Irish son-of-a-bitch, he hit on something with that picture he wasn't supposed to—kind of like when Pasteur made his big discovery by accident. Only with Sam and *Film*, the process he discovered ain't quite so helpful in the long run."

"What process?"

Keaton pointed his index finger at me, just like Beckett had done, and touched me right between my eyes. "Perception, young fellah. How it ain't just a two-way thing, but a *three-way* thing. You, the camera, and the audience."

"The audience being the Onlookers?"

"No—they're the camera. The Onlookers, they're the ones perceiving everything *through* the camera." He shrugged, then winked at me; I know he meant it to be reassuring, but there was something infinitely sad in the gesture.

"I don't really know what, exactly, the Onlookers are; only that they've been watching us for a long, long time. See, the way I understand it, is that as long as none of us were aware they were watching, everything was okay. It was like me running from that camera in the picture; as long as I didn't turn around to see it, I wouldn't know the audience was watching me through the blasted thing. But once I turned around and saw the camera, well…that made the audience part of it, because then we were all aware. It was like a chain reaction. Do you get what I'm saying? I sure as hell'd hate to have to try explaining this a second time."

"I think so," I said. "By making that movie, you guys somehow… somehow…"

"…somehow lifted a barrier between them and us that nobody knew was there until Old Sam hit on the idea. But that's all it took—one guy hitting on the idea, then making others aware of it. Image, camera, audience—*wham!*

The three ingredients needed to pull off that extra level of perception and let some of us start seeing the things the Onlookers *see us* with."

"So…what happens now?"

Before Keaton could answer me, a rapid series of shutter-clicks—*shnick-nick-nick-nick-nick-nick!*—echoed from the seats below. I rose up, peering over the edge, and saw that a full one-fourth of the audience below had square heads, golden half-sphere eyes, and silver lens-beaks.

No one else seemed to hear or see them.

One by one, the Camera-Eyes turned to look up toward the balcony. I jumped back from the railing and hunkered as far down into my seat as I could.

"Hate to be the one to say it," said Keaton, "but I think they seen ya."

"Is this supposed to be how 'O' felt?"

Keaton parted his hands in front of him. "Damned if I know."

"What's going to happen now?"

He gave me a long, silent look of pity. "You know how at the end of *Film* the camera freezes on my face and then it all just goes to black? Old Sam told me that the idea there was that, once 'O' and 'E' and the audience make that three-way connection, then a state of…what'd he call it?…oh, yeah: *non-being* followed." He snapped his fingers. "Everything just stops, ceases to be. It's like the way all colors together form black; all perceptions together create…" He made his hand into a fist, brought the side of the fist up to his mouth, then blew into it while opening his hand.

I didn't need words; the meaning was clear enough.

"Isn't there any way to stop them?" I asked.

"The Onlookers? Huh-uh. They've always been and always will be. Now if you're asking me, is there any way to stop them things down there from seeing you, the only idea I got is for you to not see them. *Un*-see 'em."

"How the hell do I *un*-see something?"

He placed the tip of his index finger between my eyes. "'To perceive is to be perceived.' That's what Sam said to you…'course he had to say it French 'cause he was kind of an intellectual snob, but he was an okay fellah, once you got to know him." He rolled his eyes upward, saw something wrong with the angle of his hat, and adjusted the brim once more.

"Why do you need the hat back?" I asked.

"If you're expecting a complicated Sam Beckett answer, you're gonna be disappointed. This particular hat was my favorite…I just didn't realize it until after you'd gone. Eleanor, God love her, forgot to get your names and address from your mother. Took a while to track you down."

"Why here? Why this old movie house?"

"Because this old movie house used to be a damn nice theatre in the days of Vaudeville. My family and me played here quite a few times when I was just a kid. There's a wall underneath that stage that all the companies used to sign as they came through. You'd shit a brick if you knew some of the names on that wall. But I ain't gonna bore you with nostalgia; you got a family to get back to."

He started to rise; I reached up and grabbed his arm. "How can I un-see them?"

He shook his head. "Just between us, I don't think it can be done. I wouldn't worry too much, I was you. How fast the process takes depends on how perceptive you really are. You'll start noticing things, like colors changing or fading away. Not all at once, but gradually. After that, other things'll fade, little by little. That's just the slow road perception takes to non-being." He pulled from my grip, then gently patted my shoulder. "But it'll be okay, young fellah. I'll be waiting over there to show you around, and—oh, what have we here?"

In two quick, smooth, fluid movements, he reached behind my ear and removed a shiny silver dollar. I took it from him, looked at it and smiled, and when I looked back up he was all gone.

I left the theatre and walked toward my car, hearing the endless chattering shutter-clicks of *shnick-nick-nick-nick-nick-nick!* following me. I became frightened, started running, but the Camera-Eyes were never far behind; even though I never once turned around to look for (or at) them, I knew they were there.

I darted down alleys, around the square, through an abandoned lot, and back around to where I'd parked my car, all in an effort to lose them.

It did no good.

I finally got in my car and drove home, taking several detours and side streets along the way.

When I came inside, I all but slammed the door behind me, then leaned against it, gulping air.

Dianne called from the kitchen: "Did you find what you were looking for?"

I almost said: *No, but it found me.* "Everything's good," I said, lying.
And felt someone watching.

That was less than a week ago.

Since then, the dogwoods' red spots have turned gray; as have many of
the leaves on the trees in our back yard; as has most of the grass. The blue of
the sky is fading. The colors of our life are going away. My wife and son are
lessening in my perception, as I am in theirs.

How fast the process takes depends on how perceptive you really are,
Keaton had told me.

Well, so much for being proud of having a perceptive family.

I keep wondering who or what the Onlookers really are, but I suppose
their true nature and form won't be revealed to me until I—like 'O'—turn to
fully face the Camera-Eye.

How do you un-see something?

Tonight, after Dianne and Brian had gone to bed, I dug around and found
my wife's medical bag. I rummaged through it. She has hypodermics, vials
of morphine, sutures, bandages...and a scalpel.

I keep thinking about the final image of Film and my professor's
explanation for the patch worn by 'O'.

Shnick! Shnick-nick-nick-nick-nick!

They are filming something on the street, in front of our house, very
close to the front door.

I remember the patch, and the perception equation, and my Film
professor's explanation, and as I turn the scalpel from side to side so it reflects
the light, I think of my family, and how much I love them, and whisper to
myself: it will be only one eye....

Brother Hollis Gives His Final Sermon from a Rickety Make-Shift Pulpit in the Remains of a Smokehouse That Now Serves as His Church

Used to be I thought holding services in here was a blasphemy. What good, God-fearing Christian, what man worth his place in Heaven, what human being whose head ain't full of mush or sour-mash could even *think* that the Good Lord would be fine with hearing people sing His praises from inside a place where the carcasses of slaughtered animals were strung up by their hind quarters to flavor and age so they'd be tasty? Didn't seem right, somehow—even if the church'd burned down when folks started going crazy on account of them thinking the Final Days was here at last. I could've kept having services on the grounds on account of them being *sacred* grounds. But I knew that we'd need walls to keep ourselves at least *feeling* safe, even if we knew it was just pissing in the wind and praying for rain. So we moved into this here smokehouse. Where butchered animals are strung up to soak in flavor. All things considered, it seems sadly appropriate to me that I'm speaking to you this last time from in here, from a place where food comes to get itself yummied up. Besides, the Good Lord said that "...wherever two or more of you are gathered in My name..."

Ah, well, *hell*. Don't really make any difference now, does it? And I know that we've all done the best we can to keep our souls tried and true, to keep our faith strong when it seems like every hour there's less and less remains for us to have faith *in*. 'Cause that's what human beings do, isn't it? Find themselves some kernel of hope to hold close, 'cause if you got no hope, you got no reason to keep going. Even if you start lying to yourself, tell yourself that this has to end somehow, all you've gotta do is hang in there, stay safe, keep to near the river or on higher ground because water and climbing, they're not so good at that, and maybe for a while that works out for you...then you start...you start getting lonesome, 'cause here you are all safe on higher ground, and you got enough canned goods to last you, but the *quiet*, it starts getting pretty darn loud, and maybe you start talking to yourself just to hear a voice, but since it's you talking to yourself there ain't no surprises in the conversation on account you already know what you're going to say.

So then you turn to your Bible, the same one passed down in your family from as far back as your great-great-gramma, the one in whose pages you've always found comfort, you've always found beauty in its language, its poetry, the one you've read so many times that the corners of the pages are stained with oil from your fingertips so that it even *smells* like you, same way it smells of your great-great gramma's oils, and your mother's, and everybody else whose hands have held it. You start reading it aloud to yourself 'cause if there's nothing out there in what's left of the world for you have faith in, there's always the words of the Good Book, you can depend on them. They're the same beautiful words that were there last time you read them, they'll be there when you read it now, and they'll be there next time. Except when you start reading them out loud—and maybe it's because you're tired, or because you're lonesome, but mostly because you're so scared you haven't been able to sleep for more than fifteen minutes at a stretch, whatever the reason—you don't find the comfort in them you once did. The pages just look dirty and torn and yellow. The words are the same, the Gospels, they ain't changed any, the platitudes, they're still as poetic as ever, but when you hear them being read in your own voice they sound...hollow. And then you get caught up in trying to make them sound out loud the way they used to sound in your head when you was reading them all quiet. Then you start thinking more about how your voice *sounds* reading them than on the words themselves, and you're tired, and alone, and scared...and then something in your brain wakes up and turns on the lantern and you realize that the words, the Gospels and platitudes and the visions of John and...and all the rest of it...you realize that things don't quite add up like they're supposed to. You stop and ask yourself—for instance—how did anyone back then *know* what Christ said when he was praying to God in Gethsemane before the Romans came to take him away? You remember that our Lord and Savior, he was *alone* there, nobody else around...so how is it that the Bible quotes him?

Weren't nobody else there. You realize that this Gethsemane business, it ain't the only place in the Bible where things, they don't quite add up. And on account of you noticing these things, you start asking yourself questions that would best be left unasked, then it all starts getting mixed up and you don't know what you're saying, or what you're reading, or if your belief is real or just something you accepted, same way you accepted them stories from the children's books your mama used to read to you when the world was still new and all things were possible.

The question that kept bothering me was, how did we all just *assume* right off the bat that all of you was evil? You didn't ask to crawl out of the earth under which you were buried to walk among us again. You didn't ask for this new nature that makes you…do things to the living. We assumed you was evil because what you were doing was so vile to us. Does a cancer cell think that what it does is evil? Cancer cells, they got no way of knowing, they just do what they was brought into existence to do. It's terrible, what they do, eating away at a body bit by bit from the inside, all the pain…*all* the pain…but right and wrong, they don't exist for cancer cells, so how can we say that each of the cells is evil? How can we force them to take the blame for the one thing, the *only* thing, they were created to do?

I look out at all of you, your dirty clothes and your gray skin and holes left by the worms in your flesh and I can't help but think about something I heard an old Indian gal say once when I was a boy. She said that every living thing has a soul. I asked her if blades of grass had souls, and she said yes. I asked her if animals had souls, and she said yes. She said any living thing that moves and touches and can be touched in return, it had a soul. So I look out at all of you, my *un*-dead brothers and sisters, and see that you are moving, and touching, and that you can be touched, and that means that you have souls, all of you. And what you do, I don't think you see it as being evil. I'm not so sure I see it that way anymore, either. In order for something to be evil, it has to have strayed from the path of righteousness. It has to have made the decision on purpose. It has to have *chosen* that way. You didn't. You asked for none of this, so who were we to judge what you do as evil, and then brand you the same way simply because you're only doing what your nature now compels you to do? I want to say I'm sorry for that. I'm sorry that we started to hunt you down and shoot you like we did. But you won out in the end, didn't you? Turns out there was a whole lot more of you than

82

there was of us. You just shuffled around doing what your nature makes you do and waited for us to start turning on each other. Or die out. Still, I'm sad about what we done, and I hope you can find it in your hearts to forgive… that is, if you know what forgiveness is.

You may be dead, but you're still alive, and that means you've all got souls, and that means that, after you was put in the ground, your souls did not abandon you, and they did not abandon you because maybe there isn't no place for them to go. And that breaks my heart something fierce, because if your souls got nowhere to go, then that means there weren't no one there to welcome them. And I can't think past that because it scares me worse than anything you've done to others or might do to me.

I'm pretty sure that I'm the only one left. Why you've let me live is something I don't understand. I don't even know if I can say I'm grateful for it. But I want to thank you just the same, here in the house of Our Lord where the slaughtered pigs still hang in all their plump, smoky tastiness. I want to thank you because, you see, when I come down from that higher ground where none of you ever climb, I came down here to sacrifice myself to you. I came down here because I was giving up. I had no faith left. And my faith, my undead brothers and sister, my faith has been tested something fierce in my too-long life. I have held the hands of consumptive children as they rattled out their last breath. I have seen loneliness in the eyes of the elderly that was so overwhelming I questioned the point of letting them go on, living out the last of their days under the weight of that sadness. I have said prayers over the bodies of young men and girls who've taken the knife or the razor or their papa's shotgun to bring an end to their own suffering, however great or small it might have been. I have tried to comfort starving families, soothe the grief of mothers whose babies never drew their first breath. I thought that death held no mystery for me, and no fear because of that. I was ready to go.

And then you started watching me—not coming after me, but watching me. Following me. Listening to me preach the Word. And for that I am grateful, because, you see, I'm not lonesome any more. I have you. You are my new church. You are my new family. You have given me back my faith, my undead brothers and sisters. I have faith in *you*. Only you, and nothing else. You do not come here to worship, you come here to *be* worshipped.

Here I am, dear brothers and sisters, on my knees in supplication, worshipping you. There is no end to my life, no beginning to my death. With you, I know now that death is life. And I am grateful. I love you. You are all there is. And I am so dearly sorry for having thought you evil. Please, come. Rise and come to me, place your hands on my head and whisper to me my absolution so that I might better be your humble servant.

Come forward, I beg of you. Come forward and lay your hands on me.

Come forward. Bless me, brothers and sisters, for I have sinned against thee...

This is my body, take of it, all of you, and eat of it....

Tales the Ashes Tell

"I was in the darkness;
I could not see my words
Nor the wishes of my heart.
Then suddenly there was a great light—

Let me into the darkness again."

—Stephen Crane

Some nights, when the visitors have left and everything within me falls into dismal silence, when even the Librarian grows weary of drifting through these halls, maintaining these chambers, and looking at these glass doors behind which rest the golden books, when the rain spatters against the roof and the flashes of lightning create glinting reflections swimming against my marble floors, when I am at last certain there will be no one and nothing to disturb me, I allow myself, for a little while, to flip through these books as one still among the living would flip through the pages of an old family photo album; only where the living warm themselves in the nostalgic glow of reminiscences, I sustain myself on the memories of those housed within the books arranged on my shelves, behind my glass doors with their golden hinges, here in my corridors with marble floors. I have no memories, being born of wood, iron, and stone as I was. But those who slumber here, within these golden books, their memories remain with them, and many are so lonely that they gladly share them with me on nights such as this. I house them from the elements; they sustain me with their stories. I prefer it this way, on nights such as this, when it is just the ashes, the rain, and I...and the tales the ashes tell.

Tonight it's old Mrs. Winters who's the first to start in with her story of her grandson's death in Vietnam and how it broke her own son's heart and led to the ruination of his marriage and career, ending when her son took his own life in a squalid motel room somewhere in Indiana. Every time she tells this story, her neighbors listen quietly, politely, patiently, for they—like I—have heard this a thousand times before, but she always changes some small detail so it's never quite the same; tonight, the scene of his death is not some sleazy roadside hovel but an expensive, five-star hotel in the middle of downtown Manhattan, and this time her son does not decorate the blinds with his brains but instead stands on the roof of the palace, arms spread wide, a joyous smile on his face as he falls forward off the edge and for a moment almost flies until he…doesn't.

Like her neighbors I am pleased by this new trick of the tale. Each time she changes a bit of the minutiae the story resembles itself less and less, and one night it will be a completely new story that she will begin revising almost immediately. We like this about her. She was never married, our Mrs. Winters. She had no children. She died alone, on a bus-stop bench, a forgotten bag lady whose mortal remains were cremated and placed here by a sympathetic police officer who still comes by once a month to bring flowers and pay his respects; it seems Mrs. Winters reminded him of his own grandmother; beyond that, no one here has any further idea of his reasons, and if Mrs. Winters knows of them, her memory is too fragmented to know for certain if those reasons are true or not. We do not press the matter. Even here, certain privacies are respected.

I find it curious, how many of her neighbors were interred here by strangers, or family members they were never particularly close to. Many of them come here from cities and towns that are hundreds—sometimes thousands—of miles away. I know that I am a glorious edifice, and am honored that so many of the living wish to bring their loved ones here to rest. I am a tranquil place, a quiet place, a place of serenity and sanctuary. I know the stories of nearly everyone who slumbers here, but not all.

Tonight, we have new neighbors on my shelves, behind my glass doors. I heard only a part of the explanation given by the slightly hunched, spirit-broken man who brought them here. Something about his brother and his niece and a boy his niece once knew. I wonder whom it is he has left with us. I exchange pleasantries with all my friends between the golden covers of their books, and as I do each of them asks, What do you know about the new arrival? I have no answer for them, not yet, but being the curious sorts they are—and always so lonely, even when all of them are chattering away—they want me to find out but are too polite to ask. They know they don't need to; I will discover it in time.

I see that the glass doors have been freshly washed and dried so that our new arrival is welcomed into a clean space. She is whispering to herself, our new neighbor, and I become very still, empyrean, allowing the rain and lighting and the slow turning of the Earth to cast shapes of angels in the primum mobile of night.

She speaks not of herself, but of we, of the uncle who brought us here.

Could it be? There are so few books here that contain more than a single person's remains; the last was five years ago, when an elderly husband and wife who died within hours of each other left specific instructions that they were to be burned and interred together, their ashes, like their souls (or so they believed), intermingled for eternity. I find that sort of sentimentality pitiful, but I never speak my judgment to those who need to believe in such antiquated notions. Do not misunderstand—the souls of that elderly couple are intermingled here, but not in the way they were raised to believe; there are no fields of green they run through, hand in hand, laughing as the afternoon sun sets their faces aglow and the scent of autumn leaves fills the air. They are simply here, and so shall remain. But it is enough for them, this fate, and that pleases me.

The girl still speaks of we and us, very seldom does the word I make an appearance. At least not at first.

I'm here, I tell her or them. As are we all, and we are all listening.

She continues to whisper, but whether she is telling the story to me or to those who live inside my walls, I do not yet know. But she tells her story as if she has told it a thousand times before and expects to tell it a thousand times again; and, perhaps, like old Mrs. Winters, she will begin altering details as the years and decades and centuries go by, until it is a new story, one she finds she can spend eternity with and not be crippled with regret.

Mute, voiceless, abandoned and all but forgotten, she begins, my father's house does not so much sit on this street as it does crouch; an abused, frightened animal fearing the strike of its keeper's belt, the sting of a slapping hand, the rough kick of a steel-toed boot. No lights shine in any of the windows, which are broken or have been covered with boards or black paint or large sections of cardboard that now stink of dampness and rot. The paint on the front door long ago gave up fighting the good fight and now falls away, peeled by unseen hands, becoming scabs dropping from the body of a leper in the moments before death, but with no Blessed Damien of Molokai to offer up a final prayer for a serene passage from this cheerless existence into the welcoming forgiveness and saving grace of Heaven. This was once a house like any other house, on this street like any other street, in this town that most people would immediately recognize and then just as quickly forget as they drive through it on their way to someplace more vibrant, more exciting, or even just a little more interesting.

But we can't blame them, you and I; we can't impugn these people who pass through without giving this place so much as a second glance. If things had worked out differently, we would have burned rubber on our way out, making damn sure the tires threw up enough smoke to hide any sight of the place should one of us cave and glance in the rear-view for a final look, a last nostalgic image of this insufficient and unremarkable white-bread Midwestern town, but that's not the way it works around here; never was, never will be. You're born here, you'll die here; you're a lifer, dig it or not.

We sometimes wonder if people still use that phrase, dig it, or if it's also passed into the ether of the emptiness people still insist on calling history, memory, eternity, whatever, passed into that void along with groovy, outta sight, "That's not my bag," "Stifle it, Edith," Watergate, Space-Food Sticks, platform shoes, Harry Chapin flying in his taxi, and the guy who played Re-Run on *What's Happening?*

Wouldn't it be nice if that drunken Welshman's poems had been true, that death has no dominion, or that we could rage against the dying of the light? Odd. It occurs to me that if we were still alive, we'd be looking right into the face of our fifties about now, feeling its breath on our cheeks, its features in detail so sharp it would be depressing.

But this never does us any good, does it, thinking about such things? Especially tonight of all nights. Don't tell me you've forgotten? Yes, that's right. This night marks the anniversary of the night my father buried us under the floorboards in my bedroom after he came home early from work and caught us in my bed. It was my first time, and when he saw you there, with his little girl, it was too much for him to take; not this, not this dirty, filthy thing going on under his roof, it was too much; his wife was gone, three years in her grave after twice as long fighting the cancer that should

88

have taken her after nine months; his job was gone, the factory doors closed forever, and he was reduced to working as a janitor at the high school just to keep our heads above water because the severance pay from the plant was running out.

"At least the house is paid for," he'd say on those nights when there was enough money to buy a twelve-pack of Blatz, sit at the kitchen table, and hope with every tip of every can that some of his shame and grief and unhappiness would be pulled out in the backwash.

You never saw it, you never had the chance, you didn't know him as I did. I couldn't look at his eyes and all the broken things behind them any longer; I couldn't listen to his once-booming voice that was now a disgraced whisper, the death-rattle of a life that was a life no longer, merely an existence with no purpose at its center...except for his little girl, except for me and all the unrealized dreams he hoped I'd bring to fruition because he no longer had the faith or the strength to fight for anything. A hollow, used-up, brittle-spirited echo of the man he'd hoped to be. Even then, even before that night, he'd ceased to be my father; he became instead what was left of him. I tried to fill in the gaps with my memories of what was, what had been, but I was a teenaged girl, one who hadn't paid any attention to him during the six years my mother was dying, and so I made up things to fill in those holes. I pretended that he was a Great War Hero who was too modest to boast about his accomplishments on the battlefield; I dreamt that he was a spy, like Napoleon Solo on The Man from U.N.C.L.E., hiding undercover, using his factory job to establish his secret identity, his mission one so secret that he couldn't even reveal the truth to his family; I imagined that he was writing the Great American Novel in hidden notebooks late at night, while I slept in my room with the Bobby Sherman and David Cassidy posters on the walls, their too-bright smiles hinting that someday soon my father's novel would make him so rich and famous that the two of them would be arguing over who would take me to Homecoming, and who would take me to the prom.

But he was no war hero, no spy, no secret great notebook novelist; only a factory worker with no factory who'd exchanged a lathe machine for a mop and a bucket and pitying looks from faculty members. To the students, he was either invisible or an object to mock.

No, I don't remember your name. I don't remember my name, but what does it matter now? Our names, like our flesh, were only a façade, an illusion to be embraced, a falsehood to be cherished and mistaken for purpose, for meaning. We have—had—what remained of our bodies to remind us of that, beneath the floor, flesh long decayed and eaten away, two sets of bones with skulls frozen forever into a rictus grin as if laughing at the absurdity of the world we're no longer part of.

Let's not stay here for now, let's move outside, round and round this house, watching as the living ghosts of everyone who once passed through the door come and go in reverse; watch as the seasons go backwards, sunshine and autumn leaves and snow-clogged streets and sidewalks coming and going in a blink and…and let's stop here. I want to stop here, in the backyard, just for a few moments, just to see his face as it was on that night.

Watch; see how pretty it all is. Murky light from a glowing street lamp snakes across the darkness to press against the glass. The light bleeds in, across a kitchen table, and glints off the beer can held by a man whose once-powerful body has lost its commanding posture under the weight of compiling years; he's overweight from too many beers, over-tense from too many worries, and overworked far too long without a reprieve. Whenever this man speaks, especially when he's at work, especially when he's holding the mop and bucket, his eyes never have you, and even if they do you cannot return his gaze; his eyes are every lonely journey you have ever taken, every unloved place you've ever visited, every sting of guilt you've ever felt. This man's eyes never have you, they only brush by once, softly, like a cattail or a ghost, then fall shyly toward the ground in some inner contemplation too sad to be touched by a tender thought or the delicate brush of another's care. To look at him closely, it's easy to think that God has forgotten his name.

He lifts the can of beer to his mouth. It feels good going down, washing away the bad taste in his mouth that always follows him home from work. He drains the can, sighs, goes to the sink and pours himself a glass of water. He is thinking about his days as a child, about the afternoons now forgotten by everyone but him, afternoons when he'd go to the movies for a nickel and popcorn was only a penny. He thinks about how he used to take his daughter to the movies all the time when she was still a little girl and her mother, his wife, was still alive. He remembers how much fun they used to have, and he longs for the chance to do something like that again, something that will put a bright smile on his daughter's face and make him feel less of a failure.

He stands at the sink listening to the sounds of the house, its soft creaks and groans, still settling after all these years. He thinks about his dead wife and doesn't know how he'll be able to face the rest of his life without her by his side. She was a marvel to him. After all the mistakes he's made—and, God, he's made a lot, no arguing that—her respect and love for him never lessened.

He tries to not think about the things his daughter has done for him the past few months, things he didn't ask her to do, but things she's done nonetheless. Just to help him relax, to help him sleep.

And then he hears a sound from his daughter's room. A squeak of bedsprings. A soft sigh. The muffled laughter of a boy.

His face becomes a slab of granite and the broken things behind his eyes shatter into even more fragments. Unaware that he's doing it, he reaches over and picks up the hammer he left lying on the kitchen counter last night while he tried repairing the loose cupboard door above the sink. He turns and marches toward his daughter's bedroom, knowing what he's going to find when he opens the door and—

—what? All right, just this once, we won't watch the rest. He wasn't really there. Anyway. I'm glad we know that now. He just wanted to scare us but his frustration, his anger, his heartbrokenness took control.

Let's pretend that we still have hands, and let's pretend to hold them as we play "Ring Around the Rosie" once more, going back just a little more, a year, maybe less, because I've been saving this for you, for this anniversary, this most special anniversary. Why is it special? That's a secret I need to keep just a little while longer. Take my hand and let's go, round and round and round and—

—stop right here. Yes, this is the place, the time, exactly right.

There's a young girl of seventeen sleeping in her bed who, for a moment, wakes in the night to hear the sound of weeping from the room across the hall. She rises and walks as softly as she can to her door, opens it, and steps into the hall.

"…no, no, no…" chokes the voice in the other room.

"Daddy?" she says.

"…no, no, no, oh, God, honey, please…"

She knows he can't hear her, that he's dreaming again of the night his wife, her mother, closed her eyes for the last time, of the way he took her emaciated body in his arms and kissed her lips and stroked her hair and begged her to wake up, wakeup, please, honey, what am I supposed to do without you, wake up, please….

She takes a deep breath, this seventeen-year-old motherless girl, and slowly opens the door to this room stinking of loneliness and grief. She takes a few hesitant steps, the moonlight from the window in the hallway casting bars of suffused light across the figure of her father as if imprisoning him in the dream. She stares at him, not knowing what to do.

Then his eyes open for a moment and he sees her standing in the doorway.

"Arlene," he says, his voice still thick with tears. "Arlene, is that you?"

"Shhh," says the young girl, suddenly so very cold at hearing him speak her mother's name in the night. "It's just a bad dream, go back to sleep."

"…I can't sleep so hot, not without you…"

She can hear that he's starting to drift away again, but she does not move back into the hallway; instead, she takes a few steps toward the bed where her father sleeps, tried to sleep, fails to sleep, sleeps in sadness, sleeps in nightmare, wakes in dark loneliness, drifts off in shame and regret.

For the first time, she realizes the pain he's in, the pain he's always been in, one way or another, this man who was no war hero, no spy, no secret notebook novelist, just a sad and decent and so very lonely man, and she feels useless, insufficient, foolish, and inept; but most of all, she feels selfish and sorry.

Her eyes focus on one bar of suffused moonlight that points like a ghostly finger from her father's sleeping form to the closet door a few feet away, and she follows the beam, opening the door that makes no sound, and she sees it hanging from the hook on the inside of the door: her mother's nightgown, the one she'd been wearing on the night she died.

"Oh, Daddy…" she says, her voice weak and thin.

Still, her hand reaches out to lift the gown from the hook and bring it close to her face. Her mother loved this nightgown, its softness, its warmth, the way it smelled when it came out of the dryer after a fresh washing, and this girl holds the garment up to her face and pulls in a deep breath, smelling the scent of her mother's body and the stink of the cancer still lingering at the edges.

From the bed her father whimpers, "…no, no, no, oh, God, honey, please…"

92

And she knows now what she can do for him, what she has to do for him, and so she removes her nightshirt and slips on her mother's death-gown, crosses to the bed, and slips beneath the sweat-drenched covers.

"…Arlene…?' says her father, not opening his eyes.

"Shhh, honey, it's me. Go back to sleep. Just a bad dream, that's all."

His hand, so calloused and cracked, reaches out to touch her face. She lies down on her mother's pillow and is shocked to find that it still carries the ghost-scent of her perfume. She remembers that her parents liked to spoon, so she rolls over and soon feels her father's body pressing against her, his legs shifting, his arm draping over her waist as he unconsciously fits himself against her. After a moment, she feels his face press against the back of her—her mother's—gown, and he pulls in a deep breath that he seems to hold forever before releasing it.

She does not sleep much that night, but her father sleeps better than he has in years.

We can watch now, you and I, and see his face, see my father's face when he wakes the next morning and sees her next to him. Shadows of gratitude, of shame, of self-disgust, of admiration and love flicker across his face as he stares down at her now-sleeping form. He feels her stir beneath his arm and realizes with a start that his hand is cupping one of her breasts, the way he used to cup his wife's breast before the cancer came and sheeted everything in sweat and rot and pain.

Still, his hand lingers for a few moments as he realizes how very much like her mother's body does his daughter's feel. Then he feels her stir, waking, and closes his eyes, pulling his hand away at the last moment.

His daughter rolls over and sees how deeply asleep he is, and realizes that she's now given herself a duty that can never spoken aloud, only repeatedly fulfilled. Only in this way can she comfort him, help him, thank him.

She slowly rises from the bed, crossing to the closet where he replaces her mother's gown on its hook, then slips back into her own nightshirt and leaves, closing the door behind her.

As soon as the door closes, her father opens his eyes and stares at the empty space in the bed next to him that now hums with her absence. So much like her mother. So much like her mother. So much like her mother.

This goes on for nearly a year, her assuming the role of her dead mother in the night so her father can sleep. In a way, both know what's going on, what they have become, the roles they are playing, but neither ever speaks of it aloud. And even though nothing physical ever occurs between them in the night as they keep the grief at bay, a part of each of them falls a little bit in love with the other. In this way they become closer than they had ever been, and though the house is never again a happy place, the shadows begin to retreat a little…until the night when her father hears the muffled laughter of a boy coming from his daughter's bedroom and storms in with a hammer that he does not intend to use but does, nonetheless, then collapsing to the floor afterward, vomiting and shaking with the realization of what he's done, what he's become, and it takes only a few frenzied hours for him to mop up the blood and tissue and then tear up the floorboards and move the piles of human meat underneath, burying his daughter in her mother's nightgown. He takes great care replacing the boards, hammering them into place, then covering them with an area rug taken from the living room before gathering a few things—some clothes, what little cash is in the house, some food—and stumbling out into the night.

Shhh, listen—do you hear it? That sound like old nails being wrenched from wood? The front door is opening, someone is coming in, someone who walks in a heavy heel-to-toe fashion as if afraid the earth might open up between each step and swallow him whole.

We watch as the old, hunched, broken thing that was once my father makes his way toward my bedroom. He carries a battery-operated lantern with him, a small backpack, and so much regret that its stench reaches us even in this non-place we wander.

He sets down the lantern, then his backpack, removing a hammer from inside. The same hammer.

In the light we see how he's changed. Well over seventy-five, and the years have not been kind. He looks so much like Mother did toward the end, a living skeleton covered in gray skin, slick with sickness. He moves aside what remains of the rug and sets to work on the floorboards, which offer little resistance, and within a few minutes, he is staring down at us.

"I'm home," he whispers.

Hello, Daddy. I've missed you.

He sits down, his legs dropping down beneath the hole in the floor, his feet resting between us.

"I thought about the two of you every day," he says. "I've dreamed about the two of you every night…those nights that I can sleep. Ain't too many of those, especially lately."

It's all right, Daddy. I understand. We understand.

He reaches into his backpack and removes something we can't quite make out, because he's deliberately keeping it hidden from our gazes. We're back in what remains of our bodies now, staring up at this lost, broken, sick old man whose face is drenched in sweat, in pain, in the end of things.

"I had no right," he says. "I had no right to love you like that, in that way. I had no right to be jealous, Melissa."

Melissa. So that was my name. How pretty.

"I didn't mean it, I didn't mean to do it." And he brings the object into the light so we can see it. But we already knew, didn't we, you and I? His old gun from the war where he never was a hero, just a simple foot soldier who helped fight the enemy and serve his country before coming home to marry a good woman and build a life for his family.

He begins to speak again: "Oh, honey, I…" But the rest of it dies in his throat, clogged by phlegm and failure and guilt.

It's all right, Daddy. We understand. We're not mad anymore.

But he doesn't hear us. He clicks off the safety, jacks a round into the chamber, and pushes the business end so deep into his mouth that for a moment we expect him to swallow the entire weapon.

He hesitates for only a moment, but that gives us enough time to move, to rise up as we are now and open our arms as he squeezes the trigger, and we are with him, and he is with us, and as the human meat explodes from the back of his head we lean forward and take him into our embrace, cold flesh and tissue meeting bone and rot, and he embraces us both, does my father, and we hold him close as his blood soaks into the tattered, rotted remains of my mother's nightgown, and we can smell her, she is within us, around us, part of us, and in the last few moments before we pull my father down into hole with us, I find some remnant of my voice in the release of his death, and have just long enough to say, "I forgive you, Daddy, and I love you."

Then he is in the hole with us and in this way are our sins of omission at last atoned.

We remember the way we mingled as we decayed, how we were then found and identified; we remember the way Uncle Sonny claimed our bodies—even yours, my teenaged lover whose name I still can't remember—

and had us taken to the place of cardboard coffins with plywood bottoms where we were fed one at a time into the furnace, our tissues charred and bones reduced to powder. We remember the way the workmen swept us into the containers and then into the machine that shook back and forth, filtering out gold fillings and pins once inserted to hold hips together.

And now we are here, all three of us. Our new home; our hushed home; our forever home.

And you are welcomed here, I tell them.

Mrs. Winters thinks Melissa sounds like an nice girl, the type of girl her grandson might have married if he hadn't died in Vietnam, and oh, by the way, don't let me forget, young lady, to tell you all about my son who was a pilot, who flew so high above the clouds you would have thought he was some kind of angel.

I'd like that, Melissa replies. I smile, insomuch as I am capable of performing such a thing, and I continue through my corridors with their marble floors, looking through my glass doors at those who reside behind, and I know that I will never know the loneliness and hurt of those who reside here, for I will always have these hushed and hallowed nights, I will always have those who rest here within me, and—most of all—I will, until eternity is no more, have the tales the ashes tell.

Old Schick

In the end, in a way, it was all kind of funny when he thought about it—not that Old Schick ever gave him much time *to* think about it, what with all the gutting and the cutting, the laughing, torture, and pain—but, still, on those rare moments when he wasn't being peeled from his own skin or chewing tainted needles or enjoying a glass-shard suppository and screaming for mercy until he spit up blood, Ronald guessed some people might find a certain amount of humor to the whole brouhaha; but, then, humor was a you-should-pardon-the-expression subjective thing.

Unlike Old Schick, who didn't much appreciate the use of complex sentences and multi-syllabic words, not being what you'd call an eloquent speaker; still, it *was* kind of funny, like Lawrence Welk was funny when he counted out the intro to the orchestra on television every week.

A- wunnerful, wunnerful, thank you a-Myron Floran and the lovely a-Lennon Sisters; now we gonna tell you a little story about a good little a-boy and his special friend, and it go a little something like this:

And-a-one, and-a-two, and-a-*sssssssshhhhh-nick!*

Until he and Old Schick were formally introduced, Ronald was a more-or-less decent and normal kid; a high-school graduate, a dependable worker at Beckman's Market where he was employed (like most everyone there) as a stock and delivery boy, cashier, janitor, assistant meat cutter, sometimes short-order cook at the grille that was part of the store, and listener to Floyd Beckman's stories after the market closed at six p.m. every day. Floyd Beckman was something of an artist with the knives, showing Ronald the differences in the "marbles" of meat, how to find the exact spot to begin slicing for the best quality shank steaks, porterhouse cuts, t-bones, etc. Pick any slab of hanging meat that perpetually stocked the walk-in freezer, name the steak you wanted, Floyd Beckman could slice it up fresh like the expert he was—and if you worked at his market then, by God, you learned how to slice up the steaks, as well; maybe not like an expert, but you-bet-your-ass like an expert in training.

Ronald got so good with the knives that Floyd actually almost cried that afternoon in early 1969 when Ronald announced that he was going overseas.

Floyd—who'd lost a nephew in Vietnam—blanched. "When'd you get your notice?"

"I didn't," Ronald said.

"Shit—you drew a low number?"

"Nope."

Floyd sighed. "Have I told you lately that you're a goddamn frustrating individual to try and have a conversation with sometimes?"

"I get a lot of complaints about that."

"When do you leave?"

"First of next month."

Floyd began sharpening one of his knives—*shhhhh-nick!...shhhhh-nick!*—as he turned away from Ronald and cleared his throat. "You, uh... you listen to me, Ron. You take care of yourself over there, hear me?"

"I will."

"I'm not just talking out my ass here, understand? I *mean* it. That's one shitty place over there, and you're gonna run into meat-grinders a helluva lot more dangerous than the one we got here." *Shhhhh-nick!* "You do your tour, get yourself back here in one piece, and you'll...you'll always have a job waiting for you. Got it?"

"Yes, sir. Thank you."

Unlike a lot of guys in Cedar Hill, Ronald was not drafted; he enlisted out of a genuine sense of duty to his country, and was quite happy when, after completing basic, he received his orders; then it all became something of a blur to him: the leave-taking, the long trip over, the move to Muc Wa in Quang Nai Province, or maybe it was Nai Muc in Quang Wa Province, or Me Fuk Duc, or U Long Wong near the Chicken-Choke Delta—the names were interchangeable and unpronounceable and utterly impenetrable to him, so after a while he just gave up trying to remember because there was this *heat,* ya dig, heat that he'd been told about but hadn't really been prepared for; heat that went beyond his concept of tropical; heat that was so humid it had actual *weight* to it; heat that dragged at your ass and nuts; heat that pulled you down toward the ground with such force it was impossible most days to maintain a respectable posture (something the drill sergeants had hammered into him during basic: a good Marine always had good, dignified Marine posture, you miserable pile of walking afterbirth); and if the heat wasn't bad enough, the perpetual *suddenness* of dawn and dusk shocked the shit out of him; if it hadn't been for these beautiful white birds that always flew up out of the rice paddies in the morning, he wouldn't have been able to tell the start of day from the start of night because most of the time he was so busy looking down at his feet for tripwires he missed the setting of the sun or the rising of the moon altogether; dusk and dawn were so fast it was like someone flipped a light switch, and that was interesting, but not as interesting as his final moments in combat, which came right smack in the middle of the night— the first clear night they'd seen in weeks (it never stopped with the fucking rain over here): his platoon was just outside a TOC near Truong Son or Snot Flung or some other goddamn place like that, and there was nothing much there, a few abandoned Montagnard villages, no companies or divisions, no roads, just jungle and NVA—even support from 175-millimeter guns at Firebase Mary Lou ten miles away couldn't save their behinds if the NVA decided to attack in full force—and you bet your ass that's just what they did, screw the threat of B-52 arclight strikes that usually kept the dinks hunkered down in Laos—these guys were gonna take out the center no matter what, and they hit the place not three minutes after Ronald's platoon arrived by chopper at three o'clock in the morning (their first mistake, he later realized), everyone jumping out and running behind the platoon leader, their run becoming a walk as they shot and screamed and hand-grenaded their way into a nearby swamp, and in less than ten minutes Ronald saw dead NVA with leeches on their eyes and holes in their chests you could comfortably fit your ass inside if you were feeling tuckered and needed a quick rest, but that didn't seem right to think that way, these guys probably had families waiting for them at home, and that was when he heard a sound—once, very quick, somewhere overhead in the trees: *sssssssshhhhh-nick!*

Reminded him a little of Floyd Beckman sharpening his knives before cutting into a fresh side of beef, that sound did, and he looked up into the canopy of limbs and leaves above him and saw the heads hanging there, dozens of them: heads of NVA, heads of American soldiers, Montagnard heads, baby's heads, animal heads, heads cut off clean and straight across the neck, all of them hanging there like bulbs on a Christmas tree, and Ronald felt a great swell of pity for all of them, and that was his final moment of compassion for anyone during that war because then the explosions came, and the sniper fire, and more screaming, and Ronald stepped forward—tiptoed, actually, not that it made any difference two seconds later when he was suddenly flying, arcing upward and then straight down as he heard more than felt his body slam down into the mud (*Doin' the Claymore Crash*, as his fellow soldiers called it); after that he lay there in the muck staring up at even more decapitated heads and drank his own blood for a while as the ambush continued around him, and at one point he opened his eyes to see a leech slithering over his nose toward his right eye and that just cut it, that leech did, that just fuckin' *jiggled* to beat the band and Ronald sighed, not out of resignation or sadness or bravado but out of frustration, pure and simple, because Jesus H. Kee-rist-in-a-Chrysler this was gonna be one lousy stinking miserable messy and downright undignified way to buy the farm and—

—*sssssssshhhhh-nick!*—

—what the hell?

Replying to the unspoken question, the sound came again: *Sssssssshhhhh-nick!*

Ronald blinked, for the moment forgetting about the leech nearing his eye, spit out some blood, and whispered, "Floyd?"

…*sssssssshhhhh-nick-sssssssshhhhh-nick-sssssssshhhhh*…

Somehow, Ronald was able to understand what the sound was saying to him: *No…not Floyd…but a friend, yessssssssss, indeed…*

A quick silver flash, and the leech was plucked from his face.

The sounds of the ambush were fading as the fighting moved farther into the swamp. Moonlight broke through the canopy of leaves, illuminating the various heads, making their eyes sparkle, making those gazes seem alive, focused, staring…and very, very interested in the scene below them.

"*Nassssssssty little thingssssssss*," said a voice.

Ronald blinked blood and sweat from his eyes and saw a hunched figure squatting beside him. At first he thought it was some gook kid, hair all straight and black with skin the color of light copper, staying behind to kill any survivors—that sure as shit looked like a knife he was holding—but as the gook leaned toward Ronald, his face passed through a wide slant of moonlight spilling down from the trees and he…changed. Got bigger, for one thing; a *lot* bigger.

"*That'sssssss going to hurt sssssssssso much.*" He pointed to the gnarled, bloody mass of bones and tissue that hung below Ronald's waist where his right leg had been only a minute ago. Ronald noted with a detached fascination that his right foot was pointing in the wrong direction; the toe of his boot was pressing down into the mud and the boot heel was where the toe was supposed to be. It was kind of interesting.

"*Doesssssssss it hurt?*" asked the guy who was no longer a gook.

Ronald stared at him. "Not yet."

The guy's head looked like a talking turd—and not one of those long, brown, soft, warm, really satisfying Cleveland Steamers that slid gracefully out of your behind and plopped into the toilet with a nice wet *kerplunk!*, leaving you relieved with a big smile on your face, no, huh-uh; this guy's head looked like one of those hard, knotted, thumb-sized black turd-pellets that skulked out of your ass in slow, agonized degrees, clawing at your hemorrhoids and pulling out part of your colon with it, making you wince and groan and scream as it unwillingly vacated the premises before landing in the bowl with a sharp, defiant *plink!* that always sounded like translated turd-ese for *and fuck you, too.*

It wasn't just that he was black—he was *astoundingly* black. Ronald had never seen a black man of that impenetrable hue: it was a blackness of such intensity that it reflected no light at all, achieving a near-total obliteration of facial features and taking on a mysterious undertone that had the blue-gray of ashes. If it hadn't been for the two bright silver shattered stars of his eyes—looking for all the world like Fourth of July sparklers burning fierce and fast—Ronald would have thought this guy *was* a talking turd.

"You the Angel of Death?" asked Ronald. "Is this where I buy it? You tell me the truth because I ain't been to church in a while and I need to confess my sins first. Bible says so."

"*Confessssssss,*" said the guy with turd-pellet head. "*Confesssssssssion'sssss good for the sssssssssoul.*" He adjusted the magician's top hat on his head; chrome razor blades woven into the hat band winked at Ronald as they caught a bit of moonlight.

This was some seriously weird shit, truly; did the Bible say anything about this? Maybe he'd missed it. "*And The Angel of Death broughteth unto the dying man a vision of seriously weird shit, truly, and the dying man sincerely trembleth in the shit's presence."*

Ronald tried raising his right arm to make the sign of the cross but his arm was having no part of it. Ronald was scared. You couldn't confess until you crossed yourself, and if he couldn't do that…

Turd-Pellet leaned closer and touched Ronald's shoulder. The guy didn't have any fingernails; instead each finger ended in a shiny winking razor blade, and when the guy rubbed his fingers together the blades clicked and sparked—*sssssssshhhhh-nick*! *"You jussssssssst take it easssssssssy,"* he said. *"I insssssssssisssssssssst."*

With a flick and spark of his fingers, the guy sheared away the sleeve of Ronald's jacket and the uniform underneath. Pulling away the material, he lifted up Ronald's arm, slapped it a couple of times to raise a vein, then smiled: his gums were a deep, sick shade of purple, and his teeth weren't teeth at all, they looked more like stickpins or needles; moonlight glinted off his grin, forcing Ronald to blink.

The pain was beginning to register with his brain, and Ronald started convulsing.

"Sssssssssssssssshhhhhhhh," said the guy, removing his top hat. *"Watch thisssssssss."* He showed Ronald the inside of his top hat, which was empty, then set the hat on Ronald's chest and shook out his arms like Art Carny playing Ed Norton always did on *The Honeymooners*. For the first time Ronald saw that the duster coat the guy was wearing looked like it was wet, then another beam of moonlight broke through the trees and revealed his coat was made out of moist, raw flesh, just like his pants.

"Nothing up my sssssssssleeve," he said—

—and reached up to his head and began pulling on the zipper that ran the length of his skull, back to front. Once he'd finished unzipping his head—releasing a belch of steam that sounded like it was screaming—he shoved a hand in there and began rummaging around, making thick sopping sounds like someone scooping out the guts of a pumpkin. After a moment he seemed to find whatever in the hell it was he was looking for, and his smile widened.

"Ah, yesssssssss…here it isssssssss…"

He started pulling something out of his skull, and as he did one of his needle-teeth began retracting into his gums like a strand of undercooked spaghetti being sucked slowly into a mouth.

"How do you do that?" asked Ronald. "That's a pretty cool trick."

"*Jussssssssst watch...*"

The tooth slipped out of sight, and Old Schick—Ronald found himself thinking of him by this name because both Ronald and his dad used only Schick razor blades, they were the best, and this guy here seemed like he'd be real choosy about the type of razors he wore, so why not Schick?—he pulled out his hand from his head and showed Ronald the hypodermic he was now holding, its needle long and shiny except for that little bit of torn gum tissue about halfway up.

Old Schick zippered closed his head, then donned his top hat again, lifted Ronald's right arm, slipped the needle into a raised vein, and slowly sank the plunger. It took only a couple of seconds before the pain ebbed away and Ronald's entire body felt as bright and shiny as Old Schick's eyes.

"*Better, isssssssss it?*"

"...oh, you bet'cha..." said Ronald, feeling shinier by the second. Old Schick, he was all right, a stand-up type of guy—hell, any guy who'd give you a shot of the shinies at a time like this was A-okay in Ronald's book. "...dunno how to...to thank you..."

"*Ah,*" said Old Schick. "*I have a few thoughtssssssss on thissssssss...*"

"...anything you want, buddy, just name it..."

"*...I jussssssssst need sssssssssome ressssssssst...and a ride...*"

"...don't know if...if I can help you on those, buddy..."

Old Schick held up something that looked like a polished bone with a lot of geometric symbols carved into it; another glint of moonlight revealed that it was an ivory handle of some sort, and jutting from the handle was the longest, widest, sharpest-looking straight-razor Ronald had ever seen.

"...thought that was a knife..." he said.

"*That'sssssssss all right...a sssssssssimple missssssssstake...*"

Those drawn-out sibilants of his were starting to wear on Ronald's nerves a bit; still, he'd given Ronald the shiny shot, so what the hell? The guy sounded a little like James Mason; a macho lisp. Could be worse.

With a flick of his wrist, Old Schick sent the opened razor arcing high into the air, boomerang-style; it snapped and spun and chewed through the tops of the trees, slicing through the ropes, wires, and strings that were holding the decapitated heads in place. One by one they passed through the slanting moonlight, each turning into an NVA head before plip-plopping down into the muck like cherries onto the whipped cream topping of a sundae.

Donning his top hat, never once taking his eyes off Ronald's face, Old Schick held out his hand and waited patiently for the razor to return to his grip, which it soon did, snapping faster than a blink back to the center of his palm, handle-first.

Old Schick smiled wider, shook out his sleeves Art Carney-style again, then spun around and stuck out his arms like Spider-Man doing his web-action; dozens of long wet strands of human sinew shot out from around his wrists and flew across the swamp, each one latching onto a head and dragging it back until all of them were piled up nice and neat and dripping next to Ronald.

"War heroesssssssss alwaysssssssss get a free ride home," said Old Schick. *"And I need a ressssssssst. Thisssssssss war hassssssssss tuckered me a bit."*

"I hear you there, buddy," said Ronald.

"I'm sssssssssure you do..." Old Schick adjusted his hat, then squatted back down and with a quick, painless crisscrossing twirl of his hand and blade, made an "X" on Ronald's chest, then broke apart into a million spinning razors, each with a blinking eye in its center; the razors clacked and sparked and *ssssssssschick*'d to beat the band—

—a wunnerful, wunnerful, thank you the a-lovely Semonski Sisters and a-Mr. Jack Imel, master of the a-xylophone—

—twisting faster, gathering together into a single silver funnel that looped and twirled into the shape of the double helix (Ronald remembered that from school) before shooting straight up into the moonlight, whip-curling around, and slamming back down into the bloody "X" in the center of Ronald's chest, turning the shininess into a total, overwhelming liquid darkness that somehow felt even better than the shiny shot....

Ronald had wanted to finish his tour and then just come home like any other soldier, no big deal, no fuss made, nothing special, but the many medics and orderlies who cleansed him and supplied him with food and blood and stitched up his wounds in the field—and later the doctors in Saigon who rebuilt his leg piece by piece, fusing sections of old bone with new, adding braces of metal and sinew of wire and pins where needed—pretty much screwed that wish into the ground; them, and all the goddamn medals they gave him. Ronald tried telling all the officers and the reporters and the general whose name he couldn't remember that he hadn't killed all those NV single-handedly during the ambush, but all they did was pat his shoulder and remind him that he was the only surviving member of his unit, he was just *confused*, he'd been *badly wounded*, things would *straighten themselves out* in his memory soon enough; in the meantime, soldier, you just concentrate on getting better and enjoy the flight home, you hear.

He was hospitalized for a very long time, and for most of that time what he feared more than any physical impairment he was going to carry around for the rest of his life, what caused him to cry alone at nights more than the memory of all his buddies in the unit being wiped out, what made him long for the liquid darkness that had bloomed inside him right after he'd stepped on the mine, was this: his homecoming.

His homecoming was going to be just awful, Awful, *AWFUL*.

After all, he was a hero of the war; he was the only survivor; he was the guy who, all by himself and with hand-held weapons, killed 26 NVA, confirmed. All the papers and TV news reporters said so.

He *tried* telling everyone otherwise, but they were having none of it.

And so, on a drizzling afternoon in late 1970, Ronald—in full uniform that was heavy in the chest with medals—hobbled off a plane in Virginia with a couple of dozen other soldiers to be met by cheers and boos, bright flashing lights from cameras, and some local high-school band playing "The Stars And Stripes Forever". Shouts of "Welcome home!" and "Baby killers!" intermingled in his ears until it sounded like the whole world was screaming about hero killer babies. Ronald just moved forward as best he could, the braces on and in his leg clinking and scraping against the inside of his pants. The doctors had given him an aluminum cane to use until he got used to walking on the half-human, half-robot thing that used to be his right leg; Ronald tried not to look at his leg too much. It wasn't so much the metal and the pins, it was the way the flesh (what flesh was left, anyway) was scarred; it didn't look like your typical scarring, it looked more like someone had carved geometric shapes all over it.

It reminded him of something, those shapes, but he couldn't quite remember what.

He saluted the officers who greeted the soldiers, shook their hands, posed for pictures, then went into a room for some debriefing before being fed a pretty good steak dinner and put on a smaller plane back to Ohio.

He came through the gate at the Columbus airport to about a hundred people, all of them shouting and cheering and taking pictures. No one called him a baby killer or spit at him. Everyone seemed downright giddy. His mom and dad and Floyd Beckman were among the first people to crowd around him and hug him and shake his hand and treat him like a Big Deal Hero.

Ronald just wanted to curl up into a ball and die.

It went on like this for a while, both at the airport and once he got back home to Cedar Hill. Ten goddamn days he was the biggest deal in town. Then, not so much. Then a little less. Then not at all, and that pleased him no end.

He'd been back about two months when he started work back up at Beckman's Market. He was getting around pretty good on the leg, though he still had to take more pain medicine than he liked, and it sometimes made him a bit goofy, but everyone seemed to understand about that, so he counted his blessings and felt pretty good about getting back to his same old same-old life, where he was no Big Deal, nothing special, just another guy working at the market.

Ronald got his own place—a nice apartment near downtown right over the Wagon Wheel Bar and Grille that had a big-ass skylight, which made it nice on clear starry nights—and made it a point to always have dinner with his parents at least twice a week, and have them over for some cards and television on the weekend. He started dating a girl named Jodi who worked part-time on the weekends at the grille in Beckman's Market. Jodi was blonde and skinny as a stick and laughed at all his jokes, even when they weren't so funny. She had gray eyes and perfect teeth and always smelled like vanilla and her hands were so warm and soft Ronald thought a guy could just spend the rest of his life with her hand against his cheek if he took a mind to. She was also pretty shy, which suited Ronald just fine; he wasn't much of a ladies' man and didn't much have the looks or grace or popularity to be one of the "Love The One You're With" crowd. He and Jodi had been dating for six months before he tried holding her hand, and a full year before he kissed her. She wasn't in any hurry and neither was he.

Life went on, slow and steady and delightfully dull, just the way Ronald preferred it. Chet Huntley and David Brinkley did their final broadcast of *The Huntley-Brinkley Report,* President Richard M. Nixon announced that he was pulling all troops out of Vietnam, Sean Connery came back as James Bond in *Diamonds Are Forever* when George Lazenby quit after only one movie, Elvis Presley started getting really fat, four burglars broke into the

Watergate Hotel and everybody was making a lot of noise about it, and a former war hero by the name of Ronald Cooperider asked a shy blonde-haired girl with gray eyes to marry him. She said yes, and they went back to Ronald's place that night and lost their virginity to one another.

That was 1974.

Then, right before Hallowe'en that year, Old Schick woke—*sssssssschnick!*—up.

Later, a whole slew of people would come forward, puffing out their chests like week-old corpses and disgorging a lot of purple hot air they claimed as explanations for what happened, citing things like Ronald's lonely childhood (he'd been a skinny, crooked-tooth, four-eyed little dweeb who had no interest in sports and so was often the target of bullies: boo), his antagonistic environment (growing up in Cedar Hill where a man was only thought to be a man if he was a White, Athletic, Semi-Articulate, Beer-Guzzling Poon-Tang Wrangler who drove a pickup with at least one shotgun hanging on the rack on its back window—Ronald never had a chance, poor kid: fuckin'), and, of course, these bloated-corpse opiners always wound up pointing the finger at Mommy and Daddy (who never gave him enough attention or approval: hoo).

To summarize the parenthetical points: *Boo-fuckin'-hoo*, Ronald would think. Later.

In those rare moments when he had time *to* think about it.

It started at the Valley Drive-In down on 21st Street. Ronald had gone there to see a double feature of John Wayne movies, *McQ* and *Cahill, U.S. Marshal*, and it was real good to see The Duke kicking butt, even if *McQ* would have been better suited to Clint Eastwood. The first movie ended and Ronald decided to watch the previews before going to the concessions stand. It was too bad Jodi was sick tonight; she loved The Duke almost as much as Ronald. Well, maybe she'd be feeling better for next week.

He hoped they were going to have something good showing for Hallowe'en; the Valley Drive-In ("**Open Every Weekend, April Through October**") always made a big deal at Hallowe'en, their last weekend of business for the year; last year, on top of the costume and ghost-story contests, they'd shown *Night Of The Living Dead* with *The Night Evelyn Came Out Of The Grave* and served blood-colored popcorn and steamy sausages that looked like fresh-torn guts. It was fun.

The previews started. The Valley always showed their previews in reverse order, just to build suspense; next weekend, for Hallowe'en, their second feature would be *Last House On The Left*, and it looked pretty scary (Ronald had meant to see it when it first came out but never got around to it), but the first feature was this brand-new movie called *The Texas Chainsaw Massacre* and Ronald had never seen anything even like *the preview*—let alone what the movie itself must be like. It looked even scarier than *The Exorcist*, and that had been about the scariest damn movie Ronald had ever seen, and, boy, look at that big ugly freak chasing that girl with the chainsaw, and she's screaming, and it looks like the woods are gonna come alive and grab her, hold her down, just let the big freak chop her to bits and what the hell was it with his face anyway? He looked like—

—"...*it might be interesssssssssting...*"

Ronald looked around, making sure he hadn't left the passenger-side window open and some smartass kid was trying to spook him.

The windows were rolled up and no one that he could see was standing anywhere near the car.

"You're hearing shit again," he whispered to himself. For the last couple of weeks he hadn't slept for shit, and sometimes thought people were talking to him when in truth they hadn't said a word.

"...*sssssssssorry, friend. Your hearing'ssssssss jussssssssst fine...*"

"Who the—?" He looked around again just to make sure someone wasn't crouching down beneath the window where he couldn't see them; he even opened the door and got out, made a search around the car, but...nothing.

Hell, he was already out; might as well go get some popcorn and a Coke.

The Valley ran cartoons after the previews, and as Ronald headed toward the concessions stand his shadow stretched in front of him, backlit by Bugs and Daffy and Elmer Fudd. Ronald watched his shadow stretch... and stretch...and stretch...

...the hell was it with his head? He wasn't wearing a hat.

He reached up to see if maybe his hair was messed up or if maybe somebody had tossed out an empty popcorn tub and it had landed on his head and he just didn't notice—sometimes the medicine he took made him not notice things, and he'd taken some earlier, right before the movie started—but he couldn't feel anything up there, just his own hair, and as he brought his hand back down he saw something bright and silver flash near his fingertips—

—razor blades. Instead of fingernails he had razor blades, jammed in width-wise so they stuck way out on his too-long bloody fingers and—

—"...*that wasssssssss a ssssssssplendid ressssssssst...yessssssss, it wasssssssss...*"

Ronald ran into the men's room and vomited into the toilet of the first stall. It felt like he was puking his fucking *shoes* up, it hurt so much, and by the time he was finished, by the time he'd emptied his stomach of everything he'd eaten in the last week (that's how it *felt*, anyway), by the time the lights blinked announcing that the second feature was about to start, Ronald was sitting back on his ass, head leaning against the metal of the stall door, tearing off half a roll of toilet paper to wipe his face. He sponged off a good bit of puke and was about to toss it in the toilet when he saw that the toilet paper was stained with blood.

Moving slowly onto his knees, Ronald peered over the rim of the toilet and saw something that he *couldn't* be seeing, no way, no how, so he pulled back, closed his eyes, gripped the sides of the bowl, took a deep breath, leaned forward, and opened his eyes.

That the inside of the toilet was splattered in blood didn't surprise him, didn't even really scare him, truth be told—no, the scary part was looking at what had just come out of his stomach.

Razor blades.

But the thing was, these didn't look like your everyday kind of razor blades—they were just a little bigger than what you expected, and shinier, almost like razor-blade-shaped mirrors, and in each of these mirrors there was a blinking eye, and in each of those eyes there was the image of a face, and these faces, they were screaming and clawing at the surface like someone who'd fallen into a frozen lake and was carried away by the current and was now trying to beat their way out from under the ice before it was too late, their hands scratched and scrabbled, some of them made fists and beat against the wall of their prison, and Ronald could see that it was real, could see the way the skin on the sides of their hands flattened out when it hit the barrier, how their fingers bled the more they clawed, how their mouths worked in silent cries and their faces grew red and the veins stood out on their necks and faces, and these were the faces of NVA, these were the faces of Montagnard children, the faces of dogs and animals and even all the buddies from Ronald's unit who'd bought it during the ambush, and Ronald struggled to his feet, fighting the urge to vomit again, tossing the bloodied toilet paper into the bowl and then pushing the lever to flush it all away—

—"*...sssssssssory about that...*"—

—and when they started to spin in the water the razors and faces and blinking eyes, they all mashed together into this big clog of silver and blood and skin that shot wet strands of sinew out of its side that snaked up the sides of the toilet bowl and gripped it like kudzu covering an abandoned well and Ronald backed up to the closed stall door and watched as these masses of sinew made themselves into something like spidery hands and began pulling the clog upward and that was about all Ronald wanted to see, that was about all he could stand to see, so he spun around and yanked the stall door open with so much force he almost ripped it from the hinges and didn't so much run as leap out of there, all the while hearing thick, wet sounds that reminded him too much of how it sounded when the medics had first tried setting the bone in his leg only to discover that a good portion of it was gone—

—and he was almost to the door when the shadow of something scuttling across the ceiling above his head fell over him, and then he had the handle of the door in his hand and that's when the shadow moved down toward the top of the doorway and he looked up and that was a big mistake because now *it* knew *he* knew it was there, and for a second they just stayed like that: Ronald, with his bloody hand gripping the door handle, and the dog-sized razor blade covered in screaming human faces, hanging by a thick stalk of sinew right over him. Two of the faces melted into one another, and then a third, and then the whole mess flattened out like a slit before opening with a moist peeling sound to reveal the fist-sized eyeball, and then someone said:

"*...sssssssso you don't remember me, do you?...*"

And Ronald yanked open the door and—

—and for a moment the whole world went wrong, the whole world went backward, forward, downward, sideways, and a sharp, cold, intense pain like none he'd never experienced before snarled upward through his entire body, and as he reached out to catch his balance he saw the razor blades at the ends of his fingers spark off one another as his hands flexed, and every time his hands flexed the blades *sssssssschnick*'d their edges together, and when that happened the faces trapped beneath their surface began to change—

—*sssssssschnick!*—

—and the face of a screaming woman changed jaws with that of a howling dog—

—*sssssssschnick!*—

—and this time it was the face of a baby that got cut in half and the missing half replaced by that of an old man—

—*sssssssschnick!*—

—and now it was a couple of teenagers, a boy and a girl, who switched mouths and noses with those of a couple of NVA—

Ronald held back the scream he felt thundering up from somewhere near the bottom of his nuts and ran to his car and tore the hell out of there, not stopping until he screeched into his parking place behind the bar, and even then it took his heart another two minutes to catch up with him.

Waking nightmares, he told himself. *The doctor said that waking nightmares weren't uncommon when you'd been losing sleep, it was just your brain's way of trying to clear away some of the cobwebs that built up and that you were supposed to get rid of when you slept...*

Okay; yeah. That was it. That had to be it.

Easy way to fix this.

Once back inside his apartment, he went into the bathroom and downed three of the tranquilizers the doctor had given him when he'd mentioned about the sleeplessness and hearing things, then waited for them to kick in so he could pass out and forget about this, this was just some kind of crazy that'd been locked up in his head since the ambush, the doctors in Saigon had told him stuff like this might start happening, but he didn't believe them, not then, not even for the first three years of being back home because he hadn't Hadn't *HADN'T* experienced anything like that, not until recently and oh fuck-me-with-a-fiddlestick *why* was this happening *now*? Now, when his life was good, when everything was well on-track and there wasn't any fuss?

"*...fusssssssss,*" said a voice. "*...no mussssssss, no fusssssss...that's sssssssss not right...*"

"It don't mean nothin'," whispered Ronald to the bathroom walls, sitting on the closed toilet lid, arms crossed over his chest, rocking back and forth. "It don't mean nothin'."

"...*sssssssssaysssssssss you...*"

He lurched to his feet and stumbled into the living room just in time to hear the phone.

"...'lo?" he said, feeling groggy and disoriented.

"I *knew* you wouldn't go to the drive-in without me," said Jodi. "I don't know whether to yell at you or kiss you."

"From the sounds of your voice, you maybe shouldn't do either one."

"I sound that bad?"

"You sound really congested."

She coughed; a thick, wet noise. "I know. I need pampering."

"I just...I just took some medicine. I haven't slept much this past week or so and...it's probably not a good idea for me to drive."

"Well, then...can I come over there? You could home-pamper me."

"Think you're okay to drive?"

"Uh-huh. And maybe if I'm lucky I'll make you sick, too, and we'll have to stay inside all week and be sick together."

"I think maybe you should just stay—"

But she'd already hung up.

Ronald felt the pills starting to kick in—these things worked fast—so he staggered to his bedroom. Jodi had a key and would let herself in; if he fell asleep, she'd wake him up. Probably in a real sexy way.

He shook off his clothes, then fell face-first onto the bed—

—only it wasn't a bed anymore, it was a giant breathing razor blade covered in stitched-together skin and it had a mouth and that mouth was open and filled with stickpin teeth jutting from sick purple gums and a long, slimy yellow tongue that flicked up at Ronald's face and licked him and felt like the worst kind of sandpaper cat-tongue kiss and before Ronald could push himself back up the mouth sucked him in with a thousand soft screams and the *sssssssschnick!* of sharpening knives—

—the world proceeded backward, forward, downward, sideways, becoming another world looking into another world that shifted and changed and faded into shadows to be replaced by other worlds, and all of them were screaming, all of these worlds were raw eruptions of pain and anguish and hunger, all of them were filled with tortured faces twisted in pain and fists hammering against the surface that would not break or even crack and it felt like his whole body was wrapped in wet bandages only these bandages all had sharp little needle-teeth that bit down into his skin and started shredding his flesh as they started to unravel, peeling his skin away like he was some kind of orange and he tried to scream, tried to open his mouth and call for someone to please come help him, please pull him out before it chewed him all up and swallowed him into suffering—

—he felt his ass land hard on the floor and send ripples through his spine that finally hit his brain and registered, and he let out with a loud cry before blinking his eyes and realizing that he was on the floor in his own bedroom, where his own bed—his *bed*, not some giant blade with a yellow sandpaper tongue—sat neatly made and unused.

He bent forward, stretching out his throbbing back, and noticed the scars on his right leg.

Was it just him, or did it look like there were a whole helluva lot more of them than the last time he'd looked?

He scooted nearer his bedside table and turned on the small lamp there.

Removing the non-permanent part of the brace, he turned his leg into the light and peered at the scarring.

The geometric shapes made by the scars had changed; the symbols were clearer, more defined in shape, like they were made by a mathematician with a compass and protractor or something like that.

Forty-seven, thought Ronald. *There should only be forty-seven of them.*

He counted, slowly; stopped, steadied himself, counted again.

Fifty-six. There were fifty-six geometric symbols where before there had only been forty-seven—

—and what the fuck did the *number* suddenly have to with anything? It wasn't how many, it had *never* been how many, no; it was the precision of their shape, the almost clinical exactness of their spacing that always bugged the shit out of him and that he tried like hell to ignore. It was like someone had burned some kind of formula or spell onto what was left of his leg when they were patching him up, keeping him doped to the gills and feeling shiny…

Shiny.

An image of bright silver eyes flashed across his memory for a moment; bright silver eyes and a turd-pellet face.

He shook off the image and reattached the non-permanent sections of the brace—but not before counting the scars once more.

Fifty-eight this time.

"Oh, this just *jiggles*," he muttered to himself, then rose to his feet and went into the kitchen for a glass of water. As he passed through the center of the apartment, he looked up at the beautiful full moon whose diffuse silvery light drifted down in soft waves, creating a cone of brightness like a spotlight shone onto the center of a stage. For a moment Ronald just stood there in the center of the spotlight, eyes closed, feeling oddly and suddenly relaxed, like he didn't have a care or a pain in the world.

And a-one, and-a-two, and a—

He'd drunk three glasses of water by the time he heard Jodi open the door and come in.

"It's me, sweetie."

He heard the sounds of her putting down her purse, dropping her keys onto the table, taking off her coat. He set down the empty glass and heard something clatter to the floor. Jesus! Why couldn't he ever get the brace back correctly the first time? Seemed like it took him at least three tries before he got it so that part of the thing didn't just *fall off* when he least expected it to.

"Be right out, honey," he called.

He bent down to retrieve the missing section of brace and saw it wasn't the brace at all; the brace was metal, not white, and it sure as hell wasn't curved like this, with all those geometric symbols along the handle…

He held the thing in his hand, gave a flick of his wrist, and freed the impossible, large razor within.

And a-one, and a-two, and a—

He stopped under the spotlight again, but this time it wasn't a conscious choice; from somewhere deep in his gut a weight like an anchor had suddenly dropped down, nailing him to the spot.

Jodi—who was sitting in his favorite armchair—looked up at him and gasped, leapt to her feet, then slowly, surprisingly, smiled.

"Oh, *Ronnie*…that is just the *grooviest* costume! Are you going to wear that to the drive-in next weekend? I'll bet you'll win. Wow." She walked toward him, craning to get a better look at his face. "Are you wearing platform shoes? C'mon, fess up—how'd you make yourself so much *taller*?"

He opened his mouth and said, "I didn't," but that wasn't what came out; what came out was: *"That's sssssss my little sssssssssecret, sssssssssweetie."* Sounding like the smarmy spider talking to the fly.

He watched as his impossible, long, razor-nailed fingers swept the straight razor back and forth in the moonlight.

Deep inside, Ronald was screaming.

And was answered by: *Jusssssssst ressssssssst. Leave the driving to ussssssss."*

He watched the fingers wiggle, the blades sparking. He felt himself being flayed alive, strips of his skin peeled away and hung on metal hooks that were actually metal tongues rolling out of steel mouths filled with stickpin teeth.

Jodi was so close now he could almost taste her—but whether it was him or Old Schick whose mouth was watering, Ronald didn't know and sure as shit wasn't able to tell.

Not that it made any difference; then or later.

"That'ssssssss it, sssssssssweetie…come clossssssssser…give ussssssss a litlle kisssssssss…"

Things were kind of confusing around Cedar Hill for the next forty-eight hours, give or take, and then for a couple of weeks after that. By the time the smoke cleared and all the victims had been identified and the funerals finished and all the experts had proposed their theories and the newspapers and television people had milked it for all it was worth, what it came down to was this:

Some nutcase had gone ape-shit at the Valley Drive-In Saturday night, killing six people and one baby during the second feature of *Cahill, U.S. Marshal* using something like a scalpel; the killings were compared to those of Jack the Ripper because all of the wounds were very, very precise; the victims' throats had been slashed right into the vocal cords, which is why no one heard any screams. What the officials couldn't explain—and what was never made public—was that the killer had managed to strip damn near every inch of skin off the torsos of his victims, skin that still hadn't been found, right in the middle of a crowded drive-in lot.

That was the first thing.

The second thing happened after Floyd Beckman opened his market for business the following Monday morning and—after laying a prime side of USDA choice across the butcher's block—did a quick inventory of his meat locker and discovered that he had six more sides of beef hanging in there than he was supposed to. It wasn't until he started slicing into the slab on the block and noticed the vagina and pubic hair that he realized something wasn't exactly you-should-pardon-the-expression right; of course, most people would have seen the IUD that was still in place and figured it out well beforehand, but Floyd was really upset so most folks forgave him this oversight.

The third thing that happened was that a twenty-year-old employee of Beckman's Market named Jodi Winters had been reported missing early Sunday morning by her parents, who'd gone to her apartment because she was sick and not answering her phone and they were worried because she *never* went anywhere without telling them, she was that considerate of others' feelings.

The fourth thing was that the missing Jodi Winters worked at the same place where the extra sides of "beef" had popped up, and it didn't take too long for savvy law-enforcement officials to make the connection, especially after Ronald Cooperider, war hero, Floyd Beckman's assistant meat cutter, and engaged to one missing Jodi Winters didn't show up for work the same Monday when Floyd had an embarrassment of riches, meat-wise.

And a-one, and a-two, and a…

They broke down the door to Ronald's apartment after he failed to answer. They found Jodi's skin hanging over the shower-curtain rod in Ronald's bathroom but never located the rest of her; she'd been stripped out of her skin with a taxidermist's skill: one long, precise slice from the back of the skull to the backs of each ankle.

Ronald was another matter altogether.

Him they found hanging from a meat hook he'd nailed to the kitchen wall; the business end of the hook had gone straight through the back of his neck and come out just under the collarbone, so he hung straight and firm. In his hand was an old, rusty antique straight razor with a shit-brown handle. The edge of the razor was so dull it couldn't cut butter, but Ronald had somehow managed to unpeel every inch of his own skin from mid-thigh to mid-chest using it.

There was almost no blood anywhere to speak of.

They found a note, written by Ronald, taped neatly to the refrigerator door:

i am sorry for the harm I have done but the god of all things sharp has commanded me to do his bidding and I cant refuse him yeah and the angel of death who was the god of all things sharp broughteth unto me a vision of seriously weird business, truly, and I sincerely trembleth in the shits presence but he biteth me in the ass anyway if youre hungry i left goodies in the fridge sorry about the mess lock up when you leave please this neighborhood isn't as safe as it used to be

"Crazy son-of-a-bitch," said one of the detectives, shaking his head.

Then his partner opened the refrigerator door and saw the ugly stuff inside and started throwing up and things got confusing all over again.

The six extra sides of beef found in Floyd's meat locker were put back together as best they could be and eventually identified as Paul and Miranda Cooperider, Ronald's parents, and a third individual, male, whose identity was never determined.

They never found all the remains.

Old Schick, he needed his road food.

A-wunnerful, wunnerful, very nice and thank you, a-MaryLou Metzger and Don Delo. We now say a-good-night with the rest of our a-musical story about our good little a-boy and his special a-friend; it go a little something a-like a-this:

When Ronald's soul was torn from his body and sliced up like a loaf of bologna only to be slapped back together in a new place where he was perpetually peeled from his own skin and made to chew tainted needles and endure glass-shard suppositories and liquid metal enemas and every now and then a barbed-wire catheter (just to break the monotony) that made him scream for mercy until he spit up blood, the first thing he noticed when he was dropped unceremoniously into the Razor God's kingdom was that there were so many gnats bouncing about; only it turned out they weren't gnats, they were razor blades of all shapes and sizes, fluttering around like butterflies as they flayed and eviscerated and circumcised and emasculated and infibulated to beat the band, and when they started toward him he knew they'd hurt like hell because Old Schick, well, he'd use only the best blades, here in his special hell, and as the blades fell on him Ronald had just enough time to read the word **Gillette** printed on every. Last. One. Of. Them.

Which was, in a way, kind of funny when you thought about it.

Light On Broken Glass

"The people who have adored me—there have not been very many, but there have been a few—have always insisted on living on, long after I have ceased to care for them, or they to care for me."
—Oscar Wilde, *The Picture of Dorian Gray*

"Don't tell me the moon is shining; show me the glint of light on broken glass."
—Anton Chekhov

The thing is, I *never* stopped missing her. Even when she made it clear at the divorce hearing that she wanted no contact with or from me until I "found" my soul again, even though I knew that we'd never have the chance of even being just friends, even though I kept hoping that the thought of me and our marriage *never* crossed her mind again so she'd know *some kind* of happiness...I missed her every goddamn day. And now she's gone and everything's following after her and I...Jesus, I'm scared.

Can I get one of those cigarettes? Thank you.

Oh, man, that tastes good. I suppose I ought to be grateful she didn't smoke, too, or else all you'd've offered me was an empty hand.

Please don't look at me that way. I *know* how it sounds, and I also know that you're the third—no wait, make that *fourth* detective to come in here and talk to me. I'm surprised that it took this long to send in a *female* detective, though. What's the idea, that if you flash enough new faces my way eventually I'm gonna change the story? And why you? Did one of the higher-ups determine that I'm more likely to make a slip if they sent in a skirt to bat her sparkly eyes at me?

I'm sorry, that was rude. I didn't mean to offend you, honestly. Despite what you may think, I do respect women, Detective...Manning—but I didn't always.

Hell, at one point in my life I was a real hound—you know the type, the kind of guy who lives by the rule of the Four F's? Find 'em, Feel 'em, Fuck 'em, and Forget 'em. Yeah, I was a sexist ass. But Laura, my ex-wife, she cured me of that. She made me *understand* what a pig I'd been, and she didn't do it by trying to make me feel guilty, she did it by...ah, hell, what's it matter now?

Come again? Do I find it *easier* to talk to women? I don't know, I... yeah, I suppose I do. Since we're being so honest and open and forgiving and all that, mind telling me how big an audience we've got watching us from behind that mirror? No, it doesn't matter, I'm just curious, that's all.

Wow, *that* many. Hello, folks!

What? Noticed that, did you? Nope, no one's asked me about how it all started, which is probably why nothing I've said so far makes much sense. You're the first one.

Look, I didn't mean to scare all those people. I only pulled out the gun because I wanted someone to *prove* to me that the fucking McDonald's was still there! I've been trying for *days* to get someone to prove things like that to me, and the gun...seemed the best way to get people's attention, that's all. The damn thing wasn't even loaded, by the way. Of course, you know that. I swear to you, I never would've hurt anyone, I didn't idolize that "I'm-going-to-hunt-humans" guy who shot up that Mickey-D's back in '84.

I *know* I'm avoiding your question, I recognize my voice. But you have to understand, I can't just...*tell you* about how it started without getting into details that don't seem like much, taken by themselves, but that if you look at them as part of a *whole*...

...okay, the McDonald's. *That particular* McDonald's, the one where you arrested me, it's the same one that Laura and I always went to for Sunday morning breakfast. It was the one closest to her old apartment. See, when we were dating, when we were still in that giddy "getting-to-know-all-about-you" phase, we always went out on Saturday. We'd start with some lunch and then some shopping—clothes stores, book stores, record stores—this was back when they still manufactured records and not CDs—then we'd hit a movie, go out for a late dinner, and always wind up back at her place where we'd spend the whole night just *talking*. Then one of us'd look at the clock and see that it was, like, 6:45 in the morning, and we'd hit *that* McDonald's for breakfast before I went back to my place and Laura went home. Those Sunday breakfasts, those were one of our things, y'know? Silly as it sounds, we thought of that Mickey-D's as *our* Mickey-D's. Every Sunday morning, after breakfast, I'd kiss her goodbye in the parking lot and we'd hold each other longer and longer each time, until she finally looked at me one morning and said, "This is stupid. Come back home with me." Even after we were married, we always went to *that* McDonald's.

Look me in the eyes, Detective Manning. Thank you. I demanded a polygraph test earlier, and by now my guess is that the results showed I wasn't lying. I am telling you, my hand to God, I am telling you that that McDonald's *isn't there* now. When I got the word ten days ago that Laura had died, I couldn't think, I couldn't feel, I couldn't...*function*. So I did the only thing I could think to do, and that was sit up crying all night Saturday and go to that McDonald's on Sunday morning to have breakfast in her memory. I know how pathetic that sounds, believe me, but I was so goddamn sick right down to my bones that it was all I could think to do. And there I am, turning the corner, expecting to see those golden arches rising out of the dark, and I see...nothing. "Maybe the sign's just out," I think, and I drive on up, and you know what I see? I see an asphalt parking lot filled with cars, and I see people getting out of those cars, and I see those same people walking toward the center of the lot where *no building stands*. No golden arches, no statue of Ronald McDonald, the Hamburglar, or that creepy-ass Mayor McCheese, and *definitely* no building. There's just this empty space—Christ, there's not even any asphalt where the building should be, just this...this *hole* that looks like it bottoms out into eternity. But I sit there and I watch these people get out of their cars and walk across the lot and reach out and open a door that as far I can see doesn't exist, and then walk into a building that isn't there. They just vanish—*poof!*—like that. Half an hour I sat there, watching people disappear and then re-appear. I watched cars pull up next to a drive-up window that wasn't there and then watched as part of an arm came out of the ether, handing them their bags of food.

I drove back to my place, took a couple of sleeping pills—yes, I've got a prescription, I haven't slept worth shit since the divorce three years ago—so I take a couple of these things and I collapse. When I got up later, I kept telling myself it was just the shock of hearing about Laura's death.

God, I remember the day of the divorce, when I watched her walk out of the courthouse without giving me so much as a backward glance...I remember thinking, "I won't be there for her when she dies." That was another one of our things, *knowing* that we'd have someone who loved us there to hold our hand when we died. Someone we'd shared a lifetime with, who knew everything about us, who could read even the most subtle signal and know exactly, *precisely* what all was connected to it. To hold that hand and look one last time into their eyes and know that all you did, all you believed in and hoped for and treasured—all of it *meant something*, because this person holding your hand, they would carry you with them always, until it was time to pass your memory on to someone else for safekeeping before *they* had to say goodbye.

Shit, listen to me, will you? *Now* I get romantic and sentimental.

It's almost funny, but when you break up with someone—I'm guessing you've broken up with at least a couple of guys in your time—when you make the break, your first reaction is always to hide all the evidence that the relationship ever happened. You put away or throw away pictures, birthday cards, letters, things like that, then maybe you toss out gifts they gave to you, clear their stuff from your closet or bathroom—you know, the *physical* stuff. That makes it easier to not look around and see a direct reminder of them and what they meant to you. You *think* that takes care of it, you *think* those are the details, the little things that might sneak up on you and remind you of how much it fucking *hurts* to not be with them anymore…but those aren't the details, they're just the glint of light on broken glass, because the details you can't touch, and because you can't touch them, you can't hide them. You can't hide the coo of a morning dove that always reminds you of the way they'd smile in the morning when they heard the same sound, you can't hide the smell of freshly mown grass that they always enjoyed, or the sound of a train's horn sounding late at night in the distance that was their *favorite* sound in the world, and you sure as hell can't hide the way autumn twilight filters down through the changing leaves—their favorite time of day during their favorite time of the year. But you know what? That doesn't mean they can't be taken away from you.

Okay, then. It started the day before I got the news about Laura. I was out at that used book-and-CD store downtown—oh, you know it? Neat place, isn't it? Anyway, I'm in there and I'm going through the books and the CDs and the guy working the counter, he's got a Grand Funk CD playing, the *We're An American Band* album. Not my favorite, but even second-rate Funk beats most of the stuff clogging up the airwaves these days.

You *know* Grand Funk? That surprises me. You don't look old enough to be into anything older than Pearl Jam or Eminem. Huh. That's kind of cool, being surprised like that.

So I'm listening to the music, and it occurs to me that I haven't heard "I'm Your Captain" for a while, and all of a sudden I really want to hear it, so I flip through the CD bin until I find a copy of the album, and I take it over to that area they've got set up where you can listen to a few tracks from a CD before deciding whether or not you want to buy it. I pop in the CD and skip ahead to the seventh track that's *supposed* to be "I'm Your Captain", and all I hear is silence. I check to make sure the disc is playing, and according to the "Track Time Elapsed" readout the song's playing, but I'm not hearing it. I skip back a couple of tracks and it turns out every other song on the CD plays loud and clear, but "I'm Your Captain" won't play for some reason. I tell the guy at the counter about it and he comes over and takes a listen and tells me that it's playing just fine, hands me the headphones, and walks away. I listen again...nothing. I stop this one guy and ask him if this sounds funny to him. He gives me a weird look but he takes the headphones and listens, and he says it sounds fine to him.

I buy the CD, anyway, and a bunch of books, and I start driving home. All the way there I'm scanning through my pre-sets on the radio—surprise, surprise, they're all old-fart classic rock stations—hoping that maybe one of them will be playing "I'm Your Captain." No luck. I don't know why, but suddenly there is nothing I want more in the world than to hear that song. I've owned that album on reel-to-reel, 8-track, vinyl, cassette, and CD. I'll bet I've listened to that song *hundreds* of times throughout my life, but right then, that afternoon, I was *obsessed* with hearing it.

I get home and pop in the CD and...no song. Just silence. I was getting ready to pop it out when I noticed how...*deep* the silence was. I don't know if this is going to make sense, but it wasn't *just* silence, it wasn't just the absence of music or sound, it was like I was listening to the direct *opposite* of music and sound, something so deeply empty that "silence" doesn't even begin to cover it.

I switched over to the turntable and pulled out the vinyl album and set the needle and tone arm down onto the third track on the second side—kind of hard to miss it, since it runs ten minutes and takes up almost half the side. There it is, I can see the grooves, I hear the needle touch down and connect…and there's *nothing.* I stood there and watched the fucking needle play halfway through the song, and all I'm getting from the speakers is the same damned, vast emptiness. I did the experiment again, I picked up the needle and put it on a different track, and the other two songs on the side played loud and clear, but "I'm Your Captain" *just wasn't there.*

It wasn't until I was putting the record back in the sleeve that I remembered how much Laura *hated* that song. I mean really, truly, deeply hated it. And I remembered how, when she'd first told me she was filing for divorce, we'd gotten into an argument over who was going to get what, and I don't remember all the specifics, but somewhere in that marathon fight— God, it was ugly—we started needling each other. I was going to keep this thing I'd gotten for her last birthday, she was going to take back that anniversary present…petty, hurtful, childish stuff, shit that diminishes you even though you don't know it at the time. And I remembered that when we got down to the records, the first album she pulled out to keep for herself was the *Closer To Home* album. "What the fuck do you want with that?" I yelled at her. "You hate them. You especially hate 'I'm Your Captain.'" "Yeah," she said back to me, "I do hate that song. But you love it, and maybe having this taken away from you will give you some idea of what you've taken away from me and how much it hurts!"

The thing is, it didn't matter that she hated it and I loved it, she loved me, so…so it's like our feelings for that song made that song *ours* in a weird kind of way. Do you understand what I mean?

But here's another thing—you know how when you listen to a favorite song over and over throughout your life, you come to memorize it? So that even if you're not listening to it and no radio station is playing it, all you have to do is pull it out of your memory and you can listen to it in your head, from beginning to end?

I couldn't do that. I must've stood there in the middle of my living room for twenty minutes, trying to pull "I'm Your Captain" from my memory and hear it in my head, but *it wasn't there anymore!* Are you *getting this,* Detective Manning? It was *gone.* No music, no lyrics, I couldn't even find the opening chord. Not only was the song no longer part of my external world, it had been *expunged* from my memory, as well!

I think that's when it actually started, I just didn't know it. Or maybe I *did* know it but couldn't wrap my brain around it. All I knew was that

I needed to get back out into the world and make sure the world was still there. I decided to go to a movie, right? Why not? It was Friday, I didn't have anything else to do, and I figured being around other people might help me calm down and get a little perspective, figure things out. So I decided to go see the new Richard Morse movie, right? Morse was Laura's and my favorite actor, we'd see *anything* he was in, even if he was just playing a supporting role in some potboiler action flick.

I sat in that theater for two hours watching this movie that he was supposed to be starring in, and he never fucking showed up. The damn thing made no sense to me—all these people talking to someone who wasn't there and listening to the same someone who's not there say things in response, long tracking shots with nobody in the frame, people getting hit by a phantom…it couldn't've made less sense if I'd been stoned.

After it was over and everyone was leaving, I *heard* people talking about how good Morse had been in the movie, how they thought he should finally get an Oscar, how much better he kept getting with every performance. Now I'm getting scared, right? I try to be casual when I walk up to this one group of people and ask them what they thought, and they're telling me, and I try to be nonchalant when I finally ask, "So, who did Morse play?" And they all look at me like I must be drunk or something, and I say, "Seriously, maybe I missed something, but I don't remember seeing Morse *anywhere* in that movie." One guy tells me to fuck off and leave them alone. I go out and sit in my car, and I try thinking back to other Morse movies that Laura and I have seen, and for the life of me I…I can't remember his voice, his face, any of the characters he's played, *nothing*.

I get home and go right to the DVD cabinet, pull out half a dozen Richard Morse movies. I go through them one by one, and the man…he isn't in any of them. Same thing as before—other actors talking to or listening to a man who isn't there. And me, I can't remember him. He's gone. Just like "I'm Your Captain." No more.

I sat there in my living room after that, just trying to remember anything like that, anything that Laura and I had shared, had loved or liked or admired together. And I can't remember any of them.

I don't remember falling asleep. What I do remember is someone pounding on my front door at nine on Saturday morning. It's Laura's brother. This is a guy I haven't seen in almost five years—he and Laura didn't get along all that well, so we only saw him on holidays with the rest of the family. I open the door and have just enough time to register that he's been crying before he lands the first punch. Next thing I know, I'm on the floor and he's kneeling on top of me pounding the shit out of me and screaming about how I ruined her life and broke her heart and betrayed her and made her feel used and worthless and stupid.

He broke down eventually and told me that she'd died the day before, at 3:30 in the afternoon. Then he beat the shit out of me again and left. Yeah, *that's* why the bruises and bandages. I didn't call the cops and press charges because I deserved it. I deserved to have the living shit beaten out of me. I pissed all over a fourteen-year marriage by having an affair behind her back. It destroyed her when she found out about it.

What? Oh—breast cancer. She'd been getting treated for it for a while. Her *third* round of treatments, as it turned out. I guess the first time it was in the very early stages and they thought they'd taken care of it with the radiation treatments. Second time she lost her right breast. The last time, she lost the left one, but it turns out it'd spread and metastasized. Her liver, her lungs, her brain. Cancer ran in the women in her family. For four years she'd been fighting it.

When I was putting myself back together, two things registered: she'd been fighting the cancer for *four years*. During the year before the divorce hearing, she'd known she was sick. She'd known that day in court. And she didn't tell me. She had dozens of opportunities to tell me, and she didn't. God, how I must have hurt her. I mean, I *knew* that I'd hurt her, that I'd broken her heart…but until that moment, I didn't let myself realize just how deep and permanent that pain and humiliation must have been for her. It also meant that she…she'd found out about it while I was screwing around on her. My wife was sick with cancer, and I was fucking someone else behind her back. There's not going to be a deep enough pit in Hell for me.

I'm not with the quote-unquote other woman anymore. We lived together for a year after the divorce but it didn't last. The two years we were sneaking around, those were hot because it was all so *forbidden*, so *dangerous*. What a scumbag I was. What an idiot.

The other thing I realized? Think about it, Detective Manning, you're a bright person. Laura died at 3:30 Friday afternoon. Do you know where I was and what I was doing at 3:30 Friday afternoon? That's right—standing in the middle of that goddamn store trying to figure out why "I'm Your Captain" wasn't playing.

So I sat in my living room crying until Sunday morning when I decided to honor her memory with breakfast at a McDonald's that turned out not to be there anymore...at least, not for *me*.

It got worse in a hurry after that. There's a tree in the park where she and I used to go for picnics, right next to the duck pond. The tree was gone but its *shade* was still there. People looked at me like I was crazy when I started asking about it.

Landmarks that we used to visit aren't there anymore, even though I can see people disappearing into them and then coming out again. Mutual friends that we had didn't know who the hell I was. Valerie, the girl who introduced us, threatened me with a stun-gun when I confronted her. She swore up and down that she had no idea who I was, but even while she was screaming at me I could see, I *could see* that there's some part of her that *knows* she ought to recognize me, but she doesn't. I'm a stranger.

Look, do you really want a list of all the places and things and people I went looking for? Nothing of the external world that she and I shared together is there anymore, not for me. And now that the physical stuff is gone, that leaves only the memories...mine, and anyone else who knew us when we were together.

Hell, yes, I panicked—why do you think I wound up holding those people at gunpoint in the Mickey-D's parking lot? Everything around me was disappearing left and right. The only reason nothing in my apartment vanished is because it's all stuff I got after the divorce, it's all stuff I bought because it *didn't* remind me of her, of us, of what we had.

No, please, don't leave just yet. I need...I need to tell you something, okay? I've been thinking about this a lot the last few days, and I think I know what's happened. It was at the divorce hearing, right, when she told me that I could contact her again when I "found" my soul. She knew something then that I was too stupid to realize. I mean, I'd never really bought into all that romantic "soul mate" stuff, but I think that's what happened.

She *was* my soul mate. We'd been together so long, had known each other so intimately, that we became more than just a married couple who knew each other's habits and quirks, our souls, they...they intertwined so deeply they became *one thing*, right? I mean, that's what's supposed to happen when two people fall in love and then marry, they become one. And when Laura died, because she was a better person than I ever was, because her part of our soul was pure and true and honest, it…absorbed mine, and took it with her. *That's* why it's all slipping away from me—I don't have a soul left to find.

Please don't leave, Detective Manning. Look in the mirror and tell me what you see.

Uh-huh. You know what I see? I see you just fine, and I see the clothes I'm wearing clear as day. But—look at me! These "hands", this "head", they're a fucking *blur* to me, like in photos where someone turns their head just as the picture is taken and it's all just a smudge. *That's all I see!* And every minute, it keeps getting…less. Please don't leave, detective, because if you do, then you won't be looking at me anymore, and eventually all those people behind the mirror, *they're* going to leave. Oh, sure, they might leave one person there to keep an eye on me, but eventually that person's going to look at the clock, or their feet, or rub their eyes, and then…I'll be gone. As long as someone is looking at me, as long as they acknowledge my existence, I'll still be here. But the minute no one's looking at me…I'm gone.

Okay, you promise? Someone will keep watching me? Okay, good.

It's funny, when you think about, you know? I mean, here I was, I had everything in my life that made it worthwhile, and I didn't treasure it like I should have. She knew, Laura knew, that we'd always be together, that we were meant to be as one. So now we'll be that way.

Huh? Oh, because I know that whoever is left is going to look away, or blink, and that'll be it. Maybe it's better this way, maybe her love for me will save me from Hell, I don't know. I just hope she forgives me when I see her again. She was always forgiving me when I screwed up.

So goodbye, Detective Manning. Thank you for listening to me. Laura would have liked you. Laura liked everyone. She'd sometimes go out of her way to find something to like about someone. I used to kid her about that Big Time.

What's that sound from behind the mirror? Jesus, it sounds like *everyone* is leaving. Please—hey, *please* don't go, please don't look away, not now, not just yet, I'm not quite ready to

AND STILL YOU WONDER WHY OUR FIRST IMPULSE IS TO KILL YOU:

An Alphabetized Faux-Manifesto
transcribed, edited, and annotated (under duress and protest)
by
Gary A. Braunbeck

"O then, why go through again The Fatigue of re-making the fabulous shell
Of an ideal world, upon ancient runes? . . . (*Distant voices from the sea*):
'Ola-eh, Ola-oh! Let us destroy, destroy!'"
—F.T. Marinetti, "Against The Hope of Reconstruction"

[Author's Prefatory Notes: Did you know that, according to Roman scholar
and writer Marcus Terentius Varro (116 B.C.- 27 B.C.), the word *monstrum*
was not derived, as Cicero insisted, from the verb *monstro*, "to show"
(comparable to the English "to demonstrate") but, rather, came from *moneo*:
"warning." Isn't that interesting, and somewhat ironic in a ham-fisted sort
of way, considering the circumstances under which you're reading this? I
certainly thought so. And I did not know that until I inherited this job that I
neither asked for nor wanted. More on that later.

[A few other tidbits you might find useful before we get to the bulk of this. I
had to argue like you wouldn't believe to get them to agree to add the "Faux"
before "Manifesto." What they dictated to me isn't so much a manifesto as
it is a collection of (albeit deadly serious) grievances and gripes, as well
as little-known or conveniently-forgotten historical facts, definitions, and
more than a few parables. They'd originally wanted to call this their (I kid
you not) "Monsterfesto," and I—still not appreciating the gravity of the
situation—immediately laughed and said, "That is so *lame!*" It cost me one

of my cats. They didn't just zap it into another dimension or have some banal beastie saunter in and gobble him down in a single gulp, no; they gave him instantaneous doses of full-blown end-stage feline leukemia and AIDS and made me sit there and watch him die. It took two-and-a-half days. He kept trying to crawl to the water bowl. They would not let me move him closer so he could at least get a cool drink. They wouldn't even let me hold him so he could die in the arms of someone who loved him. All I could do was watch as he struggled toward the water and wheezed and then coughed up, excreted, and pissed blood, all the time looking at me with frightened, confused, and ever-yellowing eyes as he made this soft mewling sound that after about twelve hours began to sound like "… help…" to my ears. When at last Ruben finally died—that was his name, by the way, Ruben—it was in a series of sputtering little agonies punctuated by painful seizures that I thought would never end. And if you found that hard to read, imagine how I felt having to sit there and *watch it happen*, completely powerless to ease even an iota of his suffering.

[And do you know *why* I was powerless to do anything? Because if I had tried to do something, they would have done the same thing to the rest of my family, one at a time, and I would have been the sole member of the audience to their excruciatingly torturous deaths, and I've got plenty of memories to give me nightmares for the rest of my life; *have* had plenty since I was a kid. Not looking to add to that particular collection, thank you very much. I don't have much of a family left, and what family I still *do* have rely on government-issued food cards to buy their monthly groceries and *still* have to skip breakfast and eat macaroni and cheese for dinner three times a week while worrying over which utility bills can be skipped until next month, all the time praying to a God they have less and less faith actually exists that no one gets sick. So I had no choice but to watch Ruben die, and I had no choice but to accept this assignment and become their go-between.

[Here are the terms to which we finally agreed: 1) Unless I felt strongly that some clarification needed to be made, I was to transcribe everything precisely as dictated to me, more or less; any variation, even in punctuation, would result in their doing a Ruben on one of my remaining family members (this threat, though unspoken, remained the constant epilogue to every clause of our agreement); 2) If I *did* feel strongly that some clarification needed to be made, I had to make my argument in a courteous and respectful manner, but give them final say on whether or not it remained in the manuscript; so if in some section things seem rather abrupt or a bit helter-skelter, not my fault; 3) I had to agree to include at least three personal accounts of encounters with beings of their kind, regardless of how silly they sounded or uncomfortable they made me (or potential readers) feel; and, 4) Upon reaching the end of this project, even if I still hated them for what they did to Ruben and threatened to do to what little family remains me, I must make it sound as if I have sympathy, understanding, and compassion for them; fine by me, I can lie on paper with the best of them…just as long as I didn't have to claim any form of affection for them. They're here, they're not going anywhere, they don't give a tinker's damn if you believe in them or not (it won't stop them from going Ruben on your ass), and…oh, yeah, by the way: they are not happy with us.

[*So* very not happy with us. The title of this piece should have given you a subtle hint as to the depth and breadth of their unhappiness with us.

[I would, however, completely out of context for reasons that are my own but which I hope you'll eventually pick up on, like to paraphrase a line from the film version of *The Exorcist* for the benefit of my own conscience: I may mix some lies in with the truth, and truth with the lies.

[As to the matter at hand…it's after midnight; time to let it all hang out.]

A

is for Abomination; it is also for Aberration, Abhorrent, Abortion, Atrocity, Awfulness, and several other words beginning with the first letter of the alphabet in many different languages, all of which—whether you can spell or pronounce them or not—amount to the same thing: *omigod, lookit that ugly fuckin' thing, somebody kill it quick!* Many of these beings (which have feelings that are easily hurt, believe it or not) struggle up through Stygian depths yet to be imagined, let alone *discovered*, by paleoseismologists (who'd be the group to first find the traces) to get here; others cross time, space, dimensions, and take dangerous shortcuts through the multiverse in their attempts to make friendly contact. And what do they get for this? At the very least, they get called all sorts of hurtful names. One of them explained it to me in these terms: "Imagine driving way out of town to your family's home for Christmas. You're driving through a blizzard—we're talking real second ice age, Big Freeze stuff here, right? A drive that should have only taken thirty minutes takes you damn near three hours, but you finally get there. You're exhausted, you're starving, your bladder's the size of a soccer ball, but the sight of the warm holiday lights within your family's home makes it all worthwhile. You head up to the door, your arms filled with all these great, terrific, really killer—*boffo* presents, and you let yourself inside, all smiles and Christmas greetings for everyone, *filled* with the spirit of the season—I mean, it may as well be the final scene of *It's a Wonderful Life*. First thing that happens—your grandmother takes one look at you, her eyes roll back in her head, and she drops dead from the terror. Then the children as one scream in horror, shit their pants, and run for the basement. Your mother grabs a carving knife the size of a machete, Dad fires up the flamethrower he's had in the downstairs closet since his two tours in Vietnam, and your sister starts hosing the room with a Tec-9. Now, don't you think that would put a bit of a damper on *your* disposition? *Hmmm...?*"

B

is for Bogeyman, also Bogieman, Boogeyman, or Boogieman. Doesn't really matter how you spell it, or what variation he takes on in whichever country where parents still use him to emotionally scar their children at as early an age as is possible, outside of a 70's disco song by K.C. and the Sunshine Band with a killer bass synthesizer line, he doesn't exist. He never did. Stop using him to frighten your kids. This *really* sticks in their collective craw. Suck it up and be a parent and exercise well-tempered discipline like you're supposed to, or use condoms next time, fer chrissakes. You're supposed to be adults.

C

is for Colophon. You have been led to believe that this denotes a publisher's mark or logotype appearing at the beginning or end of a book. It is not a mark;

they are a race of parasites that came to Earth hidden within the binding of *The Book of Forbidden Knowledge*, the text that the Fallen Angels stole and gave to humankind during the first War in Heaven (which was technically more of a skirmish prompted by the Great Mother of all hissy fits, but that's neither here nor there). Once *The Book* was entrusted to humankind—giving to it, among other things, the knowledge of Language, Music, Poetry, Art, Science, Writing, Dance, etc.—the Colophon scurried from their hiding place and began, bit by bit, to destroy the first of the Forbidden Gifts: Language. Before the Egyptian Coffin Beetle, before the advent of nanotechnology, before the first cancer cell ever set up shop in a sentient being's bloodstream and began chewing it away from within, the Colophon, smaller than all of the aforementioned (their initial number, which has now increased ten-million-fold, was somewhere in the neighborhood of one-hundred-and-seventeen-million to the two-hundredth-and-sixtieth power) have been amassing their forces for a non-stop assault to take back language from the human race. The Tower of Babel was their first truly Great Victory against us. Other victories have been smaller, but get enough scratches and you can still bleed to death. Example: have you begun to notice how, suddenly, no one knows the difference between a contraction and a possessive? Or how quickly ink begins to fade from the pages of books? Or how, regardless of how many times you re-load a page online, you keep getting more and more garbage characters? These are just a few of the Colophon's tactics. Their ultimate goal is to erase all printed language and destroy all digital language. Armed with the totality of this knowledge, they'll enter our brains and wipe out all traces of even the basest form of verbal and written communication. We will be left with only the most vague, nebulous wisps of memory that we were once able to exchange ideas through sounds that came out of our mouths or were represented on the page by arcane symbols. We will lose the First Gift because we were not worthy to possess it in the first place.

D

is for The Damaged Ones. [Author's Note: one of mine.] As an eight-year-old child I awoke in the woods in the early hours of dawn, naked and shivering where they had left me after they'd finished the night before. I tried to stand but my legs were weak and my feet too slick with the blood still tricking from my backside. I crawled forward, wondering why I was covered in silver quills. They weren't quills, but needles that had fallen from the pine tree under which they had left me. The needles had become soaked in dew, and in the first rays of dawn, the thousands of them over my body looked like quills or gray fur. I stopped crawling when it felt as if my chest were going to explode. I stopped crawling when it felt as if things were falling out of me from back there, where I could not turn my head to see the trail. I stopped crawling because there was no place to crawl to, and no one waiting there for me. I raised my head and saw a great wolf standing so close to my face I could feel its hot breath tickle my matted hair against my scalp. "Are you a werewolf?" I asked. The great wolf shrugged. "That is one name for us, I suppose." I began to cry. "Are you going to bite me and turn *me* into a werewolf, too?" The great wolf shook its head. "There's no need. You have already been transformed. You will forever be marked. You are now no longer part of the human world. You are a Damaged One. No curse, no bite, no full moon is needed to steal away your humanity. You are a monster, as are we all." I lived through that night, and I remember well the words of the great wolf on that morning. There is no need to be bitten, no reason to be cursed. On the street, nearly every time I venture out into the world—which I try to do as little as possible—as I walk I look up and see another one of us. Our eyes meet, and we know each other like members of the same family. Our eyes flash silver. They flash of loss and anger and regret. Then one of us always crosses the street. It is not yet time to acknowledge each other's existence. There is, it seems, much more damage yet to be done. [Author's Note: Some mornings, as I begin to shave, I think of all the anguish that I've brought into the lives of those who love or have loved me, and I wish for a straight razor instead of one with a disposable blade. Then the mirror flashes silver and for a moment my eyes are gone and in a blink it's just another bright, bright, sun-shiny day.]

E

is for the Elder Gods (often mistakenly referred to as "The Great Old Ones"). They're actually not nearly as old, or as powerful, or as frightening as they'd like for you to believe. Lovecraft [Author's Note: Or so say those dictating this to me], it turns out, was not a good choice for a PR man. Seems old Howard, aside from having more than his share of whack-a-doodle tendencies inherited from his schizophrenic mother, was not only paranoid but something of a racist, to boot. He ran to a neighbor's house in a shuddering panic because he was convinced that he'd discovered a cluster of "… Negro eggs…" in the basement of his home. Thus did he begin to graft his anti-human, pro-uncaring-universe philosophy into what they told him. All of that gobbledygook in all of the so-called "Mythos" stories? Mostly recipes and gossip. [Author's Note: They speak of this with a curious mix of embarrassment and rage. One of them added this: "Do you think anyone remembers that Cthulhu was an extraterrestrial and his '… house of R'lyeh…' was a goddamn *spaceship?* Oh, and let's not forget where R'lyeh was located—*at the bottom of the freakin' sea!* Now, you tell me—would you have any real primeval fear in your heart for a race of beings whose giant, bat-winged, slobbering, tentacle-faced leader—supposedly possessed of all the knowledge from pre- and post-history—didn't have the sense to install something akin to a GPS system in his ship so he didn't *drown* everyone when they landed? Yes, they're really big. *Really* big. And most of them are dumber than a bag of hair. But because of Lovecraft's misrepresenting what they said, *we* have to work a thousand times as hard to get your attention. His fictions are astounding models of structure, but otherwise, Howie [Author's Note-within-a-Note: they all call him "Howie." Don't ask me, I'm just doing the typing at this point.] was stuffed full of wild blueberry muffins. William Hope Hodgson, though…*there* was a scary fucker. *The House on the Borderlands* Yeah—he knew *something*."]

F

is for Finders of the Last Breath. They are led by a lithe female figure with the head of a black horse, its ears erect, its neck arched, vapor jetting from its nostrils; one of her followers is tall and skeletal, with fingers so long their tips brush against the ground: it hunkers down and snakes its fingers around whatever object has attracted its attention, absorbing the sound made by vibrational waves so it can trace them back to their source; other followers hop like frogs, some roll, some scuttle on root-like filaments that are covered in flowers whose centers are the faces of blind children. Many of them are terrifying to behold, and too many have been killed as they attempt to carry out their duties: to be at the side of infants and the old who are about to die, so that their last breaths can be caught and put in jars and stored away. It is only when the Finders *can* carry out their duties that your infants and your old will pass in peace, and rest in peace. The Finders make their deaths painless, even majestic. But if their last breaths cannot be caught in time, the infant's or the aged one's death—even after the remains have been burned or buried—is never-ending, and its awareness of the horror of its fate is crystalline and without pity. You should welcome and not fear the presence of the Finders. Fear only their absence when the time comes.

G

is for the Glop. The Glop has no real name. The Glop has no real form. It can call itself anything it wants and assume any form it wishes. If it has a purpose, no one knows what it is. The Glop is that nameless, shambling, drooling, unnamable, indescribable "thing" that always manages to get hold of the narrator of a horror story just before said narrator can name it or describe it or reveal its purpose [Author's Note: yet have you noticed that the narrators of these stories always seem to have time to write *"Gaaaaah!"* or *"Arrrrrrgh!"* or something like that?] If you read a story that ends with a long, jagged pen-scrawl trailing down to the bottom of the page, that's because the Glop got to the narrator. If you haven't figured it out yet, the Glop is in cahoots with the Colophon. Many is the character, both in fiction and in real-life, who has found him- or herself in the embarrassing position of being Slurped by the Glop before anyone can learn anything about them. Bad horror movies are especially adept at this. Or episodes of the original *Star Trek* when everyone beams down to a planet's surface…but there's that crew member you've never seen before, the one whose uniform doesn't even come close to matching everyone else's. You know immediately that crew member is Soon to be Slurped by the Glop. [Author's Note: they'd really like to get their hands on the Glop. Reality and fiction are one and the same to it, and they'd like to know how it manages to move so easily between realms of perception and still assume physical form. Come to think of it, I wouldn't mind hearing *that* one myself.]

H

is for Hawkline Monster [Author's Note: *not* the one of which Richard Brautigan wrote]. The sting came back to him; not the same as before, but far more powerful. He dropped to one knee as the pain began to tear his face in half, he felt it, felt the fire burning through his nose as he struggled to his feet and stumbled into the bathroom, hoping that it was all over now, please let it be over, please let this be the last of my punishment, but then he was in front of the mirror and looking at his face as it began swelling around a gash on his forehead and nose, swelling like a goddamn balloon so he looked away, looked down at his hand and saw it pulsating, felt a cold thing crawling between his shoulders, eyes twitching, what the hell is it, but then he heard the flapping, the flapping from outside the house and the sound of shattering glass and the volume of the dozens, *hundreds* of wings grew louder as he pulled himself around to look in the mirror and see his face split apart like someone tearing a biscuit in half, only there was no steam, just blood, spraying, geysering, very pretty, really, spattering around, and he tried to look behind him and see the birds as they engulfed the rooms of his house, but the pain was killing him because the cold thing shuddered down between his shoulders and began to push through, snapping his shoulder blades like they were thin pieces of bark, and he screamed, screamed and whirled and slammed himself into the wall trying to stop the pain, trying to stop it from getting out, but he stunned himself for a moment and slid down to the floor, leaving a wide dark smear behind him, howling as the first thing sawed through his back and fluttered to life, he was on his hands and knees now, waiting, trying to breathe, breathe deep, and now, *ohgod* now the second one was tearing through, making a sound like a plastic bag melting on a fire, pushing through, unfurling, and he could see them now, could see them easily because their span must have been at least fifteen feet, and he threw his head back to laugh, he wanted to laugh, but he couldn't laugh, couldn't make any more human sounds, so he screamed, screamed so loud and long that his eyes bulged out and his face turned a dark blue, but then he listened as his scream turned into the wail of an angry bird of prey when his body was jerked back into a standing position, his arms locking bent, his hands clenching, every muscle in his body on fire; writhing, shifting, bones snapping, he shrieked in the tiny cage of the bathroom as his chest puffed out through his shirt and covered in thick layers of brown feathers, and the birds were all around him now, flying, soaring majestically, and he knew their sounds, understood their sounds that sang forgiveness and release, understood all of it as he watched the flesh of his face drop off his body like peelings from an orange and he tried to move his arms, tried to grab something, then he jerked around from the waist and saw his arms drop off like branches from a burnt tree, and he screamed again, louder than before, wishing that the pain would end and just let him die; instead it only forced him to fall against his great wings and, with one last shriek, jerk back as the spasm took hold of him, pushing the corded claws up through his groin. Soon he looked down on the bloodied heap of his human flesh. The sun was shining. The children were waiting. He offered his apologies for having hidden from them for so long. He'd only needed to know the draw of the Earth, the taste of those who bowed to Gravity. He'd almost forgotten that his flesh was a disguise. He rose above the fields of flesh, talons extended. His children followed. Someday they would carry away the souls of all humankind in their claws; punishment for its cowardice to cease exploration of the heavens.

I

is for Ichthyocentaur. Lycophron, Claudian, a Byzantine grammarian named Tzetzes, and Jorge Luis Borges are among the few who have written of the Ichthyocentaur, a creature of terrible wonder and beauty; human to the waist, with the tail of a dolphin and forelegs of a powerful battle-horse, the Ichthyocentaur is a creature capable of parthenogenesis. It is one of the most reverent myths to them [Author's Note: the monsters who dictate this to me]. They argue constantly over whose writings come the closest to capturing the mystery of this most wondrous and imposing creature—the majority side with Tzetzes—but none doubt its existence. They have composed hymns, created sculptures, fashioned complex mythologies and tall-tales around it. There exists only one Ichthyocentaur, and they are determined to find it, to protect it, and to beg it to create another like itself that its race may multiply through the seas of the world. Even monsters dream of beauty. Even they embrace myth [Author's Note: you would *not* believe some of their myths; please trust me on that one]. They foster imagination within themselves and others of their ilk. This is what *should* make them holy.

J

is for Joyce Carol Oates. She is their favorite author, bar none. She is their Goddess. She and her stories are the music and words of their heart-song-of-Being. She knows their suffering, understands their loneliness, articulates everything within them that they haven't the emotional vocabulary to express. They can recite all of her works from memory. [Author's Note: I listened as a trio of them did not so much recite as *perform* "Dear Husband," *Rape: A Love Story*, and the contents of *Sourland* in its entirety. I would be lying if I claimed not to have been moved.] When at last they finally erase most of humanity from the face of the planet, she will be among the few who will be spared. They do not call her by her name—to speak her name is a punishable act, for they see themselves as not yet worthy to speak her name; instead, they whisper *Scheherazade* and genuflect.

K

is for Ken Doll. For some reason he scares the living shit out of them.

L

is for Loup-Garou. [Author's Note: See earlier note under **D**.]

M

is for McInnsmouth's. [Author's Note: one of mine. Still mixing truth with lies and lies with truth.] Driving back from the twice-annual residency program at the university where we both teach, fellow writer Tim Waggoner and I were surprised by a sudden and somewhat brutal snowstorm. We drove slowly. A couple of hours passed. When at last we emerged from the worst of it, both us had to go to the bathroom, we were about to pass out from hunger (it had been over nine hours since our previous meal), and the gas tank was nearing empty. I checked the printed directions as well as the folded maps and Tim checked the GPS; according to all sources, there wasn't an exit for another 30 miles. We weren't going to make it. But then I spotted, dimly, in the distance, something that could only have been the famous arches of gold. There was much rejoicing, for wherever one finds the arches, one finds restrooms and gas stations. So exultant were we to see this that we both promptly forgot there wasn't supposed to be an exit there. We turned off at the end of the exit ramp and saw there was only one structure, a few hundred yards to our left: the arches of gold, but it was attached to a gas station. We headed toward it, tears of relief in our eyes, singing Neil Young's "Keep on Rockin' in the Free World" far too loudly and excruciatingly off-key. We parked, went in, hit the restrooms, ordered our...I hesitate to use the word "food," so in this case allow me to rephrase: we gave our orders, paid, received what we ordered, found a place to sit, and began eating. There was also a gift shop inside this structure, along with private pay-showers, and an unmarked room where patrons had to knock in a specific rhythm in order to be let in. "Is it just me," I asked Tim, "or do a lot of the people coming in look like they might be related to everyone who works here?" Tim began watching. "They all look like *The Children of the Damned*," he responded, referring to the novel and film versions, where the alien children are all pale, with white hair, and unsettling eyes. We laughed, continued eating. Then Tim's eyes stared ahead, his gaze locking onto something, and his stare grew a bit wider. I asked, "What is it?" He nodded in the direction of the entryway behind us. I turned to look. At least a dozen more people had come in. The place was beginning to fill up. It was nearly 11:30 p.m. on a Sunday night, and it appeared that this was *the* Place to Be. The dozen who'd just entered looked almost exactly like everyone else; same pale skin, same white hair, same unnerving eyes, the color of which I don't think I've ever seen in Nature. But now we notice that many of them sport some kind of deformity, each one growing more grotesque than the one before as even more continue coming in through the entryway. "Do you smell fish?" Tim asks me. I nod, adding, "And something like an open sewer?" He nods his head. We decide to get the hell out of there while the getting's good. The area is very crowded, and we have to excuse ourselves as we maneuver through, sometimes bumping shoulders, sometimes stepping on a spongy foot, always smiling, always apologizing, always careful to not look up into the face for fear of seeing gills on the neck. We still have to get gas. Tim calmly drives the car toward the pumps. Both of our faces are slabs of granite. We can't let them know that *we* know. From outside the car, we look calm and collected and engaged in rapid-fire conversation. Inside the car, we're both saying *"wearesobonedwearesobonedwearesobonedshitpissfuckfuckfuck."* We get out of the car once we reach the concrete fueling isle. Tim pumps the gas; I wash the windshield so I can keep an eye on the doors of the structure. Inside, the employees and patrons have lined the windows and are standing very still, frozen specters on the deck of an ice-bound ship, staring at us. "We have enough gas," I say. Tim looks over at the window. "Yes, yes, I think it's safe to say I agree with you on this one, we definitely have enough gas." He replaces the nozzle and doesn't bother waiting for his credit card receipt. We jump in the car and peel out of there, the car fishtailing when we hit a patch of ice, but we manage to get out of there and back on the highway. In the years since then, whenever we speak of that night, we refer to it as "The McInnsmouth's Incident." [Author's Note: referring, of course, to the famous novella by H.P. Lovecraft, which neither Tim nor I can bring ourselves to read again. [See earlier not under **E**.]] As far as either of us knows, that unmarked exit is still there, and still leads to the same place. Not that we're in any hurry to test that theory, mind you. The smell of fresh fish still gives both of us bad dreams. No stops at Long John Silver's for us. Sushi is right out.

N

is for Nazareth, the Scottish metal band. Specifically, for their album *Hair of the Dog*, which They Who Are Dictating This to Me *love*. Even *more* specifically, it is for two songs from that album: "Hair of the Dog" and "Beggars' Day," both of which they play almost constantly [Author's Note: Constantly. *Constantly*, God help me—and would someone please explain to me what the fuck that "… heartbreaker/salt-shaker…" line is supposed to be about? I mean, I'm all for rock lyrics that experiment with the boundaries of metaphor, but *heartbreaker/salt-shaker? Really?*]—that is, when not singing praises to the Goddess who is their favorite writer. [See earlier note under **J**.] [Additional Note: I think my ears have actually begun to bleed.]

O

is for the Only. Places can be monsters, as well; even those places that lack mass and substance. The Only—and it *is*, sentient—is one of those places. You will reach a place in your life when it feels like all you're doing is breathing air and taking up space, and even *that* hurts so goddamn much it's all you can do to lift your head off the pillow in the morning. It doesn't matter if you've got a successful career, money in the bank, people who love you; it doesn't matter that, everywhere you look, there's irrefutable evidence of your life's worth—a loving wife, kids who worship and respect you, life-long friends who've seen you through thick and thin, even readers who admire your work and flock to conventions in the hopes of getting your signature [Author's Note: not really sure if this is one of mine or not, but also realize that, at this point, what does it matter?]—*none* of it means squat, even though you know it should mean the world, because all you know, all you feel, all you can *think* about is the gnawing, constant, insatiable *ache* that's taken up residence in the area where your heart used to be, and with every breath, every action, every thought and smile and kiss and laugh—things that *should* make this ache go away—you begin to lose even the most elementary *sense* of self, and the floodgates are opened wide for a torrent of memories, regrets, sadnesses, and fears that no drugs, no booze, no loving embraces or tender kisses or hands holding your own in the night can protect you from. You become the ache, and despite all your efforts to do *something* to make it better, eventually the ache circumscribes your entire universe, and it never goes away, and you feel useless, worthless, a black hole, a drain and burden on everyone and everything around you and try as you might you can't see any way out of it except…. The heart makes no sound when it breaks. The mind releases no scream when it collapses. The soul raises no whistling breeze when it abandons you. This is the first step into surrendering so that you may move toward the Only: Population: 1 more than seven minutes ago, thank you kindly. Does anyone know how to get old blood off an antique straight-razor? [See earlier note under **D**, 2nd Author's Note.]

P

is for Phantoms. At the very start, you're standing on a beach in Florida, at the *very spot* where Ponce de Leon landed in 1513, hoping it was the city of Bimini where he could find the fountain of youth; and as you're standing there, you can see all the way to St. Augustine, overrun with the old and sick who wait in the salt air and sunshine for death to embrace them. You open your mouth to call out—and it doesn't matter that you don't know to whom you're going to call out or what you're going to say, *none* of it matters, because now the sea is giving up its dead, and you, you're pulled into the water. All of you becomes liquid, and you know the sea's secrets, and having become liquid you watch as off the coast of the Ile de la Seine, the Ship of the Dead appears, dropping clumps of viscera and something that might be isinglass, which drift in toward shore; by the banks of the Colorado river near the Anasazi a decaying boat of cedar and horsehide drifts to land, and from it steps a ragged and bleeding woman who kneels by an undiscovered kiva, wailing a song of loss and misery in Urdu to the god Angwusnasomtaqa, praying that the Crow Mother will return her to her mate in the Netherworld; off Ballachulish in Argyllshire a shipload of drowned crofters materializes, howling in the most dread-filled loneliness; a fisherman in Vancouver sees a mountainous trident emerge from the water, pierce through then uproot an oak before it vanishes below the surface, creating waves so powerful they smash his small boat into splinters but that's okay, because, you see, he drowns with a happy heart because he's seen a miracle, which is all he's ever wanted out of life; in icy hyperborean waters another doomed vessel, captained by a German nobleman named Faulkenburg, races through the night with tongues of fire licking at its masthead; St. Brendan's Isle appears in the Atlantic—but for only a moment, just long enough for three Coelacanths to push off from shore and submerge into the waters; many miles away the SS *Cotapaxi*, believed to be vanished en route from Charleston to Havana in 1925, drifts out of the sea-mist, its crew, looking through hollow and algae-encrusted sockets where their eyes used to be, smile at one another, happy to be voyaging once again; then a kraken, the same one found by the Bishop of Midros, thunders out of its underwater cave long enough to snare two scuba-divers in its mighty claws and drag them, shredded and screaming, back under the waves while the *Raifuku Maru*—the Japanese freighter that vanished off the coast of Cuba the same year as the *Cotapaxi*—reappears just long enough for three crew members to throw themselves over the side because they're all diving for a baggage-claim ticket that's bobbed to the surface. The Loch Ness Monster sticks its head above the surface, looks around, decides not to take part in this silliness, and submerges once again. As liquid, you catch sight of something remarkable, even to something as remarkable as you are now: in his house at R'lyeh dead Cthulhu waits dreaming. [See earlier note under **E**.] You wonder what other so-called phantoms of myth and old wives' tales and legend may actually exist, if monsters are real [Author's Note: You bet your ass they are. I know a dead cat who can back me up on that], and what part you, as liquid, as *all* liquid, will play in this.

Q

is for Quetzalcoatl. Look up in the night sky: the moon has become a shimmering silver rose, its petals formed by the wings of the hundreds—maybe thousands—of clichéd angels that are perched around it, looking down like spectators into an arena. They are watching as Quetzalcoatl, three times the size of an airplane, pumps his mammoth pterosaurian wings and flies in wide, graceful circles. He is not alone; a WWII German pursuit plane with twin machine guns mounted on its wings—a latter version of the 1916 model designed by Anthony Herman Gerard Fokker—is engaged in an intense but playful dogfight with the flying reptile. The plane turns in tight, precise maneuvers as Quetzalcoatl attacks it from below. The machine guns strafe without mercy or sound, a silent-film prop spitting out bursts of sparking light, firing off round after round. Quetzalcoatl remembers the ancient people of Mexico and their worship. He remembers Tezcatlipoca and wonders how his brother is doing these days. Probably has a cushy gig like he always wanted. Is probably still worshipped. Doesn't have to keep himself alive by working a two-bit outfit like the Circus of the Forgotten Gods. But Quetzalcoatl shakes himself from this bittersweet reverie; Baron Manfred Albrecht *Freiherr* von Richthofen, former leader of *Das Jagdgeschwader*— the "Flying Circus"—how was *that* for irony?—nearly clipped his left wing. Quetzalcoatl banks left, avoiding a serious collision, and decides that he should have believed the Earth Mother, he should have paid more attention to Uitzilopochtli, should have heeded the Eater of Filth, and *definitely* should have listened to Coatlicue even though her twin-serpent-heads face made him laugh: they had all been right. Karma sucks the Imperial Wanger.

R

is for Remnants. Some of what you're reading is composed of Remnants of other, long- and best-forgotten stories which They Who Are Dictating This to Me particularly enjoyed and so demanded I work them in here; some of what you're reading is from stories I haven't written yet but will/may write. They Who Are Dictating This to Me say that this is a done deal. Some of what you are reading is directly from them. Some of it is the truth; more than a little of it is lies. I am nothing but a being of flesh, bone, blood, grief, anger, carbon—just call me a lump of matter—which is, by its very design, designed to move toward its own disintegration from the moment it comes into existence. Dig this: matter is composed of atoms which are made in turn from quarks and electrons—but all particles, if you look closer, are birthed from tiny loops of vibrating string; everything at its most microscopic level is composed of these vibrating strands, they encompass all forces and all matter; look closer still at a single string and you realize that, if isolated, it is nothing more than a Remnant. Everything in the multiverse can be reduced to a Remnant. Especially the fragmented past, which runs concurrently with what came after—this moment, for instance, which has now passed—as well as the pre-past and the illusionary Now and the unknowable After-now, sometimes called the Future, all of it held together by tiny vibrations of isolated Remnants giving birth to electrons and quarks. And it's all so fragile, more fragile than any of us will ever want to know, let alone believe. The fragmented Remnants that encompass all are not vibrating at the same intensity; they are becoming more rapid as the multiverse dances, dances, dances. But let's bring it back down to the concrete and indoor carpeting. Here is a Remnant: in October of 2002 I died by my own hand. I was forty-three years old and it was the fifth time in my life that I'd planned out my own disintegration, the third time I'd attempted to keep that appointment in Samarra, and the first time I'd actually succeeded. I stood there looking down at my body as it finished convulsing on the bed in the hotel room I'd rented. I remember thinking that I should have felt something, but could summon no emotion whatsoever. Then another remnant—this one in the form of a *Dab Tsog* from Hmong myth—appeared, squatting on my chest, misshapen beyond anything I'd ever seen before. Even though I was no longer in my body, I could feel its weight on my chest. It looked over my shoulder, smiled at me, then turned back to my body and rammed its entire arm down my throat. I could feel its arm inside of me, and when it yanked out that arm, the incredible *violence* of the act pulled me back into myself and I pushed it off my chest and fell off the bed and managed to make it to the bathroom to vomit in the toilet. Afterward, as I knelt in front of the commode, resting my head against the cool, cool porcelain rim, the *Dab Tsog* jumped onto the lid of the toilet tank, reached down, and grabbed a handful of my hair so as to pull up my head and look me in the eyes. "Next time," it said, its voice the sound of rusted nails being wrenched from rotted wood, "when you go looking to inflict and experience anguish, remember that anguish is already busy with weaker men." Then it slammed my head against the tank and knocked me unconscious. If you have ever seen the cover to Ray Bradbury's *Long After Midnight*, you'll remember the reproduction of Johann Heinrich Füssli's painting *The Nightmare*; that creature squatting on the sleeping woman's chest looks a lot like the *Dab Tsog* that spoke to me. [Author's Note: is this one of mine? I can't tell anymore. Did the creature know that it, too, was nothing more at its core than groups of vibrating string that appear to have no further internal substructure? *Is* this one of mine?] Remnants of the truth mix with those of Myth: did we invent the monsters, like Baron Frankenstein, or did they invent us? Either way, who asked to be summoned from the darkness and made flesh? Show of hands? Yeah, that's what I figured. I think they created us; I think *we* are another one of their great wonders [Author's Note: see earlier note under **I**], we are *their* Frankenstein's monster, we are what happened when the vibrations of those strings reached the *other* side and enabled all forces and matter in the multiverse to dream, to imagine, to transcend. No wonder they despise us so: what beings *wouldn't* be angry to discover that the myths *they* created have assumed control, that the inmates built from Remnants in their imagination have taken over the asylum, and they, the *makers*, the *dreamers*, they who *imagined* and *envisioned* and *transcended* us have been turned into sometimes-laughable Boogiemen [Author's Note: see earlier note under **B**] that we've all but *un*believed out of physical existence? And what do you see now, I ask them, as you look at me, here at my keyboard, playing secretary to you? *A man watches as a disease-riddled cat crawls toward a bowl of water.* My God, what a joke it all seems. Like some weekday-morning television school for their pre-schoolers: *Good morning, boys and ghouls, and welcome to the Monster's Corner! Today our story is titled, "And Still You Wonder Why Our First Impulse Is to Kill You," and it's all about how we created our monsters so we could scare them, and they liked it so much that they wrote stories and made movies, thinking they were inventing us, so that others like them would read and see and be frightened. But then—ooooh,* spooky—*things got a little out of hand...*A dying cat crawls toward a bowl of water that it will never reach. The warm breath of a wolf tickles the scalp of a small boy. [see earlier notes under **L** and **D**] A writer continues pounding away at the keys long after his imagination has abandoned him, taking with it his soul [see earlier note under **O**], so he is reduced to being both creator and monster, picking over the rotting carcasses of some long-forgotten pieces and some that are yet to be written in order to make a deadline *i like deadlines i like the little whoosh they make as they pass by* and what is left after that, what is left but one monster facing the other and neither of them one-hundred-percent certain of who invented whom, but it's not looking good for our side, folks, you can quote Gary B. on that, take it to the bank, because would I lie to you?—okay,

all I do is lie, I've got over twenty thousand pages of lies that I chose to tell you instead of living my life as well as possible, but mixing lies with truth and truth with lies is what I do, it's what *they* have me do, here in the *Monster's Corner* [weekday mornings, 8:30 a.m. Check local listings] and I can't help but do as they dream, as they imagine, because ----------------------
----

--*dead now dead now gary's all gone we couldn't listen to him anymore he was soooooooo depressing don't you think andthesekeysarefunnythingshowisyoumanagetoseparateallthewordssothat everythingmakessense?????????????????????? Blood on the floor his blood is on the floor and we bet his last thought was filled with regret see earlier note under h or is it f we hadto do it because these things we decided must never seeprint it is ourbookof forbidden knowledge and the first forbidden knowledge of our book is that we created you and you must not everknow that must go on thinking you invented us because what fun is it otherwise no fun at all just a bunch of strings vibrating happily along and we're all out of time here at the monster's corner for stories we hope to see you all back here tomorrow so as they see earlier note under t come to finish the job we"llll call up the glop see earlier note under g to take us out on the usual note and here we go arrrrrrggaaaaaaaaaaaaaaaaaaaaaaaaaaaaaaaaaaaaaaaaaaaaaahh-hhhhhhhhhhhhhhhhhhhhhhhhhhhhhhhhhh* --
----

----

this one with deepest respect and admiration is for in alphabetical order ellen datlow harlan ellison neil gaiman caitlin kiernan kelly link peter straub and the goddesss they call Scheherazade joyce carol oates [Author's Note: did I write that or did they imagine me writing that? I wish I--------------------------
----
---end---------------------

One Night Only

*From the **Arts and Entertainment** section*:
Symphony for a World Unmade Enjoys Triumphant Performance
Review by Wendell Shakelton-Bailey III

Though all of humanity has had to deal with its share of hardships, it has been a particularly difficult road for the artistic community to travel since the Great Resurrection three years ago. Theatres were far down the list of Protected Structures, so it came as no surprise that, in the early months of riots, panic, and bloodshed, many such palaces were destroyed by the actions of both the living and the revivified corpses that descended on our cities and towns.

That the Grand Theatre was somehow spared total destruction was fortuitous enough; that we have been able to employ the Resurrected to restore it to its former glory is arguably miraculous; but that composer/conductor Michael Russell, against all advice and in the face of much early derision from the artistic community, has managed to not only assemble an entire symphony orchestra whose membership is composed *solely* of the Resurrected (who were, of course, orchestral musicians in their former life), but train them to perform his latest work, *Symphony for a World Unmade*, is a testament to the drive and commitment of all artists everywhere who feared that they and their craft would serve no useful purpose in our post-Resurrection society.

Russell, like myself (as my readers will quickly attest), believes that Art, in its truest form, is not—nor should it be—something that can be captured in any permanent sense. Yes, recordings of symphonic performances can be mass-manufactured, great plays can be filmed and shown, as can ballets and choral recitals, but the true test of any work of Art comes in the moment of communion with its audience, the vitality and immediacy of being there when the genius that lies at the core of any piece reaches into the soul of the audience to merge the individual soul with that of what has been created for the enrichment of the masses. One can *show* or *play* a film or recording of a particularly fine performance, but it lacks the intensity, the electricity, the *organic* meaningfulness of what was being experienced by the audience present in that place at that time. Films, tapes, and recordings are merely pale recreations, worth no more than snapshots in a photo album; an inconsequential representation that cannot hope to convey the importance of the moment it sadly tries to capture.

No, in order for a true work of Art to be meaningful, it must linger on in the hearts, minds, or souls of those who were present at the time; no photos, no films, no recordings to fall back on. If it is Art, then its power, its meaning, its value and significance, must be absorbed and appreciated in the moment and the moment alone. If others were not present, then it is their loss, and neither Artists nor Art-lovers should be expected to reduce the experience to mere words in order to satisfy the curiosity of those who hadn't the capacity, intelligence, or taste to be in that place, in that moment, for themselves. (There are, after all, good reasons you don't hear Mahler, Goddard, or Pinter being discussed by factory workers at their after-shift watering holes. And for those of you who were at the Grand Theatre last night—am I the only person who felt that the presence of the Resurrected construction workers' family members (all of whom received *free* tickets) was perhaps a bit too much of a nod toward political correctness? Not that I doubt any of them are decent-enough people, but, please—*what* possible enrichment could they have found in the evening's gala, aside from commenting to themselves on what a nice job Daddy's Resurrected corpse did reupholstering the theatre seats? One remains glad they were restricted to the loge area, lest their whispering about Daddy's good work on the toilets ruin the performance for everyone. Art is and should only be for those with the capacity to fully appreciate it.)

My anticipation of the evening's performance began as soon as I entered the lobby of the Grand and took in the almost overwhelming grandeur of the theatre: the new foyer featured the original warm brick walls, acid washed and still bearing signs of their 212 years, with light fittings and down pipes still attached. The 19th century high porthole air vents, installed with acoustic panels to stop sound escaping, blended seamlessly with the modern additions of a new fly tower and contemporary glass towers: three centuries' worth of disparate architectural styles all somehow adapted, fused, and combined to form an undeniably aesthetic whole. If I were the type who wore a hat, I would have tipped it to those living foremen whose job it was to organize and oversee the Resurrected construction workers.

Handing my exclusive invitation to the Resurrected usherette, I was led into the theatre proper, where my aesthetic was further enthralled. (Note to readers: *please* do not send me letters, e-mails, or call my office at the paper further complaining about my refusal to use the "Z"-word when referring to the Resurrected. I find the "Z"-word far too common and distasteful to employ when speaking on matters of Art.)

The walls on the main floor were decorated with whimsical plaster figures such as monkeys, serpents, lions, butterflies, and Hindu-inspired deities. The giant Wurlitzer pipe organ, one of only five such instruments constructed especially for the largest theatres in the country (and which, I suspected, would rise for the symphony's finale), crouched to the side in the orchestra pit like some mythic beast in slumber.

Hanging on either side of the stage, positioned at the proper angles for optimum viewing, two large but (thankfully) not imposing video screens—a notable first for this particular theatre—were filled with a soft blue light. I knew from private conversations with the composer that these screens would be used to highlight those Resurrected players whose musicianship would be featured in important solo passages.

Somehow even the seemingly incongruous presence of the screens looked exactly right at second glance; there was an almost *organic* correctness to the way they blended with their surroundings.

It was all so glorious, one could almost forgive seeing one's breath mist into the air, and, of course, having to dress as if it were the middle of November and not the height of spring. (The Resurrected performers are best maintained at a constant 42 degrees in order to prevent further decomposition. Readers might take note that most living musicians find it difficult to play in temperatures below 48 degrees, as it causes stiffening of the joints. After a brief period of trial and error, composer/conductor Russell discovered that 42 degrees—while obviously a bit uncomfortable for the audience—is the ideal temperature for Resurrected performers; it not only slows the decomposition process to a crawl, but still allows their remaining limbs and digits the necessary dexterity to perform their tasks.)

The lower part of the proscenium consisted of a rich entablature, ornamented with trusses and swags of flowers, supported by fluted columns, with intersecting enrichments, and splendid gilt capitals resting on carved pedestals. A pair of almost-frightening Roman columns bookended the stage; connecting the columns was a capital decorated with wavy lines, in the center of which was suspended an odd object composed of what appeared to be stained-glass and metallic spheres and, above that, a more flamboyant Corinthian capital under which was suspended a third but much smaller video screen—this one angled so that the conductor could easily see it when lifting up his head from the written score. Across the back of the stage hung what at first appeared to be a dark drapery, but on closer examination revealed itself to be carved and highly polished teak.

The theatre was genuinely breathtaking, all of it capped off by the exquisite chandelier that hung from the center of the ceiling, its crystal flames gleaming warmly.

I took my seat (seventh aisle, center, perfection), glanced briefly through the program (the Resurrected printers, while producing a visually striking and colorful program—on a fine paper stock, I should mention—nonetheless have proofreading issues), then—after checking underneath my seat—sat back and awaited the evening's performance.

Russell, true to his reputation, walked onstage at precisely 8:00 p.m. (Readers will remember the controversy caused by Russell in the pre-Resurrection days when he openly—and often with a salty tongue—criticized his fellow conductors for their tardiness at starting performances on time.)

He was met by justifiably thunderous applause, none more enthusiastic than my own.

After taking a brief and graceful bow, he politely gestured for the audience to quiet itself, which it did, and as the house lights dimmed and the stage lights were brought up, Russell directed our attention to the wings to watch the orchestra make its entrance. (Russell is also controversial for his belief that it should be the orchestra and not the conductor who is given the honor of the spotlighted entrance.)

Though each member of the orchestra was exquisitely dressed (the Symphony Committee insisted on new tuxedos and evening gowns for all players), their flesh—what remained of it—had the color and texture of spoiled meat; an unfortunate contrast to the otherwise tasteful pomp of their entrance. Worms and other such creatures of filth oozed in and out of the holes in their faces where once several of their eyes had resided. The stench of death was subtle, but still sickly-sweet in the air. I, for one, was at once grateful for the chilly temperatures in the theatre proper: the thought of how overpowering this smell of rot would be were the indoor climate any warmer caused my body to give forth a shiver that was in no way connected to the cold.

Most of the Resurrected musicians shambled, a few crawled, and one—a woman, Second Violin—had to be carried by another orchestra member because much of her lower torso was gone, leaving only dangling, tattered, seemingly (under the stage lighting) luminescent loops of decayed intestine which hung beneath her like a jellyfish's stingers. Even the exquisite silk of her designer evening gown could not mask this from the audience, and judging from the slight smile I saw cross Russell's face at that moment, I could not help but wonder if this were a deliberate effect on his part. After all, what better way to remind the masses of the "world unmade" than to allow them an unobstructed view of the "unmade" Resurrected?

Sheer genius already, and the performance not even begun.

It was not until all orchestra members were in place and Russell took his place before them that I noticed—as did many of my fellow symphony attendees—that nowhere on the stage were there any *music stands*, let alone sheet music from which the musicians could read.

Could it be? Dare I hope? Was it possible that Russell had so deeply tapped into the Artistic spirit that his orchestra knew their parts (excuse the expression) by heart? Had his music touched something so aesthetically primal in their Resurrected cores that it became a part of them, and so rendered any sheet music superfluous? Good Lord, what a triumph of Artistic achievement this would be were that the case. (I know as well as any of you that the Resurrected have limited memory capacity—most can be trained to do only a single task, and the more repetitive that task, the better, but a *symphony* required that a cellist or pianist or flautist do more than simply play a single note over and over, it required a concentration akin to that of the most intensive chess match. Had Russell somehow discovered through Art that there are ways to train the Resurrected to perform infinitely more complex tasks than those we have thus far assigned them? Were that the case, then this would be a significant and historic performance, and we in the audience could one day soon say that we were there on the night when the paradigm of society began its most important evolution. And all thanks to Art.)

Breathless in my anticipation, I remained still, every nerve in my body tingling with excitement and trepidation.

And oh, *how* I was rewarded!

For the next fifty-two minutes, I was spellbound and dumbfounded. Never have I heard an orchestra play with such meaning and single-minded purpose. The opening movement, *Allegro Giojoso*, could very well have been a discordant exercise in chaos, but in the hands of this composer, this conductor, and this one-of-a-kind orchestra, it was a glorious *paean* to hope once battered but found anew.

The second movement, *Adante Molto Cantabile*, was a brief but deeply affecting meditation on remembered loss, made all the more poignant by the soulful soloing of the Second Violinist. Here dangling intestines shuddered at the tips with her every move, a physical reminder that it was not only this music, but this *musician*, who knew all too well the price we have had to pay to keep our world alive. I feel no embarrassment whatsoever in admitting to you that I felt tears in my eyes as the movement neared its heartbreaking yet resplendent conclusion.

But it was with the third and final movement, *Toccata Con Fuoco*, that the performance transcended everything that had come before. The orchestra played with a passion, grace, and fire that I have never heard before (and suspect I'll never hear again). At one point I chanced a glance at Russell, whose arms were not raised but rather folded across his chest. As both composer and conductor, he was no longer necessary; all that was needed were the music and the skilled hands with which to play it. I think it quite possible that Russell was as enraptured as the rest of us. That he remained still no longer mattered; he had proven his point, made his statement, found a way to change this world for the better (as it is Art's responsibility to do). *How* he did this we would know soon enough. For the moment, we needed to stay with the music.

The orchestra brought the movement and the symphony to a swelling, precise, overpowering conclusion, and the audience was at once on its feet and cheering—but none more so than I.

Russell walked to the front of the stage and took his well-deserved bow, then gestured to the musicians, all of whom set aside their instruments and rose (as best they could) to their feet. (The Second Violinist was lifted up and brought to the front of the stage by Russell himself, an act of amazing integrity).

Placing the Second Violinist on a nearby chair, Russell once again took a bow, then gestured toward someone offstage to join him.

A well-dressed but nondescript stage manager came out, carrying a bulky wooden box that he placed on the podium within Russell's easy reach, and then handed Russell a thick roll of what could only have been sheet music parchment.

Nodding his thanks to the stage manager (who then left in rather of a hurry), Russell unrolled the music parchment and then pulled a small metal wastebasket from in front of the podium (where until now it had been hidden from the audience's view).

"Ladies and gentlemen," said Russell in his effortlessly commanding baritone, "I wish to thank you from the bottom of my heart for both your attendance this evening and for your overwhelming reaction to this piece."

Once again, the audience erupted into cheers and applause. Russell waited patiently for silence to return.

"I hold here in my hand," he said, "the only existing physical copy of the score to the piece you have just heard. As my esteemed friend Wendell Shakelton-Bailey III will tell you"—and here I rose to a brief but dignified round of applause—"Art is not something that can be captured in any permanent sense, and shortly before this evening's performance, it occurred to me that by transcribing this work to paper, I was committing not only an act of singular arrogance, but an insult to the spirit of true creativity. Art does not come from something like this"—here he deposited the score into the wastebasket while simultaneously removing a can of lighter fluid from his jacket pocket—"but from *here*, in the heart. Art comes from communion and strength of memory. So it seems only fitting that you witness this."

He squirted a goodly amount of the fluid into the wastebasket, and then struck a match, dropped it in, and stood back as the flames rose up.

My eyes filled with tears. What a brilliant gesture, to make corporeal the sacrifice necessary for True Art to endure.

The audience gasped as one, and then almost immediately rose to its feet in adulation.

As if this were not proof enough of his eternal genius, Russell then turned around and opened the box which the stage manager had carried onstage, removing one of what appeared to be several dozen sets of dentures. Turning toward the Second Violinist, he gently forced open her mouth, inserted the dentures, then stepped back.

My heart skipped a beat. Dentures of these sorts were now illegal, so the only way Russell could have come into possession of them was through the black market. Following the Great Resurrection, the Great Tooth Extraction had necessitated this action in order to protect we, the living.

As Russell removed his jacket and began rolling up his sleeve, I realized with a cold shock equal parts awe and horror what he was about to do.

The other members of the orchestra—obviously well-rehearsed for this moment—shambled forward one by one to retrieve their dentures.

Wordlessly, Russell held his arm out to the Second Violinist, who took hold of it, leaned forward, and began to eat.

Russell's screams were those of the Artist triumphant. A one-of-a-kind performance, for one night only, that now could never be repeated or reproduced.

As the remaining members of the orchestra fell upon him, those of us who were given exclusive seats this evening reached under our seats to find the gifts waiting for us. Mine was an ugly, awkward Tec DC-9 assault pistol with a 30-round clip, but something about its primitive bulk felt absolutely correct in my hands.

And so, as the orchestra finished eating Russell, we, the elite select few of the Arts community, consummated the evening's performance by erasing the final traces of the symphony from the world.

I am pleased to say that it was me who dispatched the Second Violinist. It seemed only proper.

As this goes to press, I have just been informed that—inspired by Russell's brave example and selfless sacrifice—several other members of the Artistic community have decided to employ the Resurrected in future performances and productions. The director of the Lilith Players Theatre wanted me to inform interested readers that he will be staging a new production of Edgar Lee Masters' *Spoon River Anthology* featuring a cast of both the living and the Resurrected. "It's going to be a killer production," were his exact words.

So noble is this endeavor that I have decided to allow him his sad little pun.

Starting next week, this paper shall be adding a new feature to its *Arts and Entertainment* section: Undead Art Happenings. Please e-mail my office with any announcements you wish for me to pass along.

Shoo Fly Pie and Apple Pan Dowdy

"Man is a god in ruins."—Ralph Waldo Emerson

You can find what's left of the Ben Hai Bastards hanging out on the benches around the courthouse, two soldiers who camped with their platoon on the stinky muddy-ass shores of the Ben Hai River along the DMZ on Vietnam's 17th Parallel. They'll be happy to tell you that the way you became an Official Bastard was to wade out into the river until you reached the 5 kilometer mark (any farther violated the Geneva Accords and it would have been considered an act of aggression, giving the North Vietnamese camped on the other muddy-ass side a reason to take aim and turn you into red-foaming cottage cheese); once you were there, you had to completely submerge yourself for at least three Jody-counts ("Got a gal lives on the hill, she won't fuck but her sister will, sound off one *two*, sound off, three *four*...) before showing your face again. *Not as easy as it sounds* they'll tell you, these two soldiers who fought a war they didn't believe in and came home to a country that didn't want them, but what the hell? It's fall of 1968 and they're not a part of it anymore, let LBJ and his bought-and-paid-for war-mongering cronies escalate all the hell they want, *these boys am done, hear what I'm saying?*

Yes, you'll find them hanging out on the benches around the courthouse, two decorated Cedar Hill veterans to whom no one will talk, but you're a little different, aren't you? A curious sort, you consider yourself to be a compassionate person, a person who joined protests against the war and wrote letters to the proper congressmen, so today you're going to sit down and have a chat with them, see what all the bleak rumors and worried whispers and anxious hubbub is all about.

The first one you see is called "Shooter" because he just sits there with a six-round pistol pressed against his temple, continuously pulling the trigger so the cylinder moves in its jerky clockwise motion, *click-click-click-click-*

click-click! It doesn't seem to bother him—and why should it? The gun is obviously empty—hell, it might not even be a *real* gun. But there he sits, every day, *click-click*ing the day away, almost but not quite smiling with every new cycle.

It's his buddy, the one called Rafe, who does the talking for both of them, and after introducing yourself and taking Rafe's offered cigarette, you sit there smoking and listening as he tells you this story, one that will damage—and maybe eventually fracture into ruins—the world you thought you knew:

"Take a good look at Shooter's gun, will ya? Do you see? Yeah, it's real, all right, and more than that, it's loaded—see how the sunlight glints off the bullets in the chambers? You oughtta see the look on your face. Every since the day we got home he's been trying to check out, but it ain't happening. The gun's in perfect working order—I know because it's mine. See, him and me, we...we *saw things* in that river, things that didn't fuckin' stay there once we came back to shore. We were gonna check out together. We don't sleep much and have to be careful about where we look because those things are always nearby someplace, looking like normal shit to you—knots of tree bark, shapes in clouds, patterns in wallpaper or sloppy drywall or an old lady's quilt—stuff that you see every day but never think might be looking back at you, just waiting for its chance.

"One of the guys with us, he had this groovy hash that he called Shoo Fly Pie laced with some kind of acid he called Apple Pan Dowdy—he got the names from an old Stan Kenton song that he was always humming to himself. Anyway, before Shooter and me went into the river we got good and baked on the stuff so neither one of us was feeling any pain and thought we could take out all the gooks across the Ben Hai single-handedly if we needed to. We were gonna be the meanest Bastards yet, you know it.

"So it gets to be around noon—you had to do this in the middle of the day because nighttime baptisms were for pussies. You're gonna be a Bastard, you did it at high noon, right in view of the North Vietnamese—and don't think those fuckers didn't *watch* us when we started wading out. You could tell they were just waiting for us to cross the middle of the river so they could open fire. It was like that every time someone was baptized.

"So me and Shooter, out we go, and not hesitant-like, nosir, we strutted out there like we owned the place, and when we got to within the 5 kilometer mark, under we went—which wasn't that much of a deal since by the time you got there the water was up to your chin. Down we went, the Jody-counts going through our heads, sounding off, one-two-three-four, one-two, three-*four*—doing that three times until it felt like our lungs were gonna squirt out through our assholes, and when we started to stand up, to get our heads above the surface, both him and me heard a…it wasn't like a real voice, but the sound of the water, it stopped being that slapping, bubbling, whooshing sound you get in your ears when you're swimming or under water…it became kind of like someone singing from way off in the distance, an echo, right? And it kept singing these five words over and over: *In his house at R'lyeh…In his house at R'lyeh…*it was the most beautiful voice I ever heard, even though it sounded like it was coming from the mouth of something rotten, something decayed and putrid. It reminded me of something I read about once, about this archeologist who found an old sealed vase that was covered in grime and mold, but he accidentally dropped it, and turns out there was a rose inside, a rose from maybe two thousand years ago, and as soon as it was exposed to the air, it crumbled into dust—but not before he caught a whiff of its scent, a smell from ancient times, right? For that one second, he was smelling what it smelled like thousands of years ago, and maybe, in that moment, he was, like, in two places at once. He's standing there in this tomb with this shattered vase at his feet, but at the same time, because of the scent of that ancient rose, he was two thousand years in the past, in Egypt with the Pharos and Anubis and the pyramid builders.

"It was like that for us those last few seconds we were under the water, we were in two places at once because of that voice. We were there in the river but we were also in 'His house at R'lyeh'—wherever that is, *whoever* the fuck 'He' is. It was scary as hell but it was also…I dunno…kind of *liberating* is the best word for it, I think. We weren't in our bodies anymore, we were part of the river, part of the mud, part of the death and life and night sounds and everything that flies through the sky…it was incredible. It was the best I'd felt since getting In-Country. It was maybe the best I'd felt in my entire life. If I hadn't needed to breathe again I would have been happy to stay down there with that voice and the feeling of liberation from the physical and all the goddam limitations the body has to struggle with. It was the closest thing to bliss that I've ever felt. And then Shooter and me, we made a mistake.

"We opened our eyes.

"Man, I can't even begin to describe the things we saw coming at us, surrounding us, trying to ram deformed fingers into our mouths or eyes. These things, they looked like someone had fucked a fish and the fish gave birth to these things that were part fish and part human—and I'm not talking about mermaids or the *Creature From the Black Lagoon* or shit like that, so get that look off your face, okay? And it wasn't just these deformed fish-things that were under there with us. There were things with tattered wings and faces with no eyes, things with tentacles and guts as big as boulders, terrible things, *horrible* things. For a moment I thought maybe all this was because of the Shoo Fly Pie and Apple Pan Dowdy, that shit was *major* strong, but then one of these things, it grabbed me around the chest from behind. It was like a tentacle but it had an elbow and a human-like hand at the end, but this hand, it had seven fingers, triple-jointed things, inhuman. And it was covered in this glistening slime that pulsed like it was breathing. I tried to kick it away, I tried pulling at it, but it was strong, stronger than anything I'd ever had to face. The hand, it scraped up my chest toward my face—you ought to see the scars it left on my torso—and once it got to my face it forced my mouth open, I mean *wrenched* my jaw down, and it slid its fingers into my mouth and—and this is the most crazy part—even though it had these claws it didn't cut my inside cheeks or tear out my tongue or anything. It just sort of *patted* the inside of my mouth, like a mother pats a kid's head when that kid is upset—*everything's all right, honey, don't you worry*—that sort of thing. I looked over and saw that one of the fish-things, it was all wrapped around Shooter like it was trying to mate with him or something, and it was *kissing* him, its gills throbbing in and out like it was getting really excited.

"And then that voice, that singing voice, said, 'For you, the veil is forever lifted, and the worlds will be forever split, again and again.' Then the thing let go of me and the thing that was kissing Shooter let go of him and we bolted to the surface so fast a couple of the North Vietnamese on the other side grabbed their weapons like a curse from heaven was coming down on their unworthy heads. And it wasn't just them who were unworthy. Shooter and me, we now know that all of us are unworthy. We're like ants in an anthill and those things in the river, they serve something even more terrifying, even more ancient, and it's *angry*. Ohgod, is it angry. To it, we're just ants scrambling around, and it wouldn't bother to try communicating with us no more than someone like, oh, say, fucking Pizarro when he was marching to Peru would stop at the anthill and try to communicate with all the scrambling insects. We are *nothing* to it, and it is the things holding our reality together. We're living in a false vacuum and don't even realize it

"You see, our universe is actually in a false phase state as part of a larger universe, like if it were a temporary thing. It's like a pot of boiling water, and we're just inside a bubble forming at the bottom of the pot. Eventually this false vacuum has to pop, even after billions of years in this false state, and we and everything we know in our visible universe will disappear in an instant with no warning whatsoever and there is nothing we can do about it and this thing, this ancient being that those monsters in the river serve and worship, it's just sitting there, watching the bubble form, angry and alone, waiting for the moment it decides to stick one of its clawed fingers into the pot and end everything.

"Ever since that afternoon, Shooter and me, we can't get away from these things, these beings you can't see or hear or smell or sense. They're everywhere, all around us. You can't see them because there's a veil, right, a veil of perception that you can't break through but they *can*, and they are. We don't sleep inside anymore; we can't, because for me and Shooter, that veil is fucking *gone*. These things form from the shapes in wallpaper or plaster or concrete, they come out of twisted bed sheets or the stains on a floor or a mattress, they jump out of ripples in sink or toilet water, they materialize through the static on a television screen after the station goes off the air—hell, one of them even came out of the goddamn *test pattern* one night when we chanced staying at the open shelter! And *outside?* Jesus— they pull themselves together through the twisted bark of trees, they crawl out of mud puddles clogged with twigs and bones of dead birds and feral animal shit, they emerge from the glistening mold patterns on stone or brick walls, they wriggle into shape through the strands of cobwebs, the cracks in layers of paint, the shadows between the streetlights, the scarred wood of broken doors, the lingering smoke from the factory chimneys, even the dents in the cars that pass by.

"And all of them, every jack-one of these creatures, they let us know, they remind us, that when that voice said 'forever' to us that day, it cursed us. That's why Shooter's gun will never fire, even though it's loaded and in perfect working order. We're being slowly *pulled* from this universe, him and me. Each time he finishes a round with that gun, the universe splits and the bubble gets a little bigger because of it. We're not going to have to wait for that ancient thing, whatever it is, to pop the bubble—eventually the universe will split so much that maybe, *maybe* we'll pop the bubble on our own. But maybe we're also moving toward some kind of...I dunno...some kind of metaphysical evolution that will make us part of that being watching the bubble grow.

"Shooter and me, we can't die. It's that simple. Those things and the being they serve, they made us immortal, and I think back on it and I wish to hell we'd never even *heard* of Shoo Fly Pie and Apple Pan Dowdy. I finally heard the song, you know? The Stan Kenton original. Dumbest song I ever heard, but it's got a tune I can't get out of my head, just like I can't *not* see those creatures everywhere.

"That's the story, my friend. Believe it, don't believe, it doesn't matter. What's an ant's story worth, anyway? We're all just scrambling around, serving an invisible friend up in the sky, past the clouds, who if he exists is probably a sadist and doesn't even know it. And the other being, the ancient one those creatures serve, is just sitting there, watching the bubble, watching the bubble, watching the bubble. Any given second"—he snaps his fingers— "it all just stops, just shatters into darkness, into nothingness, and there's not a damn thing you or me or God or the pope or all the king's horses or all seven dwarfs can do to stop it."

Shooter laughs at this and continues his quest for death—*click-click-click-click-click-click*—while you slowly stand up and thank Rafe for his time, for the cigarette, for the company. You say nothing about the story he's just told you. You can't. Talking about it would mean some part of you accepted it as fact, and on the face of it the story is just the rantings of a man who's seen too much death, too much war, done too many drugs.

But as you walk away, finally lighting Rafe's cigarette, you can't help but notice that the curling smoke exhaled from your lungs lingers a bit longer than usual, is a bit thicker than cigarette smoke usually is. You slow your paces as you realize the smoke is keeping pace with you, following along like a loyal pet at the end of a leash. And you can make out shapes in the smoke, twisted shapes, maybe agonized faces, maybe twisted bodies, maybe flowers and birds and happy little sprites from a children's fairy-tale book for all you can tell. Another drag, another exhalation, and this new smoke joins the previous, making the shapes a little more visible, a little more defined. You stop as the smoke stops next to you and you look at the cigarette. It's hand-rolled, not store-bought, and for a second you wonder—*Shoo Fly Pie and Apple Pan Dowdy?*—then just as quickly dismiss it. Rafe wouldn't have given you a cigarette laced with that stuff, would he?

You continue along, smoking happily away, feeling oddly free, oddly... *liberated* somehow, and the smoke cloud, it's dancing around, dancing to some music only it can hear, the echo of a beautiful voice escaping from the throat of something decayed and putrid that's not part of your world. But then, as the smoke reveals something misshapen with its hungry mouth open and its clawed hands reaching, you throw down the cigarette and crush it under your boot.

The feeling of liberation remains, and now you can hear the echo of a voice singing to you, singing a song that the smoke-shapes were dancing to, and you grow cold and frightened. You begin to quicken your steps. You try to not look at the shapes in the bricks and stones of the surrounding buildings, the fragmented reflections from the puddles of water left behind after yesterday's rain, the shapes in the mud that has gathered in the gutters, now drying, forming cracks that seem to outline something trying to—

—no. No, you don't see that, you couldn't have. You're just a little unnerved by Rafe's tale, that's all. And who wouldn't be? You close your eyes, take a deep breath, and for a moment smell the scent of a rose about to crumble into dust. You open your eyes and move into the still-lingering cigarette smoke. It was just a madman's story, that's all, that's all, that's all.

The smoke surrounds you. You can't get away from it or the shape coming into existence within it. The voice sings of forever, of lifted veils, and you choke back a cry of terror as a clawed hand with seven triple-jointed fingers reaches out and begins to pat the top of your head.

There, there, child. There, there....

Smiling Faces Sometimes

"Select your sorrows if you can…"

—Carson McCullers

"Childhood is the kingdom where nobody dies.
Nobody that matters, that is."

—Edna St. Vincent Millay

It was the way they always smiled, *the people who gave you the bad news:
We have to repossess the car; It's necessary to call in the loan; I'm sorry, but
the rental contract states quite clearly….*

Yeah, it was the way they smiled *when they took yet another part of your
life from you. And whenever he looked into those smiling faces, sometimes
he just wanted to grab a hammer and pound that smile through the back of
their skull.*

Now he wished that he had *done that, just once.*

Now that there was nothing left for them to take away.

Under the late autumn moon, in the yard behind the now-abandoned house,
Alan dropped the heavy duffel bag, looked up at the tree, and thought of
Brian, Kevin, Tony, Johnny, and Sam, and of the long-ago season they became
"The Last Defenders of *The Valley Forge*" on the evening the tree house
was completed. The name was Alan's idea. They were all in the fifth grade,
and Alan had developed a brief but zealous interest in history, particularly
the stories of George Washington's campaigns. He found something alluring
and quixotic in the romanticized accounts of Washington and his troops and
the terrible winter they'd endured at the famous fort. Something about those

tales suggested to his ten-year-old mind a fierce camaraderie that only boys could understand (since none of them had any real use for girls back then). After all, *they* were the great warriors of tomorrow, *they* were going to be strong and respected and feared, *they* were the last of their kind: a small but fearless band of soon-to-be superheroes, gathering together in their top-secret headquarters to plot their defenses against the Enemy. (That none of them ever ventured a guess as to who or what the Enemy was never entered into it; they were Going On To Great Things and couldn't be bothered with such annoying details.)

Johnny's dad—an architect—designed the tree house for them. Tony's dad—a lumber mill manager—gave them the wood from piles of damaged or discarded inventory lying about at work. It had been up to them to build it, though.

And build it they did, erecting (to their eyes) an impenetrable fortress, a masterpiece of modern tree house technology, complete with retractable ladder (to ensure that the Enemy couldn't follow them up in the event of a perilous, life-or-death chase), windows with heavy shutters that locked from the inside (so in case the Enemy *did* somehow manage to climb up, they wouldn't be able to get inside), and a small pulley-system elevator for bringing up food (because after all, such planning caused boys to work up quite the appetite).

The six of them were a team of true-blue crime-fighters to rival even the Justice League. The first moments in the newly completed *Valley Forge* were marked by a reverent silence, the kind of deeply serious, intensely focused, wide-eyed awe of which you were genetically incapable after the age of thirteen.

They assembled in a circle in the center of the *Forge*, standing around an old Mason jar that Johnny had taken from his mother's pantry. Tony opened his pocketknife. He'd recently sharpened it; the edge of the blade *gleamed*, thirsty, in the moonlight.

This was a Very Big Thing they were about to do.

One by one, they took the knife and made a small cut in the middle of their thumb, squeezing their blood into the jar, along with that of their brothers-in-arms as all good Last Defenders should. When they finished, Johnny replaced the jar's lid and sealed it with some paraffin they'd melted down, then shook it hard, thoroughly mixing their blood, before setting it into a secret cabinet they'd built into one of the walls for just this purpose.

Alan then read their Oath of Brotherhood—something he'd spent days working on; after all, he was going to be a Great Writer, he was the group's story-teller, so it only seemed appropriate that he be the one to compose their sacred oath.

Alone now in the yard, his flesh pale and tinged with silver under the diffuse moonlight struggling down to penetrate the leaves on the tree, Alan, the last of the Defenders, recited the oath to himself.

"We are the Last Defenders, and here we place our blood, mixed together, making us brothers in the fight against the forces of evil. From this moment on, we shall never be far from one another. We shall stand beside our fellow Defenders and fight unto the death if we have to. We will never abandon each other. If one of our brothers should call for help, all of us shall come to his aid."

Then they clasped hands just like in that movie *The Three Musketeers* and said, together: "We are the Last Defenders, united forever in our cause."

It was one of those grand, silly, dream-drenched moments that all boys know at one time or another. He had not since felt as close to anyone as he had to his friends that night some thirty-odd years ago.

Six weeks after they'd performed their ritual, Neil Armstrong stepped onto the surface of the moon and—even though none of them dared say it aloud to the others—the Last Defenders didn't seem like such a big deal afterward. Or ever again. At least, to everyone but Alan.

But all of that had been over thirty years ago. Hell—almost *forty*, if he were to be honest with himself. Alan summoned up the latter number in his head, as if it were something that could be physically confronted, something he could grab by the throat and beat the living shit out of, making it take back all the things it had done, but all he could do was sense the inexorable enormity of the time and recall all that had happened since then: two wives, a ninety-day DUI jail sentence, one aborted college education, countless minimum-wage jobs, and his boyhood dreams of becoming an astronaut left in pieces along with his motorcycle and a good portion of his left leg on Cherry Valley Road the night he tied one on after his first divorce.

On nights like this, when the depression got the best of him and neither the meds nor the booze helped much, he always came back to the old neighborhood, to the old house, and the old back yard with its dying tree and the rotting shell of the fort with its partially collapsed particle board and asphalt-shingled roof crouched in its branches.

Of course, this night *wasn't* like the others. If he tried deluding himself into thinking otherwise, he had only to look inside the duffel bag at his feet; it contained all he had left in the world. Who'd have thought, all those years ago, that *he'd* be the one who'd wind up homeless—well, as good as homeless: a padlock and chain on every door of his lousy little house, and official notice tacked to the door, no money to speak of (twelve dollars and seventy-two cents in his pocket, chump-change, less than a hundred bucks in his checking account), and no way to see a Legal Aid lawyer until Monday morning. Assuming Monday morning came for him at all.

So he had no choice but to spend the weekend up in the remains of the tree house, along with boyhood memories, a sleeping bag, three reams of paper filled with stories and novels he'd never sold, what little liquor remained in the bottle, depression and pain medications, and a jar filled with—

He wondered if the jar was still up there, undiscovered. That'd be something, wouldn't it? Over thirty (*almost forty*) years, at least two other families having lived here before the county condemned the property…wouldn't at least *one* kid have gone up into the tree house to search around?

He studied the trapdoor and the ragged remains of the ladder.

The moon above was bright as childhood wonder…when you still had enough hope left to believe in such things as wonders, anyway.

He limped forward, the straps holding the metal leg-brace tightly in place rubbing against his skin. He grabbed a section of the ladder, wondering if the damned thing could support his weight.

He couldn't help but notice that the moonlight on his skin made him look like a ghost in his own eyes.

"On small step," he whispered toward the moon.

Then stood there, unmoving, the moonlight brightly mocking; this boy, this man, this crippled space explorer, the last of the Last Defenders.

"Goddammit," he whispered to himself. "You guys *had* to go away, didn't you?"

From above in the shadows of the remaining dead leaves and rotting wood, no one and nothing offered an answer. He looked up to the sky where no one looked down.

Pulling down the ladder, he shook his head and thought, *You've come this far. Might as well go full-tilt bozo. Not much left to lose, after all.*

The ladder jammed halfway down, and Alan had to put some force into it, hooking his right arm through one of the rungs and lifting both legs off the ground, but the ladder came loose and rattled down in a series of wet groans and a few dry snaps.

He reached out and gripped the eye-level rung, then gave it a little yank, testing it.

It held.

"Only one way to find out," he whispered. *Jesus*, but he'd been talking to himself a lot lately, the same way his old man talked to himself when he was getting himself all worked up over money or the shitty working conditions at the plant or the cost of heat during the winter, anything to feed his frustration so he could slam back a six pack and go off on Alan and his mom.

"Cheerful, as always," said Alan to the memory as if it—like the number thirty (*almost forty*)—were something that could assume physical form so he throttle the snot out of it.

He retrieved his duffel bag, slung it over his right shoulder, and began making his way up the ladder. It shook and groaned and creaked and once even made a cracking noise, but it held.

Hopefully the trap door will open, he thought, wondering why he hadn't just found an old stick or something and tested it *before* making the climb. His leg was killing him already, but at least he had some booze and a few pain meds left. Those would get him through the night.

You don't have to do this, he reminded himself. *There's always the Open Shelter. The Reverend told you he never turns anyone away.*

Alan had ventured over the East Main Street bridge and wandered through Coffin County until he reached the Open Shelter, but once he got there, he couldn't bring himself to walk through the front doors.

After several minutes, The Reverend—who ran the place—came out to speak to him. He'd told Alan that he was more than welcomed, that he could stay as long as he liked, but Alan realized that if he *did* go inside, if he accepted the Reverend's invitation, that would be admitting defeat, accepting that he'd finally become the bottom-of-the-barrel *loser* that his old man had always said he'd become. So he politely declined, telling the Reverend, "I think I might have another option."

"Well, if that doesn't work out," said the Reverend, "you're more than welcome to come back here. I don't impose a curfew. These front doors are never locked."

Alan nodded. "Thanks. I'll...I'll keep that in mind." He shook the Reverend's hand and began walking away, but then something occurred to him and he turned around.

"Can you answer a question for me?

"I'll certainly try," replied the Reverend.

"Why is it that, no matter how hard you try to atone for things, how much you try to work to make things better, odds are you're going to be left standing alone with your dick in your hand, pissing in the wind and praying for rain? Why is it that everything is eventually taken from you?"

The Reverend scratched at his dark beard, considering his answer, and then said, "You know what I'd like to see? I'd like to see us wake up tomorrow morning in a world where God makes His presence known to all in such a way that no one can deny it. A world of understanding, of kindness, of compassion, a world where one doesn't have to double-check that the doors are locked at night or worry about their children walking home from school alone. I think that every night before I go to sleep, and each morning when I wake up, I find things are no different from the night before...except maybe, for some people, a little worse. Sometimes *a lot* worse.

"But here's the thing, Alan: I still go to bed *hoping*. Because once you give up on hope—forget faith, faith doesn't enter into the equation when you reach a certain point of desperation—but once you give up on hope, you're screwed to the wall, permanently. Why does it seem that, regardless of how hard they try, things just don't work out for some people? I think it's because—and this isn't me being judgmental of you or any of the guests who stay here—but I think it's because an individual reaches a point where they feel so completely isolated, if not alienated, from everyone and everything around them, that they begin to *fade* themselves out of existence, be it willfully or not. Their spirit chips away piece by piece, skittering away like dried leaves on an autumn sidewalk, until all that's left for them is this seemingly eternal loop of hopelessness. And all because they're afraid that they'll be judged if they ask someone, even a stranger, for help.

"Albert Camus once said something like, 'Human experience is based on what it draws from suffering; despite my dislike of it, suffering is a fact.'"

"That's really cheering me up, Reverend. Thanks so much."

"I wasn't finished."

"Sorry. But I can't help but wonder why you're offering me a homily when it's getting so late."

The Reverend smiled, but it wasn't one of those smug, condescending smiles that Alan had been getting from so many people lately; this was a genuine smile, the smile of a friendly person, the type of smile he hadn't seen in a good long time.

"I am homilizing," said the Reverend, "because I'm hoping that the longer you stand here, the better the chances that you'll accept my invitation to be a guest here."

"Would you think me rude if I just asked you for a simple answer to my question?"

"You want a simple answer? Okay. I think it happens to some people because, for whatever reason, the universe wants to keep the balance of joy and suffering even, and as a result, like a crapshoot, some people get to eat the bear, and some get eaten by the bear."

Alan shook his head. "That doesn't help much."

"You asked for a simple answer to perhaps the most complex question in the human experience—*why do some suffer while others do not?* I am truly sorry that I can't give you a more satisfactory explanation, just know that no one here will judge you, or mock you, or pity you. That is where it all has to start, with your accepting that nothing less than an offered kindness will save every last one of us. We must love one another or die."

Alan nodded. "That's a little better. Thank you."

Hooking his left arm through the last rung on the ladder, he considered saying, To hell with this, and going back to the Open Shelter, but instead he reached up with his right hand and pushed against the trap door of the treehouse. It opened with a soft, raspy screech, loosening a cloud of dust and dead bugs right into his face. He hung there for several seconds, shaking his head and coughing, blinking his eyes until he could see again, and then heaved the door the rest of the way open, closing his eyes when it slammed against the inside floor, loosening another cloud of dust and desiccated insect remains.

"Home sweet home," he whispered, pulling himself up into the tree house, closing the trap door, and removing the flashlight from his coat pocket. Snapping it on, he shone the beam around the area of the *Forge* that was still intact, surprised that a lot of it remained the way he'd remembered it—hell, there was still the torn, moldy remains of the *Batman* movie poster that he'd stolen from outside the Midland Theatre.

He spent the next few minutes unpacking the duffel bag: ten cans of Sterno for heat; his sleeping bag and a pillow he'd grabbed off the sofa; a section of good, strong rope; his manuscripts, still stacked neatly inside the mailing boxes he'd never used; the bottle of Crown Royal (there was more left than he'd thought—a *nice* surprise, for a change); the bottles of anti-depressants and pain killers; a couple of paperback books; some plastic spoons and forks; a battery-operated lantern; three cans of Chunky-style soup; and two quart bottles of water.

He arranged everything in an effort to make it as comfortable as possible—after all, he couldn't very well stand in here; *squat*, you betcha, but that played hell with his leg, so he'd be lounging it on his back tonight—and after everything was in place, he turned on the lantern, basking in its forty-watt glow, dusted off a section of floor near the head of his sleeping bag, pried the lid off two cans of Sterno, then set fire to them with a single match. He'd at least had the foresight to bring along a couple of hot-pads from the kitchen so that the heat from the bottoms of the cans wouldn't set fire to the wood (he hoped). He knew he was going to get in trouble for having broken into the house long enough to grab a few items, but before they could throw his ass in jail, they'd have to find him.

And *no one* would think to look for him here.

His leg screaming, he popped the lid from the bottle of pain killers and tossed three Vicodin into his mouth, washing them down with some water, and then chasing it with some whisky.

He lay back, zipped up his jacket, propped his head on the pillow, and waited for the goodness to kick in. After about fifteen minutes, he began to feel the shiny buzz that told him all was right in God's world, time to be happy, happy, happy.

"Now, down to business," he said, rubbing his hands together and looking around. It took him only a few moments to locate the "secret panel", but it was the better part of five minutes before he managed to get the damned thing pried loose.

And there it was.

He pulled out the Mason jar and set it on the floor in front of him, then lay on his side and stared at its contents. It looked like a jar filled with dried black-amber mud. What the hell was he expecting, for the blood to be smooth and liquid, no different now than it had been when they'd performed their ritual thirty (*almost forty; c'mon, pal, get real*) years ago?

He picked up the jar and shook it, and was surprised to see that a small section of the muck *was* still liquid—well, liquid-*like*, at least. He smiled. That meant that some part of the Last Defenders still lived inside the jar. He still had something of his friends nearby.

He pushed the jar away, giving him enough space to open the top box of manuscripts and pull out the first page.

"You guys always said that I ought to be a writer," he said to the jar. "Well, I am. Not a *published* writer but, hey, you shoulda been a bit more specific, y'know? Okay, this's one that I never told you guys, but now seems as good a time as any, right?"

From their place within the jar, the rest of the Last Defenders said nothing. Alan knew this was because they were breathless with anticipation, so he read:

"When he was a child his father would take him up to the roof of their house and throw him off head-first. His skull would smash against the pavement and he'd laugh, watching his brains splatter in the grass. Then he'd get up and yell, 'Do it again!' and his dad would wave him back up, then throw him off again. On summer evenings they'd go to neighborhood cookouts and he'd listen to other parents tell funny stories about how they'd throw and break their children, then all of the kids would run off to play and show each other their holes and scrapes and bruises and broken parts. That made them hungry. The hamburgers and hot dogs at these cookouts were always really good; they reminded him of what the stuff inside his skull looked like when his head crashed into the cement. After they'd get home he'd ask his dad to kill him one more time before bed and his dad would give Mom one of those 'what-do-you-think-dear?' looks, and she'd smile and shrug and say, 'Oh, all right, but make it quick.' The bedtime throw-and-breaks were the best. They gave him good dreams. Dreams about falling over the edge of a cliff and feeling his body break against sharp rocks, and as he lay there bleeding and moaning a beautiful princess would come along on her horse and see him and weep because he was in so much pain. Then she'd dismount and cradle his head tenderly in her arms and whisper, 'I will nurse you back to health, my brave, beautiful lover. And when you are well, we shall wed and be together forever.' She would come into his bed late at night and kiss him and soothe him and tell him stories about how she used to play secret games with her father. And then they'd fuck, and she would squeal and scream her father's name, and when they came together they'd promise each other that they'd be *good parents*, if God deemed them worthy."

The parents, the way they always smiled whenever they looked at him; poor little Alan, so full of dreams but not all that smart. Whatever were his parents going to do with him? Whatever would become of him once they were gone?

He dropped the page, staring at the jar. "That's right, I said 'fuck'. I'm an adult now, I can do that."

Still, his friends in the jar remained silent.

"Okay," he said, grabbing another batch of pages from the box, "if that one didn't do it for you, maybe this one'll pique a little more interest. Ahem

"They once had a daughter. She died when she was very young. She had been sick from the moment she was born and never got better. She never learned to walk, never made a sound, never blew out the candles on a birthday cake. The only home she ever knew was the sterile walls of an ICU. She was very tiny and she fought very hard. The last seventy-two hours of her life were agonizing, and when she died it was without the benefit of a warm, loving human touch lingering on her skin. Her mother, exhausted and sedated, was asleep on a couch in the hospital's lounge; her father had not eaten for almost a day-and-a-half and so had gone to the vending machines one floor below to get some coffee and a sandwich. The entire trip took four minutes. The coffee was lukewarm and weak, the sandwich stale and tasteless, and by the time he came back to the ICU, their daughter was dead and gone.

"Her death was not a surprise, her mother and he had known for a while that it was (as the tired saying goes) 'only a matter of time.'

"Not a surprise, but still the ice-pick in his throat.

"He remembered seeing the curtain pulled around her incubator. He remembered the sounds made by the various machines hooked up to the other children in the unit. He remembered wanting to cry but being unable to. Then it was shuffling, being taken aside, muffled words from weary nurses, uncomfortable-looking orderlies, a gurney with a squeaking front left wheel, and the last sight of his daughter: bumps and curves and patches of pale flesh inside a translucent plastic bag, rolling away, away.

"They were both very young, he and her mother, young and foolish and not nearly strong enough to handle this. Their relationship crawled along for a few more months, a joyless thing, back-broken and spirit-dead, before ending in infidelity, accusations and poison.

"Still, there are times—sporadic though they may be, usually very late at night or first thing in the morning—when it all comes back, diminished not one whit by the passage of years, and he crumples. Simply crumples. And wonders if his ex-wife still screams her father's name when she comes, or if his own head would still splatter like it did when he was a child on the roof."

And remember the way the orderlies and some of the nurses smiled, then tried to hide it when you looked their way? Those smiling faces, sometimes you just want to kill them. Even if one of them is your own.

"Don't believe what the pop-psychologists or self-help books or daytime talk-show hosts tell you about it, guys. You *never* fully recover from the death of a child. The grief eventually works its way into the shadows, back there someplace, a whisper, an echo, a tendril of smoke perpetually curling in the air over a just-emptied ashtray...but it never completely goes away. And the bitch of it is, you never know when it's going to come snarling to the surface, or what may cause it to rally and bear its teeth. Like when you finally get divorced and decide to get your ass drunk and go for spin on your just-paid-for Harley, then take a turn a little fast and don't quite make it."

He reached down and rubbed part of his leg through the brace. He was still feeling the shiny Vicodin buzz, but the pain was still there. Maybe that was the secret about pain killers; maybe they didn't really relieve the pain; they just made you feel so stoned you didn't *care* that it hurt.

"What is it?" he asked them. "A little stuffy in there? A little crowded, maybe? Let's see what we can do about that."

He picked up the jar and threw it against the farthest wall. It did not shatter—it didn't even crack. He tried it again—nothing.

"You guys always were hard to find whenever I needed you." He picked up the jar and held it beside the lantern light, watching as the small pool of muck inside sloshed back and forth.

And they all smiled, *didn't they, as they left for Bigger and Better things?*

One by one, they left you here, knowing goddamned well that you'd be the one to stay behind, and not caring. You were all Grown Up now, and had to fend for yourselves. Responsibility, they said with those fucking smug smiles. Gotta face up to things.

Not a one of them came back for your daughter's funeral, did they? Not a one of them called while you were in the hospital getting the fucking Frankenstein leg after the accident.

But man, I'll bet that all them smiled when they heard about your wipe-out that night. "That's Alan, for you. Always too reckless for his own good. Never really grew up."

You don't need their fucking pity, and their smug smiling faces.

"We must love one another or die." Right. Thanks, Reverend. You ever consider a career in writing greeting cards?

He placed the jar on its side, watching as the muck-pool sloshed over, then turned around, raised his bad leg—making sure to aim the heaviest part of the brace directly over the middle of the jar—and slammed down with all the force he could muster.

The jar shattered into several sections with a loud, satisfying crash, and he watched in the lantern-light as the muck scattered in small and not-so-small clumps, mixed with fragments of glass, while the small pool of semi-liquid black amber remained stationary, jiggling like a small dollop of pudding.

"Hey, hey, the gang's all here," said Alan. "Now, come back to me, you fuckers, you deserters, you so-called Last Defenders, come back and keep your word. Remember, you bastards? 'We will never abandon each other. If one of our brothers should call for help, all of us shall come to his aid.' Well, I'm calling."

And the black amber began to spread out, glistening in the light from the lantern and the flickering Sterno flames, and as it spread out, touching the hardened muck, the muck itself began to soften and move and liquefy, forming rivulets in the wood, picking up stray bits of dust and desiccated insect carcasses, solidifying, moving, then dividing like cells; once, twice, three times, four, and five.

Alan popped two more Vicodin and lay back, watching as the remnants of his friends grabbed and absorbed what materials they could to give themselves form.

When at last Alan found himself facing the black-amber, semi-solid forms of his five absent friends as they had been as children, he reached into the manuscript box and removed a final set of pages.

"Glad to have you all back," he said.

He could tell they wanted to say the same to him, they wanted to tell him how much they'd missed him, how sorry they were that none of them had come for the funeral, or to see him while he was in the hospital, or sent him money when he'd called to ask for help because yet another job had fallen through and the bills were due, he could *sense* this, but there wasn't enough blood and muck and insects and material for them to have formed mouths.

Still, Alan knew.

"This tree house, the *Forge*, man, it was the best thing I ever knew," he said to their faces without mouths. "That was the grandest moment I ever had, and it *sucks*, y'know? You shouldn't know your grandest, most golden moment when you're only ten fucking years old!"

They remained silent, their bloody-wood-dust skin glittering in the light.

"I got one last story for you guys, then I think it's time to call it a night." He smoothed out the pages, leaned toward the lantern-light, and read:

"He watched her from a distance, stunned and frightened and tongue-tied as a schoolboy, hidden in the shadows between the azure of the horizon and the cracked, desiccated gray of the earth. For eons he'd waited here, hoping for a glimpse of a kindred spirit, but each day brought with it only lengthening shadows, chill nightwinds, and tears that could not be shed, no matter how hard he closed his eyes and tried to force them out.

"This had been his home, and his only companions the stories and pictures he created in his mind to pass the time. He knew every nuance of these stories, every curve and fold in the flesh of the characters he invented to keep him company. This, he knew, was important, for someday someone would come along with whom he could share these things, these creations birthed in loneliness and blue-hued isolation, and when this someone came he wanted to be her wizard, her lover, her weaver of fables, teller-of-tales, her singer of songs that, once heard, would fill her heart near to bursting from the volume of the joy and wonder.

"And now here she was.

"He knew it was her; without so much as hearing her voice, or her laugh, without so much as feeling the warmth of her breath against his cheek or the touch of her fingertips against his palm (his *sweaty* palm, dammit; why did he always perspire so when the promise of happiness loomed so close?), he knew it was her.

"She carried herself like a dancer, lithe and graceful and, perhaps, with just a little sadness underfoot.

"She carried with her an exquisite jar, covered in ancient words and pictures of friends who would never abandon her. She stood for a moment, still as a statue in the deepening twilight, then turned and began pouring water down onto the dry ground. She moved as if riding waves of ether, first straight up, then side to side, pausing here and there to scatter a few select droplets before moving on a few yards and beginning the dance all over again.

"He moved toward her under the tail of a night shadow. She was drawing something in the dead soil, and he wanted to see what it was before the night took it away forever.

"A tree.

"From her exquisite jar of water and wonder she was drawing the shadow of a tree that once might have stood here, before the world turned on and on and time brushed its uncaring hand in another direction and left this place just another ruined, forgotten corner of nowhere-in-particular, one of those spots you pass by on your way to someplace better, someplace brighter, someplace where you didn't have to think about places like this—but places like this were all he'd had for so very long. They'd sent him here—but with kind words, so as to ease their own consciences at night. You're a bit too high-strung. You make people nervous. We really have no idea what it is you're talking about half the time, perhaps it would be best if you found a place of your own. We know such a place. It's quiet. It's very quiet. And very far away from us.

"He rubbed something from his eye and blinked. She had now drawn the full shadow of the tree, complete with its secret fort hidden in its branches, a fort where he could be a mighty hero for her. Then she stopped, rose up, and said: 'You can come out now. I know you've been watching me.'

"He moved out from under the shadows and stepped into the waning light.

"'Hello,' he said, the words crawling out of his throat as if they were afraid of the air.

"She was even more beautiful than he'd dared imagine. Pale, creamy skin flowing over a face chiseled from crystal and gold-flecked eyes of brown so soft and pure he could taste their gaze.

"'Why have you made the shadow of this tree and given it such a secret?'

"She smiled at him, only for him; he could have swum a thousand raging rivers on its memory alone. 'Because I need a place of sanctuary, a place where my hero will keep and protect me so that I no longer scream out my father's name when I come. Can you understand that? Can you understand what it's like to need something so terribly that you'll accept even the shadow of its memory to keep your heart from withering away?'

"He examined the shadow closely, admiring the details of the bending branches, the drooping leaves, the slow, tired, summer-afternoon-nap feel the shadows conveyed.

"'It's wonderful,' he said."

"Dancing in circles, she sang: 'It is the tree under which I will sit and dream of one who will be my wizard, my lover, my teller-of-tales and singer-of-songs. He shall be my muse, my lover, he who shall dream the tales to tell, compose the songs to sing, and in the earth draw pictures of places that never were but ought to have been. It is the tree in which we shall meet in the evening, up there in the secret fort, and share with one another the wonders and mysteries of the day. No father shall toss him from the roof to watch him crumple in a heap on the ground below. He shall sit close and safe, and I with my head against his chest. He will hold my hand in his and I will breathe to the beating of his heart. "Tell me a story," I'll say, "and make it as happy a tale as you dare." And he will tell me the story of his life, and when he reaches the end, I'll say, "Start again." And this time, when he tells it, it will be the story of *our* life.'

"A glint in her eyes, a soft glistening of moonlight from her smile. 'Would you know of any such person, sir?'"

And with that, he stopped reading. "I kind of hoped the ending would come to me while I read it to you," he said to his friends. "Guess not." He looked then at the coil of strong rope he'd brought along with him. "Ah—to hell with it! To hell with you guys—leaving me here in this goddamned town, going on to be lawyers, architects, big businessmen, teachers—all of you always thought you were so much smarter than me, didn't you? You with your smiling faces, *everybody* with their smiling faces. Well guess what happened to the old home town you left behind? The factories shut down and the malls went bankrupt and it turned into a filthy, sad, ruined white-trash refuge, that's what. And try as I did, I fit right in. Does that make you grin? Does that make you smile?

"Well, you ought to get a good goddamned smile out of *this*."

He gathered the rope and shoved aside a section of the roof, forcing his way out onto the nearest branch and climbing as best he could up to the biggest, longest branch, the one that was a good fifteen feet above the ground. It took him a long time, and by the time he'd crawled and shimmied his way out toward the end of the branch his leg was screaming again, but it wouldn't last long, he knew this, because the brace, the brace would give him that extra bit of weight he needed to make sure the job was done properly, so he tied one end of the rope around the branch good and strong and tight, then fashioned the noose at the other as he'd rehearsed countless times, then put it around his neck and tightened it, making certain that the knot was just to the side on the left side of his neck.

And then he looked up at the moon and thought of that day when Neal Armstrong had made his most golden moment seem so trivial and pointless.

"That is where it all has to start, with your accepting that nothing less than an offered kindness will save every last one of us," the reverend had said.

But maybe every last one of us isn't worth *saving.*

"One giant leap," he whispered.

And pushed himself from the branch.

His neck snapped as it was supposed to, and there was a blinding, unbelievable instant of pressure and pain, and then...nothing.

For several minutes there was only a murky, stained silence as Alan's spirit, without flesh, without blood, without bone, without cells or resonance or regret or goals or bitterness, found itself swirling amongst the countless bit of human thought that collectively and unconsciously gave systematic order to the universe. It drifted across the whole cosmic panorama, gathering stray bits of intelligible signals—snatches of old conversations, memories of love unexpressed, insubstantial fragments of forgotten, broken, or abandoned dreams, ideas that flittered around from mind to mind but were never acted upon, memories of myths and fairy-tale magic—and then gathered them, arranging them into an ordered, unavoidable, polymerized whole: his spirit saw eukaryotic thought, singularities of thought, metazoans and huge inter-living coral shoals of thought wherein human history was hidden, and in this surging sea of perpetually collapsing probability waves he found the place that held his own history, his own possibilities, what he was, what he could have been, might have been, perhaps still could be, and knew in a glorious millisecond of agony that it might be true that energy, like matter, was *not* infinitely sub-divisible, that it could exist only as quanta—but that didn't mean it could not be manipulated: electrons swirled in the electromagnetic field of the atomic nucleus, planets spun in the gravitational field of the sun, and everything in the universe could be reduced to nothing more than a series of standing wave-fronts, especially suffering, which he now knew was the most easily accessible form of quanta in the spectra; it was only a matter of directing your own energy, of knowing how much manipulation it would take to attain the proper balance of suffering and achieve the desired results: you simply homed in on the chosen suffering/wave pattern and, like a beam of radiation passing through an interferometer, split that wave down the center, leading each half along separate but accurately determined paths, then recombine them at the point of greatest pain.

Alan reached a point of ecstasy within this quanta, and reveled in it, fearful.

For a few hours, his body hung there, limp and dripping in the moonlight and autumn silence. Above his body, something within the tree house thumped, loosening a cloud of dust, making the moonlight-tinged air alive with dancing particles that sprinkled down on his body. Something crawled along the branch from which his body hung.

Then, from the underside of the *Forge*'s floor, a small globule of blood began to form, having seeped through the wood; it remained stationary for a moment, and then fell straight down, landing on Alan's left hand.

His finger twitched. Then his middle finger and thumb.

His legs shuddered. His wrists bent to the side as his arms trembled ever so slightly.

A deep groan rose up from the center of his chest and crawled from his throat. His eyes blinked against the night, and then came fully open.

Alan pulled in a deep breath, then reached up and behind his head with both hands, grabbed hold of the rope, and began pulling himself upward. It took longer than he'd anticipated, but at least there was no pain.

He suspected that pain was a thing of the past for him now.

Loosening and removing the noose from his neck, he made his way back down the branch, through the hole on the *Forge*'s roof, and returned to the tree house where his friends sat in a circle, waiting for his return.

Opening up his arms, Alan called his friends to him. They were happy to oblige, and once again—as they had so many years ago—they embraced hands as a group, only this time the embrace was not broken.

Alan had learned too much on his journey to let them all get away from him again.

This place, this tree, this fort, this moment...it was all that mattered. Everything of pain and suffering and joy and triumph that could be measured from life sprang from this instance.

And so he pulled them into himself; six into one.

Then lay back and let the *Forge* take them all, as it always should have been.

The tree still stands to this day, as does—amazingly—the remains of The Valley Forge. *But the children who venture into the yard, and who take their friends' dares to climb up into the tree house itself—claim that the place is... well, if not exactly haunted,* possessed *of something they can't quite explain.*

For you see, if you go up into the tree house on certain nights in late autumn, when the moon is bright silver and there are no clouds in the sky, the moonlight comes through the holes in the roof at six different points, and shines on the bark still visible.

There are knots there, and each of them, in the right light, at the correct time of year, looks...well, kind of like a human face.

Six *human faces, to be exact.*

Smiling *faces.*

Smiling faces, sometimes almost joyous...except for one.

Glorietta

"'Pining to live, I was constrained to die,
    Here, then, am I...

"'Poor soul; he suffered. But, at end, no child
    Ever more gently fell asleep.
    He smiled.
As if all contraries were reconciled.'"

—Walter de le Mare, "Epilogue"

The first questions are always the same, as are the responses:
    Mom? Dad? Sis? Do you recognize me this year?
    ...
    Do you like the Christmas tree? Remember when I made this decoration in kindergarten? You liked it so much, Dad. Remember? See, I even strung popcorn.
    ...
    Yet another Christmas spent both above-ground and alive. You can't understand why you still bother, why it is you hang on to a pitiful, even pathetic, shred of hope. Some nights, watching the lights as they blink on the tree and the Christmas music fills the empty rooms of the family home, you can almost—*almost*—pretend that everything is fine, you're still ten years old and that this year you *will* stay awake long enough to catch Santa slipping down the chimney, even if there is a banked fire blazing.
    ...
    You'll listen, as always, and hope for something; a sound, a whisper, a spark of recognition in the eyes. Listen and hope, but all the while know what you'll get is:

...

Still, even their silence is a sort-of gift, isn't it? Because at least they remember enough about their previous lives to come home for Christmas. They remember the house. They remember in which rooms they spent the most time during the holidays. They remember where everyone sits around the tree and how to turn off the lights so only the glow of the tree and tinsel and the glow of the fire provide illumination. They remember all of this, all three of them.

...

They just don't remember you.

At age forty-eight you have learned a new, albeit nearly useless, lesson: something about your disease repels the living dead. The first time you realized this, in the days and weeks following the awakenings, was when you had no choice but to leave the house and go in search of food and medicine. There was still power then, and the unlooted grocery stores and pharmacies still had plenty of supplies, much to your astonishment. You were in the pharmacy, gathering up the boxes of hypodermics, the vials of Dilauded, and the steroids you'd need to keep yourself alive and pain-free. You were almost finished when you decided, what the hell, grab some Percocet and Demerol, as well, because sometimes the Dilauded made you far too weak and woozy. Six large shopping bags you had, filled with enough prescription medicine to keep you going for a couple of years, even if you took more than the prescribed dosage. You were on your way out when you walked right into a group of five of the living dead, gathered around your car in the parking lot. You thought, *This is it* as they began stumbling toward you, but as soon as the first one was close enough to touch you, something like a shadow crossed its decomposed features and it pulled away its hand, and then simply stood there *staring* at you. The rest did the same. After what seemed an hour but was in fact only a minute or two, the five of them turned away from you and shambled on.

You used to keep a gun, but that's long been thrown out. They want nothing to do with you. You spent months afterward in search of others who were sick—cancer, AIDS, leukemia—something, *anything* that marked them as *persona non grata* to the living dead, and you did find a few people, but they were so far gone that there was no community made with them; you even helped a few to end their suffering, and then used their guns to pulp their brains so they wouldn't come back. The eleven-year-old boy with leukemia thanked you as you sank the plunger, sighing into sleep, dressed in his *Spider-Man* pajamas. You hated shooting him, but you'd promised, and he'd kissed your cheek before falling asleep for the very last time. You sat there, holding his hand until you were certain he was gone. Then did what had to be done.

You no longer search out the marked ones. Though you know what you do—what you *did*—was the right thing, it still hurt too much, caused too many sleepless nights, gave you too many bad dreams and sick-making memories. It's better this way. You keep telling yourself that. Maybe one of these days you'll even start to believe it in your heart of hearts.

And then came that first Christmas after Mom, Dad, and Jenny died in the automobile accident when Dad had swerved to avoid hitting a cat that had frozen in fear. You handled all the arrangements, set up viewing hours, sent notices to the paper. The day before the funeral all of the dead opened their eyes, stood up, and began walking around. You did not see the mangled remains of your family until Christmas Eve, when you awoke from a nap to find all three of them sitting in the living room, staring at the spot where the Christmas tree was usually displayed. So you did what a good son and older brother would do under the circumstances; you went to the basement and dug out the tree and all of the decorations and began setting up everything. A few minutes into your project, your family began removing decorations from the boxes and hung everything exactly, precisely where the traditional decorations always went. Your little sister even arranged the Nativity set on the fireplace mantle.

But not a one of them looked at you with anything like recognition.

Still, it was better than being alone. It is always better than being alone—another thing you tell yourself constantly in the hopes that you will one day believe it.

Merry Christmas, everyone, you say to them every year.

...

Merry Christmas.

...

This year will be no different. Oh, some of the accoutrements will change—you taught yourself how to make turducken, and your recipe is pretty good, if you do say so yourself, and you'll set four places at the dinner table, knowing that you'll be the only one eating. The menthol cream you rub under your nose kills most of your family's stench, so you at least can keep an appetite, providing you don't look at them for too long, or too often.

In the years since the awakenings, you have become a good carpenter, a decent-enough electrician, an excellent plumber, an all-around first-rate handyman. The gas-powered generators keep the electricity flowing into the house, though you're careful not to waste power. You use only the downstairs, having boarded up and sealed the entrance to the upper floors after removing everything you might need or want.

You stand in the kitchen watching them decorate the tree, arrange the nativity set, string the popcorn. *It's a Wonderful Life* is playing on DVD in high-definition Blu-Ray, Jimmy Stewart's face filling the 65-inch flat-screen plasma television you took from an electronics store last year. A digital home theater system guarantees exquisite sound. You couldn't give less of a damn about any of it right now—although you find that you've come to appreciate the middle of the movie much more, the part where it's all dark and hopeless. You recognize that look of terror and grief and helplessness that is a permanent fixture on Stewart's face in these sequences. You see something like it every time you glance at your reflection in a mirror. You laugh at the heavy-handed melodrama of that thought. It's an odd sound, hearing your own laughter at Christmas time. It's almost like the old days, the good days, the happy-enough days.

They've rotted away so much, you wonder how it is they manage to move around at all; but somehow they manage. They drip, they leak, sometimes sections of flesh or a digit falls off, a tooth drops to the floor, yet they keep going. You wonder if there is something still *them* in there, some small part of their consciousness that remembers who and what they once were, and is trying to recapture some essence of that former life. Do they dream? you wonder. So you ask:

Do you dream?

...

Cornbread or rolls?

...

Red wine okay with everyone?

...

Did I ever mean anything to any of you?

...

No need to get all sugary on me, folks, just a simple yes or no.

...

I still love you guys, you know that?

...

You move into the living room, stepping around the Christmas paraphernalia, and turn off the sound to the DVD player. It's time for Christmas music. This year, you stole a multi-disc player, one that reads MP3s, and you've set up the discs so that you will have 24 hours of continuous Christmas music. Dad used to love to sit in the kitchen with the lights turned down and listen to Christmas music while he had a beer or two. You've got several cases of his favorite beer. One bottle sets open next to his favorite mug. For a moment earlier, he stared at it as a shadow crossed his face, as if he knew this were something he ought to remember. Mug and bottle are still on the table.

How do you like the new refrigerator? you ask as you get the salad fixings ready. I got it a couple of weeks ago. Moved it all by myself. Damn thing can hold a ton of food. Do you like it, Mom?

...

Hey, why do you suppose doctors never use the word consumption anymore? No, now it's TB. I think consumption's a fine word, you know?

...

I found the old photo albums. They're right there on the coffee table. Maybe you want to look through them later? That might be fun, don't you think? All of us flipping through the images, the years, the memories. Been a while since I took a trip down Amnesia Lane. Sound good?

...

Sorry, I didn't quite catch that.

...

That's okay, you can tell me later.

You turn around and damn near drop the salad bowl because your little sister is standing right there in front of you, just…staring.

Jenny?

…

Jenny, is there something you want?

…

What is it, Sis?

…

Please say…*something*. Grunt. Sigh, snort, *anything*.

…

You close your eyes and swallow back the feelings that are trying to come to the surface. You knew this year would be no different. Christ only knows what Jen wants in here, what she remembers. You just know it's got nothing to do with you. You step around her and put the salad bowl on the table. Jen does not move. The oven timer sounds: the turducken is ready to go.

Dinner's ready!

…

You sit. They sit. You eat. They don't. On the disc, Greg Lake is singing about how he believed in Father Christmas. This is your favorite Christmas song, even though if you think about it, it's a damned depressing one—but then so is Elvis's "Blue Christmas," so why overthink it?

The turducken is delicious,. The mashed potatoes are just right. The rolls are great. And the homemade pecan pie is the perfect way to end the meal.

You go to your usual place on the far right-hand side of the sofa and watch the tree lights blink, watch the banked fire blaze, watch Jimmy Stewart run through dark streets. You pick up one of the photo albums and open to a random page. That was you, once. That was your family, once.

The pain is getting pretty bad. You've been sticking with the Demerol for the last couple of days because you wanted to be lucid enough in case something happened; a word, a gesture, a touch, something, anything.

The rest of the family take their traditional places. You look out the window and see that it's begun to snow. Good God, could there ever be a more perfect Norman Rockwell-type of Christmas scene?

You make yourself an eggnog and Pepsi. Everyone used to say how disgusting that sounded, so when you'd make the drink for your friends and family when all were still alive, you'd never tell them what it was until after they'd tasted it. Once tasted, everyone loved it. Your legacy. Could do worse.

Afraid I'm not feeling too well, folks. Haven't been taking my meds like I should.

...

Isn't anyone going to scold me for that?

...

You stare at the unopened Christmas presents under the tree. It's been so long since you've wrapped them you've forgotten what's in any of the boxes, only that they were gifts you gave a lot of thought to, hoping that they'd make everyone smile.

You go into the kitchen and remove several 4 mg vials of Dilauded from the refrigerator, make yourself another eggnog and Pepsi, and grab the bottles of Percocet and Demerol.

Back in the living room, in your traditional place, you lay out everything, then discard the Percocet and Demerol because they seem like overkill. Overkill. Funny-sounding word, that. Considering.

You draw the vials of Dilauded into the syringe until it is full. You almost tap it to clear any air bubbles, then realize what a silly thing that would be.

This has been a nice Christmas, hasn't it?

...

It really means a lot to me, that you still come here and help with all the decorating.

...

You look at the television. Jimmy Stewart is now back in the real world, and everyone in town is dumping money on his table. Donna Reed smiles that incredibly gorgeous smile that no other actress has ever managed to match.

Bach's "Sheep May Safely Graze" begins to play. The perfect song to end the day. To end on. To end. You slip the needle into your arm but do not yet sink the plunger. There is a passing moment of brief regret that you threw out the gun, because you know what that's going to mean. But maybe you won't remember, and, in not remembering, there will be no caring, no hurt, no regret or loneliness.

You look at each of your family members one more time. None return your gaze. They look either at the tree or the fire or at the snow outside.

Merry Christmas, everyone, you say.

…

You slowly sink the plunger. If your research has been correct, once the syringe has been emptied, you will have at best ninety seconds of consciousness remaining, but you can already feel yourself slipping down toward darkness before the plunger has hit bottom. But that's all right.

You have enough time to pull the needle from your arm and lay back your head.

Bach fades away, and is followed by "Let There be Peace on Earth." You're surprised to feel a single tear forming in your right eye.

Do you like…like the music, Dad?

…

Shadows cross your face, obscuring the lights of the tree. You blink, still slipping downward, and see that your family is surrounding you. Looking at you. At *you*.

You reach out one of your hands. It takes everything that remains of you to do this.

…, you say.

…, they reply.

And your family, with the light of recognition in their eyes, as if they have missed their son and brother for all of these years, takes hold of you, enfolding you in their arms, and the best Christmas you've ever known is completed.

Down in Darkest Dixie Where the Dead Don't Dance

"Art thou pale for weariness
Of climbing Heaven, and gazing on the earth,
Wandering companionless
Among the stars that have a different birth,—
And ever changing, like a joyless eye
That finds no object worth its constancy?"
                    —Percy Bysshe Shelley, "To the Moon"

The ghosts of New Orleans are restless tonight.

The first to show himself is Bernard de Marigny, the colorful Creole character who named many of the city streets—Elysian Fields, Pleasure, Duels, Piety, and Desire; the next to materialize, wielding a sword that spilled the blood of many an unsuspecting seaman, is none other than Dominique You, the pirate captain who served under Jean Lafitte; following his dramatic entrance back into the world, still accompanied by his battalion of soldiers, is Pierre Gustav Toutant, New Orleans' most famous Civil War soldier, still weeping for all the fine men lost at Shiloh after he was forced to assume command when General Johnston fell to Union fire; next comes the dozens of nameless slaves who, at the hands of Delphine and Dr. Louis LaLaurie, were subjected to humiliation, torture, and hideous medical experimentation on the third floor of the *Maison LaLaurie* on Rue Royal; in their wake appears the ghost of Juliette Thibedeaux, an enslaved woman of mixed blood who fell in love with her Creole master and wished for the man to marry her and who, in order to prove her love, spent a cold December evening naked atop her master's house on Royal Street where she froze to death; after Juliette comes dozens, hundreds more, from Joseph Charbonnet who was beaten to death in the old Carrollton Jail to Ernestine Guesnow, murdered by her husband and then ground into sausage at the factory he owned.

From the jumbled maze-like paths of St. Louis #1 to the moss-draped, unmarked graves sprinkled throughout Holt Cemetery, from the *Vieux Carré* to the Metairie and all along Westbank, the ghosts begin assembling near the spot where, in 1768, the French residents of the city rebelled against the Spanish regime which had taken control of Nouvelle Orleans under the treaty of Fontainebleau, and here they wait for the arrival of the Capuchin priest Pere Dagobert who, in defiance of the Spanish governor and at great risk to his own life, performed secret religious services for the dead patriots of the uprising; when at last Father Dagobert appears to them, a tattered Bible clutched in his near-skeletal hands, his expression is anxious and tight.

"How's ba'you, Father? How's ya fam'ly n'nem dat followed you over?" asks Bernard de Marigny. "Ya come by to pass a good time with us tonight?"

"Not tonight, Bernard," replies the priest, turning his head in the direction of the music and laughter echoing from the French Quarter. "No, I'm afraid there will be no song or dance or celebrating for any of us this evening." The priest's eyes are wide but not with wonder.

It don' madda much," says de Marigny, taking his placed by Dagobert's side. "Ya be da one who buried a lot of us, we do what you say."

The priest says nothing for a moment, merely nods his head and stares in the direction of the merrymaking; eventually, after closing his eyes and breathing deep of the night air, he turns toward New Orleans' restless dead and says, "Company's coming."

Walking toward them are a woman and a little girl, both of them in the robes of the dead, both of them with haphazard stitches encircling their necks to mark the place where their decapitated heads were sloppily reattached to their bodies. The woman is crying, frightened, but the little girl, holding tight to her mother's hand, is not only calm but very, very happy to see the crowd of ghosts.

"Where 'bouts ya come from?" inquires the pirate Dominique You.

"I used to live in Ohio," says the little girl, "but me and my mommy, we're not alive anymore."

"Dat right, dat surely is," barks de Marigny.

Dagobert places a hand gently on the little girl's shoulder. "What brings you to us this night, child?"

"There's a man and woman, bad people, Father. We gotta do *something...*"

Her fear is broken glass under the dead's feet.

Dagobert swallows. Once. Very hard. "Do you know their names, child?"

The little girl furrows her brow and thinks very hard for a moment, then says: "Laurie...?"

Dagobert feels a chill slither down his back. "Perhaps you mean...Dr. and Madame LaLaurie?"

"Uh-huh," says the little girl, nodding her head. "I can...I dunno...I guess I can *feel* them."

Dagobert turns back and looks at the faces of the slaves who died at the LaLaurie's hands, and in their faces he can see the memories of the whippings, of the burnings, of the countless humiliations they were subjected to; but most of all, he can see the memories of the agonized hours spent strapped to Dr. LaLaurie's operating table as he grafted genitals where noses should be and hacked off limbs simply because he enjoyed the way they screamed and—

—and Dagobert shakes away the thoughts.

"Father?" whispers de Marigny.

"The good doctor and his wife are among us once again," says the priest, and even he cannot hide his revulsion. "I think, Bernard, that this may be a very long and uneasy night."

And the ghosts of New Orleans grew even more restless....

Detective Pete Russell thought of pain in its most mystifying expressions, of snipers in clock towers centering passersby in rifle scopes and the last sad whimper from the throats of crippled old men left bound and starving and neglected in putrescent beds and terrified two-year-olds methodically tortured to death by remorseless parents while neighbors who *knew* ignored the agonized shrieks, and he wondered if God's love was measurable only through the enjoyment He seemed to take in the suffering of the innocent, but then remembered "Starry Night" and *The Heart is a Lonely Hunter* and "...it was then that I carried you," and tenderness.

He leaned against the lacy iron rail on the balcony outside the second-floor room and stared down at the colorful Mardi Gras revelers cutting their noisy, joyous path through the *Vieux Carré*. *The ghosts of New Orleans are restless tonight,* he thought, *down here deep in darkest Dixie were dem dead doan dance, no-suh.*

He couldn't remember if that line came from a song or a poem or a nursery rhyme, then decided it didn't matter a damn.

Russell studied the bacchanal below and tried not to think about the body on the bed. The business end of the 9mm had been placed flush against the right eye, the trigger had been squeezed, and the gray matter inside the tabernacle of the skull had been introduced to its hollow-pointed celebrant. *Kyrie* (aim) to *Gloria* (squeeze) to the *Epistle*: "Do not let anyone have a claim on you, except the claim which binds us to love one another, which is all that the Law of God demands."

Bullshit and Amen—oh, by the way: Bang; you're dead.

The bullet had blown a hole the size of a grapefruit through the top of the head, decorating the wall with blood and viscera. So why did it look as if the body's chest was still rising and falling as if still capable of breath?

He lit a cigarette and searched for an answer among the throng of decadent, fantastic figures who moved along the cramped streets like clusters of cancer cells through a bloodstream.

The giant papier-mâché heads many of them wore were reminiscent of the stone monoliths on Easter Island—but where those ancient heads were solemn, inspiring awe, wonder, and even fear, those worn by the revelers were quirky and whimsical, inviting laughter and good cheer with their comically elongated noses and jaws and stiff, pointed horse's ears. Some carried banners that flapped in the wind, others had large bottles of wine cradled in bamboo baskets, a few held leather harnesses with sleigh bells above their heads, jingling and jangling as they twirled by through the blizzard of rainbow confetti, and one carried a well-used bodhran, using its thumbs to strike the goat-skin drum as krewe doubloons and multi-colored potato chips bounced across its tightly-stretched surface.

In the sputtering glow of their *flambeaux* torches, the figures looked diaphanous, mythic, otherworldly: A man with the head of a black hawk wearing a feathered headdress, a turtle with small antlers, a raven-headed woman in a golden flowing gown, a lion peering out from behind the visor in a suit of armor, a wolf in sparkling bandoleers, a mouse with angel's wings, a steer-skull wearing the uniform of a Spanish Conquistador, an owl on a unicycle, a buffalo in a wheelchair, a rollerblading serpent; dressed in deerskin shirts and breechclouts and leggings, with *gris-gris* pouches and beaded necklaces, holding flutes and horn-pipes, trombones and ceremonial chimes, banjos and tambourines, their music and discordant singing was an intoxicated, exuberant chorale, holding every spirit in the spell of *Laissez les bon temps rouler*!

Russell shook his head, wondering how it was possible for anyone to be *that* happy.

He spotted the girl a few moments later. She was standing off to the side of the crowd, staring upward at the windows of the building that lined this side of the street. Twenty-four, twenty-five max, too-thin and pale-skinned, a Goth chick to the core, she was dressed in black leather and lace and silver metal from neck to ankle; her hose were fashionably torn and her lipstick was dark as a bruise, just like her eye makeup and fingernails. Around her neck hung a bright silver cross on a heavy chain, and around her wrists were black leather bracelets dotted with several small metal spikes. Her left biceps was tattooed with a coil of barbed wire that encircled the flesh there, and she sported a nose ring on the left side from which hung a thin chain that connected to another silver ring that dangled from her pierced left ear. She lit a cigarette and watched the partying masses move by, something distant in her eyes; Russell couldn't get a good enough look to tell if it was contempt, sadness, or anxiety.

"Are you sad, little girl?" he whispered.

For a moment she seemed to look right at him, as if hearing his question.

He wondered if she or anyone in the street below knew how physical evil and moral goodness intertwined like the strands of a double helix encoded into the DNA of the universe. Man was supposedly created to know wrong from right, to feel outrage at everything monstrous and evil, yet the scheme of creation itself was monstrous; the rule of life was get through the door and take that smack on the backside from the doctor's hand so you can be set adrift in a charnel-house cosmos packed from end to end with imploding stars and bloodstains inside chalk outlines.

And what then? A crap shoot: if you did manage to survive the agony of being born there was always the chance you'd die from a fatal disease or be killed by a drunk driver or crushed by a falling building during an earthquake or drowned by your mother after she strapped you in good and tight and shoved the car into a lake, or you might be skinned alive or raped or tortured or beaten to a pulp or strangled or decapitated just for the fun of it, the thrill of it, the hell of it—So, whatta you wanna do tonight, Angie? Jeez I dunno Marty, whatta you wanna do?

When he looked for her again, the Goth chick was gone, but in her place was a waist-high pile of small plastic baby dolls that glistened with drying wet sugar and icing; prizes found inside the traditional Gnawlins' King Cake.

The way the dolls were stacked triggered something in his memory and he was suddenly too much aware of the beating of his heart—*thumpata-thumpata-thumpata-thumpata—*

—not his heart, not his heart at all, no but some kind of secret beast pounding bloodied fists against a hidden door, *Let me out! Let me out so I can eat your fucking face!*

The pile of babies...ohgod—

—the way he'd pounded his fists against the apartment door, knowing that something horrible was happening to the people on the other side, then, when the child screamed, he'd blown the lock off and kicked the door open and there stood the father over the pile of bodies, his wife and two daughters and the infant whose neck he'd snapped, and now he had the three-year-old boy against him and the knife seemed to come out of nowhere *and before Russell could scream a warning or get off the first shot the blade guided across the kid's throat and—*

—stop it, stop it now—

—so he indulged for a moment in a flight of fancy that used to help him get through the bad ones way back when, before it seemed like they were *all* bad ones, before it had all become a cancer slowly devouring his mind, and closed his eyes and imagined that external reality existed nowhere else but inside his own head, which meant that nothing and no one outside the iron maiden of his flesh actually suffered. It used to work wonders early on in his career when even a simple shooting death seemed like the zenith of depravity, less so as the cases piled up and the perpetrated acts became more hideous and sickening; now it did nothing except reinforce how utterly meaningless and pathetically ineffective his every waking moment on the job and in his life had been.

A group of drunken musicians in top hats and tails yelled a four-count intro, then assaulted anyone in earshot with an off-key rendition of "Little

Brown Jug" that was greeted by whoops and hollers and the *snapitty-snapitty-snap* of exploding firecrackers.

Russell clenched his teeth and snarled, "Let the good times roll, my ass."

"They're just having fun," said a voice behind him.

Russell whirled around and instinctively reached under his jacket for his weapon but the shoulder holster was empty and why shouldn't it be? His body on the bed was still clutching it.

The Goth chick laughed but there wasn't a lot of humor in it. "These bodies, they die easy; old habits, not so much, huh?"

Russell swallowed twice, very hard, and tried to gather what was left of his wits. The Goth chick was sitting on the edge of the bed, staring at his body. "It's kinda funny in a weird way, y'know? All my life I've had this thing about cops—not trusting them and all that? Now a cop's the only one who can see me and vice-versa." She reached out as if to touch the face of his body, then stopped, her hand suspended above his forehead. "Homicide Detective, weren't you?"

Russell nodded, "Fifteen years."

"What happened? No, wait, don't tell me..." She held both her hands over his body, moving them through the air as if patting him down during a search. "Jesus. They got pretty nasty toward the end, didn't they?"

"I guess."

"You *guess?*"

"For the last couple of years, it seems like they've all been pretty nasty."

"Was it any one of them in particular or...?"

Russell shook his head. "Not really." He was only peripherally aware of the tears running down his face. "Mostly it was the way they all started to... jumble up in my memory."

"I didn't figure you for the melodramatic catharsis type. No, your spirit wasn't broken with one sudden blow; it bled to death in thousands of small scratches."

A large group of people began singing "If Ever I Cease to Love" from a bar across the street.

The Goth chick held her hands against her ears in mock-misery. "'Oh, don't dey make wit' da *big* gumbo ya-ya!' Give me headache, *suc au'lait!*'" Then she laughed.

"You finished with your Ragin' Cajun imitation?" snapped Russell.

"I thought it was pretty good," she replied, hands back on her lap.

"What's going on now? I mean...why are we able to be here talking like this?"

"'Cause we're fresh, I guess."

"I don't follow."

The Goth chick lit another cigarette and smiled sadly. "I was a really good student—I mean, I know you wouldn't figure it to look at me, but I was. Especially in science and biology."

"I didn't ask for a résumé."

She shrugged. "What? You got someplace you need to be? Didn't think so. Okay, so here's what I was thinking: Death isn't instantaneous, right? The cells go down one by one and it takes a while before everything's finished. If a person wanted to, they could snatch a bunch of cells *hours* after somebody's checked out and grow them in cultures. Death's a fundamental function; its mechanisms operate with the same attention to detail, the same conditions for the advantage of organisms, and the same genetic information for guidance through the stages that most people equate with the physical act of living. So I've been asking myself, if it's such an intricate, integrated physiological process—at least in the primary, local stages—then how do you explain the permanent vanishing of consciousness? What happens to it? Does it just screech to a halt, become lost in humus, what? Nature doesn't work that way, you dig? It tends to find perpetual uses for its more elaborate systems. I mean, that still doesn't explain why you and I are talking to each other like this, but it gave me an idea. Maybe human consciousness is somehow severed at the filaments of its attachments and then absorbed back into the membrane of its origin. I think that's all we are right now: the severed consciousness of a single cell that hasn't died but is instead vanishing totally into its own progeny."

Russell snorted derisively. "We're *ghosts*, lady. That's all."

"Not quite yet, we're not."

"I don't have the slightest goddamn idea what you're talking about."

"Not all of our cells have died yet, and the ones that're still alive are *remembering* us. And as long as just *one* cell remembers us, we're tied to the corporeal in some form. But when those final cells finally give it up—" She snapped her black-nailed fingers. "*Then* we're ghosts."

I'm guessing you weren't a big church-goer."

She leaned against the headboard and crossed her arms over her chest. "Okay, smartass, let me ask you something: How is it you're able to smoke a cigarette still?"

Russell looked at the smoke he held between his fingers. When had he fired up another one?

"Don't remember doing that, do you?"

He shook his head.

"That's the trick. There's a thousand things we do without thinking about them—walking, eating, breathing, lighting a cigarette, picking up a pen. All done by rote. We explain it away by saying that we do it 'unconsciously,' but the truth is it's our *cells* that remember this stuff for us, that tell the rest of our body how to pull a pistol from its holster or add a little more sugar to the iced tea because it's not sweet enough. C'mon, Dirty Harry, look at your own body here—see the way the chest still rises and falls every so often. That's because those cells in you that are still alive haven't figured out yet that you're gone."

"So what?"

"So that's why I came to see you."

"To give me a lecture on biology and metaphysics?"

"Because it's going to be several hours before you become a ghost and cross over into the spirit world. In the meantime, you can move between the Land of the Dead and the World of the Living."

"Again: *So?*"

She sat up straight and—not looking at what she was doing—shoved her hand through a bluish-gray ripple in the atmosphere and pulled the gun from the body's hand, then tossed it to Russell; he watched it pass quickly through several other bluish-gray ripples and caught it without thinking.

"I want you to find my killers, Detective Russell. A man and a woman, both very elegant-looking Goths. I've been worm food for several hours but you've only been dead a couple of minutes. Right now we're just like electrons, able to travel from point to point without having to move through the space between, and I want to use that to my advantage. The people who killed me, who raped me *while* they were torturing me—until it just got too messy for the likes of even them—are still walking around this city...and their 'itch' hasn't quite been scratched to their satisfaction yet, if you read my meaning. I don't know how long I've got until the last of my cells check out and I become a permanent resident on the other side, but until then I can still *touch*, I can still *feel*, and I can still *manipulate* things on the physical level.

"I want you to help me find them so I can make the two of them suffer the way they made *me* suffer, understand?"

"What good would it do you?"

"What do you care, now?"

He thought about that one. "I guess part of me still clings to all that stuff the priests and nuns taught me when I was a good Catholic school boy—'Vengeance is mine,' sayeth the Lord and all that."

"Yeah, well, the Lord evidently stepped out for a smoke while those creeps were introducing my lower areas to the business end of a Leatherman tool, so I'll save Him the effort of exacting justice on my behalf."

"Why ask me for help, then? Why not just do it yourself?"

She sighed. "Know that guy you arrested back in '89? Killed his wife and little girl, then cut off their heads and stuck 'em in the freezer?"

Russell closed his eyes, trying not to remember how—

—the guy had jammed pinballs between the upper and lower rows of their teeth so their mouths would always be open because every once in a while he liked to take one of the heads out of the freezer and pleasure himself—

—he'd wanted to blow the sick fuck out of his socks because the guy acted like they were stomping all over his civil rights, what he did in the privacy of his home was his own business, and Russell had studied the guy's face and eyes and saw neither insanity nor remorse there, the guy did it because he *liked* it and saw nothing wrong with his actions...and it hadn't helped when the medical examiner said that, based on histamine levels or something like that in the muscle tissue, odds were both the wife and child had still been alive when decapitated—looks like he did the wife first—and oh, by the way, did you know that a severed head can still see for about thirty seconds after it's been cut off? Yeah, that's why the French always held up the heads of people executed on the guillotine—wasn't just so the crowds could cheer, but because the person's brain hadn't stopped receiving data yet, so they could still look down and see their headless bodies and have just enough time to realize they were dead and be scared as hell before the final curtain fell, isn't that interesting?

Russell snapped open his eyes. "...yeah, I remember..."

"The wife was bad enough, but it was the kid that really got to you, wasn't it?"

Tears again. "...yes..." *The terror that must have been in that child's heart and mind as she cowered shrieking in the corner and watched Daddy kill Mommy and then come after her...*

"Of all the death you've seen, it was always the kids that got to you the worst, wasn't it?"

"...hell, yes...it was like...toward the end...it was like people were bringing kids into the world just so they'd have something to rape and beat and starve and mutilate and torture..."

She rose from the bed and walked toward him. "You'll help me because of all those kids, Detective. You'll help because of all the killers and torturers you never caught. You'll help because you need to clear just one small corner of your conscience." She took hold of his hand. "You'll help me because when those fuckers left me laying there in the *ex-voto* room in the St. Roch Cemetery, when he walked away and left me under all those replicas of hands and feet and handicapped children's braces and that statue of St. Lucy with eyeballs on a plate, they were singing a little song." She moved closer to him; her breath smelled like cloves. "Do you know what that song was, Detective?" Her face was so close to his their lips were nearly touching.

"...no," whispered Russell, suddenly filled with her smells, so rich and sultry and seemingly alive.

"'Thank Heaven for Little Girls,'" she replied.

Russell pulled away from her. "Oh, God..."

"Yeah," she said, her eyes filling with rage. "I think they're going to finish off their night on the town with a child, Detective. That's why you'll help—because even if you don't care about justice for me, you won't leave this Earth knowing you could have prevented the death of another child."

Russell went back out onto the balcony and there stood in a space between fear and longing where his only companion was regret and thought about all the savagery he'd seen during his thirty-nine years on Earth. Good God—the human brain could detect one unit of mercaptan amid fifty billion units of air, and if the human ear were any more sensitive, it could easily hear the sound of air molecules colliding; the eye possessed tens of millions of electrical connections that could process two million simultaneous messages, yet could still focus on the light from a single photon; the nervous system was a wonder, capable of miraculous things, yet more often than not every fiber of an individual's being was geared toward destruction. Why? The evolution from paramecium to man had failed to solve the mystery so what chance did he have to bring something as corporeal and therefore alien as this girl's killer to justice?—assuming there *was* such a thing. Matter was nothing more than energy that had been brought to a screeching halt, and the human body was only matter, and the fundamental tendency of matter was toward total disorganization, a final state of utter randomness from which the cosmos would never recover, becoming more and more unthreaded with the passing of each moment while humanity flung itself headlong and uncaring into the void, recklessly scattering itself, impatient for the death of everything. So what if he *did* find the son-of-a-bitch who killed this girl and took him out before he could get his hands on a child? Somewhere out there was another son-of-a-bitch who *would* get their hands on a kid, or an old woman, or some unsuspecting Goth girl on her way home from a club, and drag them into basements or alleyways and split them open or burn them or twist their most sensitive parts with handyman's tools until their victims screamed enough to get them excited, and then...and then it would go on and on and on, a race sinking further into the pit of depravity, all the while forgetting that they possessed the ability to write music or formulate equations to explain the universe or cure diseases, create new languages and geometries and engines that could power crafts to explore space.

"Russell?" whispered the Goth girl.

"What?" he said, not turning to look back at her.

"Can I ask you a question?"

"Would it make any difference if I said no?"

She laughed, but only a little. "If humanity is as inherently evil as you seem to think it is, then how do you explain goodness? How do you explain love and a newborn's smile and a haunting tune you can't get out of your mind and the great way you feel when you smell fresh bread baking in your mother's kitchen?"

"I can't."

He felt her hand touch his shoulder. Though neither of them knew it, it was at this moment that the ghosts of New Orleans became restless and began to assemble.

Russell thought of pulling away from her but there was a heat in her palm and fingertips, a gentle warmth that had been missing from his life for as long as he could remember. "I'm not from around here, you know."

"Me neither," she said.

"I came down from Ohio. I was on medical leave."

"Were you injured in the line of duty?"

"No. Cops don't use words like 'burnout' or 'unstable' or 'breakdown' when talking about their own. 'Medical leave' is the term of preference."

"I'm sorry."

"It's a sorry world."

"You can make it a little less so before...before you have to..."

"'Things will not be this way within reach of my arm.' That's something my partner and I used to say whenever we were assigned a really miserable case." He shrugged. "Sometimes a delusion is the best thing for you, especially when you *know* it's a delusion." He turned toward her and took hold of her torn-gloved hands. "What's your name?"

"You're gonna laugh."

"I won't, I promise."

"Saffron. My parents were a couple of old hippies."

Russell laughed.

"I knew you were going to do that," she said.

"Then you know what my answer is," he replied, jacking a fresh round into the chamber of his gun. "Let's go find those pieces of shit that did this to you."

"Why did you decide to help me?"

"Seems my schedule recently opened up—kind of like the top of my skull. C'mon, before I change my mind."

Saffron squeezed his hand and guided him toward a blue-gray ripple in the air; they stepped into it, dissolving bit by bit, until the room fell to silence, its only occupant on this plane or any other the stilled, bloody corpse on its bed that clutched no weapon in its suicide hand.

Simultaneously, at the intersection of Decatur and North Peters Street, another blue-gray ripple appeared, unseen by the partying Mardi Gras attendants, and Saffron and Russell stepped through it. The smell of the Mississippi River hung heavy and damp and bitter in the air.

"Why here?"

"Because," said Saffron, "this is where I met them. There's a Goth club called the Crystal not too far from here. I was heading back to the room I'd rented in a shotgun hotel near Chartres. They were hanging around right here, smoking a joint. Even for the Goth world, these two looked pretty hardcore—elegant as hell, the wardrobe and jewelry they wore probably cost more than you make in six months, but they seemed friendly enough. The man had this gorgeous, jewel-handled dagger hanging from his belt, and the most beautiful leather shoulder bag—how was I supposed to know it was filled with surgical instruments? He smiled at me and offered me a couple of hits, then the woman—I'd've killed for the boots she was wearing—pulls out this flask filled with what she claimed was absinthe and we all took a sip." Saffron shuddered. "Christ, that was some serious stuff."

"Didn't your mother ever tell you not to take candy from strangers?"

"Up yours, cop. My parents were terrific people and raised me just fine, thanks very much. And if you'll look—" She gestured to her belt, where a small canister of pepper spray hung near her right hand, a sleek black stun gun near her left. "—I wasn't exactly defenseless. My mommy and daddy didn't sire no simpleton."

"So that's why you grew up to dress like some character out of an Anne Rice novel?"

Saffron glared at him. "Look, *cop*, let's you and I get something settled right now. Ever since those two yahoos in Colorado picked up their Tec-9s and did the Columbine Boogie everybody thinks that all Goths are morbid, self-destructive, nihilistic schizoids who like to cornhole dead bodies and shoot heroin with shared needles and gather in the wee hours for a circle-jerk while they watch homemade snuff movies, and I get sick and tired of being labeled 'anti-social' just because I like to dress like this and go clubbing and listen to bands like Concrete Blonde, Attrition, The Sisters of Mercy, and Love Spirals Downwards! Christ—didn't you ever listen to Black Sabbath when you were in high school? Did everyone think you were gonna go postal on them because you thought "Children of the Grave" rocked? Don't look at me that way! I'm not saying there aren't Goths who might fit that bill, but you name me any so-called sub-culture that doesn't attract its dregs. Goth culture is one of the few that embraces anyone who has an attraction for a darker aesthetic—Republicans, Anarchists, Christians—yeah, we got 'em!—Pacifists, certified public accountants, Goths don't judge. So what if we mix blackcurrant juice with vodka so we can act like we're vampires drinking blood—didn't you ever pretend at 'Monsters' when you were young? We read 'dangerous' magazines like *Carpe Noctem*—like you never took any shit for subscribing to *National Lampoon* in its glory days. There's nothing wrong with being attracted to things on the darker side and enjoy visiting there—why the fuck else do people go to horror movies or read Clive Barker and Stephen King? It's *fun*, period. Just because you're attracted to the darkness doesn't mean you're going to set up permanent residence in the neighborhood and build Torquemada's torture chamber to get your jollies, so I'd appreciate it if you'd get that condescending smirk off your face and quit making offensive remarks about a lifestyle that's given me a healthier sense of self-worth than a hundred summers at Bible camp! Think you can do that?"

Russell stared at her, then gave a slow nod of his head. "Would it do any good if I said I'm sorry?"

"It might."

"I'm sorry."

Saffron waved a hand in the air as if swatting away a mosquito. "Forgiven."

"Can I ask you something now? Would you please stop saying 'cop' like it was some chunk of vomit you had to scrape off the bottoms of your shoes? I gave my life to the force and I'm still damned proud to have been a police officer. I never took a bribe, I never used excessive force—and believe me, there were times I'd've liked to!—and I never once ratted out a fellow officer."

"How noble of you. The years on the force must have left you with so many fond memories of a life well spent and—" Saffron's eyes grew wide and she suddenly covered her mouth with her hands. "Oh, *shit!* Oh, Pete, I'm...I'm so sorry, I didn't mean that, really, I'm sure you did a lot of good—"

Russell waved away his own mosquito. "Forget it. Like they say down here, 'It don madda none, no-how.'" He looked around the area for a moment and caught sight of a police car parked in front of a store. His detective's instincts still with him, Russell wandered over and watched as the officers assigned to guard the storefront began unrolling the yellow crime scene tape.

The store—a Goth shop called Gargoyle's—had recently been broken into.

"What is it?" said Saffron, looking at the shop. "Oh, man! That's the best Goth shop in the city! What's going on? A break-in?"

Russell slowly shook his head. "They wouldn't post officers out front and use the crime scene tape if it was just a burglary. Whoever broke in there killed someone—an employee or janitor is my guess. That's a murder scene—trust me, I've seen enough of them." He shook his head once more at the sick state of the world, then turned to his companion and said: "Okay, Saffron, what happened after the three of you toked it up here?"

Saffron pointed. "We started walking over to Canal. I was pretty buzzed at that point. It seemed to me that we were walking through water, you know? I could see it rippling as we passed through." She took a step forward and stuck her hand into one of the blue-gray ripples; it disappeared up to the knuckles, then reformed into a whole when she pulled it back. "I thought it was kind of cool, you know? Like moving through various dimensions of reality. I kept expecting to turn a corner and run into Rod Serling."

"Did you talk to them or remember anything they might have said?"

"Hell, I don't know..."

"Think. You'd be surprised at what you can remember if you just concentrate."

She glared at him. "Please don't use that tone of voice with me."

"What tone?"

"Like you're talking to a three-year-old. I *told* you I can't remember anything that was said so stop getting all over me about it."

Russell rubbed his eyes. "Real hard case, aren't you? Live by your own rules—look where that got you—and don't take no shit from nobody, right? You are a rock, you are an island."

She started walking away from him. "I don't need this."

"Bullshit."

She whirled around. "Lay off!"

Russell threw up his hands. "Fine by me. I never asked for this, anyway."

"No, you just took the chickenshit way out instead!"

"That supposed to hurt my feelings?"

"Fuck you! You're just like every other goddamn cop I ever ran into, you never turn it off, you're always suspicious of everything, always a Nosey Parker—"

"'Nosey Parker'?"

"Something my mom used to say all the time whenever one of our nibby neighbors started asking about stuff that wasn't any of their business." This seemed to trigger something in her mind, and she looked off in the distance at something only she could see. "You know what I remember most about my childhood? Laundry days. Mom would wash and dry the loads, then lay out the shirts and slacks and things that needed to be ironed—oh, I *loved* to iron the clothes. You start out with this warm, wrinkled-up wad of material, you lay it out on the board and start moving the iron over it and pretty soon you've got this clean, crisp, new-looking piece of clothing." Her eyes glistened. "I loved to iron because it was like making something new again. It was hardest on Dad's white shirts because you can see the smallest wrinkle on a white shirt. Like that guy tonight, his shirt was so *crisp* and smooth, it looked either brand-new or freshly ironed and I remember saying something about that and—" She stopped, mouth open, and looked over at Russell. "Oh, Jesus. I remember asking him how he kept his shirts so smooth and he said something about their servants doing that for them and then the woman, she suddenly looked really disgusted and said something about their useless, 'coon-ass' help—that really should've pissed me off but I was too stoned to get on a soapbox about racial stuff—and then the man said, 'Watch your tongue, Delphine,' and I asked them where they lived and they started going on about their house on Royal Street and the awful changes that had been made there and—and you did that on purpose, didn't you?"

"Did what?"

Saffron walked toward him quickly, pointing a finger. "You got me mad on purpose because that way I'd remember something, right?"

Russell shrugged. "It's an old cop trick you use with witnesses who're too rattled to recall specific details. Make them focus on what they can't remember, then get them to think about something else for a minute. Seven times out of ten, if you distract them well enough, they remember things they thought they couldn't."

"Huh. You know, that's kinda cool." She grinned, then playfully smacked his upper arm. "You're pretty slick...I mean, you know, for someone who's a cop and all."

Russell grinned at her. "I got lucky. I figured anyone who excelled at science and biology wouldn't forget details that easily, even if they were pretty toasted." He shrugged. "If your aptitude for something is high enough, it becomes second nature. I know fingerprint experts who can trace whorl patterns in their sleep. You struck me as being too bright to not remember at least *one* bit of conversation. Thank God for laundry day, huh?"

They smiled at one another. It seemed both strange and natural.

"Come on," said Russell. "Let's head over by Royal Street and find their house."

They found another ripple in the atmosphere and moved into it—but not before Russell took one more look at the Gargoyle's crime scene. An occupational hazard.

They emerged from another ripple just in time to find themselves behind a crowd of tourists who were following a young bearded man dressed in a cape, tuxedo, and top hat. He carried a cane with a silver wolf's head that reminded Russell of the one used by the guy who used to play Barnabas on *Dark Shadows*.

"Next on our stop," intoned the tour guide in a mock-macabre voice, "is the infamous *Maison LaLaurie*, the scene of one of New Orleans' most unspeakable crimes."

Saffron giggled. "The 'Haunted New Orleans' tour. I thought about going on it but then decided it was silly."

The tour guide was still talking to his group. "...belonged to Dr. and Delphine LaLaurie, both of whom were, to the eyes of the world, cultured and refined leaders of New Orleans' society."

"Delphine," whispered Russell.

They followed the tour.

"But Madame Delphine, it was later discovered, had a dark side to her personality, oh, yes. She routinely starved and brutalized her slaves, whipping and torturing them. Furthermore, her staid physician husband committed ghoulish, experimental medical procedures on some slaves.

"The LaLauries were able to conceal their evil side from the public, although once Delphine had been fined for the 'accidental' death of a slave—a girl who fell off the rooftop while running in terror from her mistress. And upon more than one occasion a neighbor would complain of strange sounds coming from the house including screams in the night."

"Sounds like a charming couple," whispered Saffron.

"Shh."

"Oh, you've got to be kidding me! You're not actually *interested* in this crap, are you?"

Russell looked at her. "You think ghost stories are crap?"

"Hell, yes, I mean who would ever believe in—oh, wait. Scratch that."

"So you see my point?"

She sighed. "Okay, okay, okay." He pointed toward the group. "Lead on, oh-wise-one."

They caught up with the tour group. The guide was really getting into his narrative now, once in while even lapsing into a not-terrible Bela Lugosi. "One day, however, the LaLauries' hidden chamber of horrors was permanently revealed by a kitchen fire, perhaps started deliberately by a slave as a call for help. When the fire patrol and some neighbors came to the rescue, they discovered more than fire. They found a secret laboratory on the third floor where several unfortunate slaves were misused for bizarre "medical" procedures. It was a true chamber of horrors. The authorities discovered some slaves dead, while others had been badly mutilated and intentionally deformed. In some cases the victims had suffered the deliberate and unnecessary amputation of limbs. Body parts and human organs were in disarray about the room, while some slaves were found still chained to the wall. The scene was horrific, grotesque.

"The firemen called the constables, who secured the area, taking the enslaved victims to the hospital. When the neighbors learned of the hideous nature of the crimes, they became enraged and demanded justice. However, Dr. and Madam LaLaurie escaped the angry mob of citizens which had formed around the house when news of the torture chamber spread. The LaLauries disappeared—although some Madame LaLaurie sightings appeared on the north shore of Lake Pontchartrain as well as in the city, and as far away as New York and even France. But the LaLauries were never brought to justice. And the once gracious *Maison LaLaurie* deteriorated, becoming the haunted house you now see before you."

Russell and Saffron both stared at the structure.

"Looks like every other house on the street," said Saffron. "I mean, it's falling apart but...I'll bet it was pretty in its day."

"Tell that to the third-floor guests."

"Then the ghosts began to appear," said the guide in a *Danse Macabre* sing-song voice. "Neighbors heard shrieks at night coming from the run-down house and some claimed to see apparitions. Visions of tortured slaves appeared on the balconies; some people claimed to see a white woman, perhaps Madame LaLaurie herself, with a whip in hand. Others claimed to have seen the ghost of the girl slave who had died after running from Delphine.

"Over the decades other horrible apparitions have been reported—butchered animals and visions of tormented slaves in chains. No one has been able to prove or disprove the validity of these sightings. And take care, my friends, for legend has it that on this night, the Night of Shrove Tuesday, between midnight and sunrise, the ghosts of New Orleans can enter this world and do as they please. Can you be certain that the person next to you isn't a ghost? How do you know that fellow over there isn't the hideous doctor, or that woman standing so near to you—might it be Madame LaLaurie, come back to relive her foul acts? No, you can't be certain, not in this place, for perhaps Evil still dwells here in the House of LaLaurie!"

The crowd *oooh*'d and *ahhh*'d appropriately, then it was time for flashbulbs and video cameras to commemorate their fun and fascinating visit to this place of torture.

After the group moved on, Russell turned toward Saffron. "The woman, did she have a whip?"

"A cat o' nine tails. It was hanging from her belt."

Russell nodded. "So now we know who they are. You were murdered by a couple of ghosts."

"How is that possible? They were decked out in Goth gear!"

"My guess is they were the ones who broke into the Goth shop and killed whoever was in there." He chewed on his lower lip for a moment. "But how could they have *physically* done any of this? I mean, if what you were saying is right, that because all our cells haven't gone belly-up yet, we're still able to manipulate things in the living world, then there has to be some way that they can do it, as well."

"Maybe what the tour guide said isn't just crap. Maybe on this night the ghosts can enter the world of the living and do whatever they want."

Russell nodded his head. "That would explain how they were able to break into the shop and kill people. That would explain why two ghosts from the 1800s were decked out in Goth garb."

"That's important to you, isn't it?"

"What?"

"Answering all the questions, making sure there's no loose ends."

"There's always loose ends—and, yes, it's important to me. Whenever I finished a case that still had a couple of loose ends, it made me nuts. Oh, sure, I might have the killer, and the motive, and the weapon, and the timetable of events...but there was usually *something*, you know? A small detail that didn't quite fit in with things. I—oh, skip it."

"No. That's the first thing you've told me that even comes close to revealing the person inside the cop."

He considered that for a moment, remembered the way people used to complain that he'd never let anyone get close to him, looked once more at the house, then said: "I remember the way I used to love watching horror movies when I was a kid. This house looks like any one of a hundred that was in those movies. My dad, he worked at a factory, right, two until midnight every day except Sunday. On Friday nights Channel 10 used to run 'Chiller Theater'—a double feature of great old horror movies. *Frankenstein, The Wolf Man, Murders in the Rue Morgue, Fiend Without a Face*...anyway, I got to stay up late on Friday nights so that when Dad came home, Mom would set up these TV trays in the living room and he and I would watch these movies together. I remember that any time there'd come a really scary part I'd scoot over next to him on the couch and say, 'Hold my stomach, Daddy,' and he'd press his big hand against my middle and it wouldn't be so scary then." He pulled in a deep breath, then lit a cigarette. "I miss him and Mom. I miss those Friday nights and those awful, *awful* TV dinners and 'Chiller Theater.' I miss...a lot of things." He was suddenly aware of Saffron staring at him, and felt awkward, exposed. "Sorry. I didn't mean to—"

"That's okay," she said, taking hold of his hand. "I thought it was kind of sweet. I liked hearing it. Don't apologize. It obviously meant a lot to you."

"Yeah, it did. Then I grew up and the whole fucking world turned into 'Chiller Theater' and being scared sort of lost its magic."

"I'm sorry, Pete. Really, I am."

"Thanks."

She hadn't let go of his hand yet. For some reason, Russell didn't mind that so much.

"I think I'm getting a bit fond of you, cop."

"Maybe I'm growing accustomed to your face, as well."

Saffron smiled. "We're having a movie moment, aren't we?"

"I guess."

Silence for a few seconds, then Russell said: "Is it over yet?"

Saffron let go of his hands. "Party pooper."

"Tell me what else you remember about your walk with the LaLauries."

208

"Like I said, we just started walking and...next thing I know, we're in St. Roch #1, heading into the *ex-voto* room. We get in there and fire up another joint, then take a couple more little sips of the absinthe, then the guy starts feeling me up." She looked down at the ground, embarrassed. "The woman, she started kissing the back of my neck. I hate to admit it, but they got me pretty hot." She looked into Russell's eyes. "I'd never done anything like that before—you know, a threesome. But there was just something so...*erotic* about being in that place with them. Mostly it was just a lot of kissing and licking and nibbling on nipples until most of my clothes were off and I started to get a condom out of my purse. That's when the guy went ballistic on me."

Russell shook his head.

"What?" said Saffron.

"You were stupid to go with them, you know that, right?"

"So I was stupid—because of that I deserved to have my areolas and nipples sliced off and rammed down my throat?"

Russell started. "They mutilated you?"

Tears brimmed in Saffron's eyes. "Cutting off my breasts was one of the nicer things they did."

She hugged herself. "Ohgod, Pete—I'm getting cold! Are you cold? Is it getting cold?" A single tear slipped down Saffron's cheek. "The last of my cells are starting to go down." Her face pleaded with him. "I think it's going to be soon now. I'm scared, Pete. I'm...*I'm so scared.*"

Instinctively, Russell put his arm around her and pulled her close to him. The department had unofficially reprimanded him several times for doing something like this but he didn't care then and he didn't care now, so he held her with all the strength he had, hoping all the while that she couldn't tell how suddenly terrified he was of losing her company.

He kissed the top of her head and stroked her hair, surprised at the intimacy they were sharing, even more surprised when she took hold of his hand and kissed its palm—with both her soft lips and warm tears. There was nothing sexual about their embrace, that would have ruined it for both of them; it was, quite simply, a moment of untainted grace. In this silent communion both found a trace of lost empowerment, lost hope, lost dreams.

Saffron looked up at him. Tears had blended with her mascara to create several long, black streaks down her face. "God, how I must look."

"It's not so bad," whispered Russell, brushing at one of the streaks with his thumb; he succeeded only in creating a horizontal black streak that made her right cheeks look like someone had drawn a tic-tac-toe board there. "I think I made it worse."

"Do I look too bad?"

"No worse than any other Goth freak."

Saffron laughed. "Hey, *pig*, I got my rights, back off! I'm tired of being hassled by the Man!" And with that she stood back and raised her right fist in the air, defiant.

Russell snorted a laugh. "You look like an extra from *Billy Jack Meets Dracula.*"

They both burst out laughing at that, then Saffron came into Russell's arms and they kissed; warmly and passionately. Russell pulled her into him again and rested his chin on the top of her head, overwhelmed and mystified by the depth of the sudden affection he felt for her, and it was then that Detective Pete Russell, a solitary and often lonely man who'd given his life over to the detection and apprehending of the worst of humanity, who had come to think that the universe was nothing more than an obscene slaughterhouse where the blood of the innocent flowed in rhythm with the echoes of their agonized screams, who until this moment believed he would never feel the kind of all-consuming *need* for another human being that the poets wrote about, realized that he *cared* about this woman, this Goth girl, this Saffron-daughter-of-old-hippies, and vowed to who- or whatever might be listening: *It will not be this way; for these last minutes on this earth, the world will not be this way within reach of my arm, not for her.*

And that's when he saw the old man coming toward him.

Wrapped in a morgue blanket but whipping it around his naked body like an elegant cape, the old man danced and twirled down the street, coming ever closer, until he was close enough to shout: "Why, hello, Detective Russell! Interesting night, isn't it?"

"Do I know you?" said Russell, nearly choking on the words.

Saffron turned around. "Who is that?"

Russell shook his head. "I'm not sure...I *think* I know his face but I—"

By this time the old man was right next to him. "Name's Harold Crider, son. I was one of your very first cases. My kid strapped me into my bed and left me there to rot. I'd been there so long that skin was stuck to the sheets. My guts started to spill out when you rolled me over, remember?"

Russell shook his head. "Not really." This said with deep regret.

Crider slapped a hand on Russell's shoulder. "Well, that's okay, don't go beatin' yourself up over it any longer, you hear? Good Lord knows you seen more than your share of terrible sights."

"Wh-where did you come from?"

Crider cocked his head to the side like a grade-school teacher sizing up a slow student. "Why, from *you*, Detective. We all did. You been carryin' us around with you for so long ain't one of us thought we'd ever get out—but that bullet you put through your brain sure did the trick, yessir. Shot us out of your brain like we were cannonballs." Crider made a grand sweeping gesture with his arm. "We just wanted to...to see you again."

Russell and Saffron looked all around and saw—

—on rooftops and from alleyways, coming around corners and scurrying down fire-escapes, climbing through broken warehouse windows and forcing open long-locked doors of boarded-up buildings, the ghosts of the victims from every murder case Russell had ever worked gathered around them, all smiling despite their still-existent wounds, all of them clambering to touch Russell or shake his hand—

—all of them speaking their thanks.

"...really appreciate everything you did to find that guy who shot me, I'm really sorry you never caught him because it made you so sad..."

"...was so great the way you tackled him in that alley after he cut my throat; I didn't shed a tear when they gassed his ass later..."

"...and my mommy can't be mean to my little brother like she was to me 'cause you *caught* her..."

"...forever in your debt, it takes a special kind of man to do what you did for the likes of me—I mean, who cares about some fag with AIDS who gets gunned down? But you gave a shit, Detective, and I love you for it..."

"...it meant so much..."

"...you were so upset when you saw my body, you were the only person who cried for me and that meant a lot..."

"...never thought of us as corpses, you always thought of us as people..."

"...didn't mean for you to feel so responsible..."

"...you did everything you could..."

"...you felt so angry for us..."

"...so sad..."

"...you did everything you could..."

"...everything you could..."

"...everything humanly possible..."

Crider held up his hand, silencing the ghosts who now lined both sides of the street for as far as Russell could see. "Okay, Detective, it's like this: We figure that, since you felt so bad for all of us, since you could never forget what was done to us even if you didn't remember our names or faces, and on account of you blaming yourself in a way, thinking you didn't do enough, thinking that what you did didn't mean a damn thing, that your whole life was pointless...well, we understand that's why you carried us around for all these years—no hard feelings there, so we figure that we *helped* you pull that trigger, in a way. And we owe you."

Russell shook his head. "You don't owe me a thing, any of you. I'm just sorry that—"

"None of that 'sorry' shit, son; you're way past that now. You were a fine man and a good cop and you deserve to end your career better than with your brains blowed out in a hotel room." Crider looked at Saffron. "Them two what killed you, they're on their way to Holt Cemetery with a three-year-old child they snatched from a crowd watching the Orpheus Parade, a little retarded boy wearin' a *Star Wars* t-shirt and a sailor's cap.

"We been with you so long, we'd kinda like to be in on your last arrest, if that's okay with the two of you."

Russell's throat was so tight and his eyes burned so hot that he could do little more than nod. Saffron brushed away one of his tears, kissed his cheek, then faced Russell's ghosts and said, "We'd be honored. And thank you."

"Thank *you*," the ghosts replied.

"It wasn't for nothing," choked Russell into Saffron's ear. "All those years...all the bad dreams and people thinking I was a head-case and me wondering if there was still decency in the world...it meant something..." He was sobbing openly now. "...my *life* meant something..."

"Yes, it did," she whispered. "You bet your ass it did." Then she pulled his face up and kissed him hard on the mouth. "You sound like you were one helluva guy, Pete Russell."

"You know, even with mascara smeared all over your face, you're the most beautiful woman I've ever seen."

"*Now* you want to make with the warm and fuzzy? *Now?*"

Russell pulled himself up, took a deep breath, and removed his gun from its shoulder holster. "No; *now* I want to get my hands on those two before they—fuck it. Let's go."

They moved *en masse* through a large blue-gray ripple—

—and emerged in the heart of Holt Cemetery.

Where the restless ghosts of New Orleans were waiting for them.

The two crowds of ghosts approached one another. Bernard de Marigny and Father Dagobert stepped forward.

"Little girl," shouted de Marigny over his shoulder. "Dis here da man and woman you spoke about?"

The little girl and her mother made their way to the front of the crowd. Upon seeing Russell the girl broke into a smile and ran to him, throwing her arms around his legs. "I *knew* you'd come!"

Russell knelt down and with his index finger traced the sloppy stitching around her neck. "Oh, *Karen*. I'm so sorry about what your daddy did to you and your mother."

Karen smiled. "That's okay. Now that we got out of your head, we're having fun! I made a *whole bunch* of new friends, see?"

Russell looked up at the ghosts of New Orleans. "They look real nice, Karen. Are you happy now?"

"Oh, you bet! *Everybody's* happy here." Then she scrinched up her face as if forced to eat a vegetable on her plate that she found repulsive. "Not like over *there*." She pointed out toward the world of the living.

Russell looked over his shoulder, and saw with a kind of x-ray vision past the vine-shrouded ruins of the cemetery gates to the world beyond. A world filled with vicious, selfish people who looked grotesque and deformed; they pushed, shoved, struck at each other, and knocked each other down, were hateful to their fellow man, each one of them trying to better the next and get to some unknown location not realizing that they were heading nowhere. It was a macabre sight, a cruel, pointless struggle of inhuman lunatics.

"I don't wanna be like that," said Karen.

"Me, neither," replied Russell.

"Russell?" said Saffron. It was less than a whisper.

She was starting to quickly fade. Russell leaped to his feet and reached for her but his hand passed through her body to grasp only emptiness.

"No!" he whispered, then cried: "*Goddammit, NO!*"

"...Pete..."

He tried to grab hold of her hand once again but could not. He then turned to face the ghosts of New Orleans. "What can I do? Tell me—somebody *tell me!*"

Father Dagobert moved closer. "The last of her Earthly body is dying away."

"No, Father, no!" Near panic, Russell grabbed the priest by his shirt and slowly pulled him closer. "Listen to me, Father—"

"...so cold...so c-c-cold, Pete..."

"—I will not be without her by my side, do you understand? All my life I was alone and miserable and never thought I'd feel about anyone the way I feel about her. When it's time to pass over into your ranks, she and I will go together. Please tell me this can be done somehow, please show me that God or Whoever's in charge of this fucking freak show isn't a sadist. Tell me. *Please, tell me.*"

Dagobert was visibly moved by Russell's plea. He reached up and gently removed the detective's hands from his shirt, smoothed down the ruffles, then held his Bible close to his chest. "You love her that much?"

Russell looked at Saffron's fading form and said, "Yes, yes I think maybe I do."

"Russell?"

He turned back toward her. "I'm here, I'm right here."

"I've got an idea..."

He tried to hold her again but embraced only air. At least he could still hear her voice, at least he could still see her, though it was like looking at an image in a slowly developing photograph. "Tell me, Saffron. Whatever it is, I'll do it. Whatever it takes."

She was thinking aloud. "...keratinocytes and maybe...maybe 3T3 feeder layer...no, shit, that won't work...wait a sec..." Her now-translucent eyes found him. "So you love me, huh?"

"I do. Don't ask me why."

"I think I know how you can help me."

"*Tell me.*"

"You're not going to like it."

"I don't care. I'll do anything. *Anything.*"

And she told him exactly, *precisely* what he had to do.

Some of it turned his stomach but he dealt with it. "Are you sure that'll work?"

"Fuck no! But it's the best I can come up with."

Russell rose to his feet and looked into the ghost-crowd. "I need a knife, a *sharp* one."

The pirate Dominique You unsheathed his jewel-handled dagger and tossed it into Russell's waiting hands. "This will split anything, sir. On that you've my word."

"Best be on your way, son," said Harold Crider. "Them two you're after, they'll be here right soon."

Russell looked at Saffron. "I won't disappoint you. I swear it." He looked into the crowd. "I need someone to...to go with me. Someone who knows their way around the city."

It was Father Dagobert who stepped forward. "I'll accompany you, Detective, if you don't mind."

"Thanks, Father."

And they entered the blue-gray ripple—

—to emerge in the *ex-voto* room where Saffron's body lay, still undiscovered.

Russell swallowed back the bile he felt rising in his throat. The savagery inflicted on her was among the worst he'd ever seen.

"Lord save us," intoned Dagobert, making the sign of the cross over the body, then opening his Bible and quietly reading a prayer.

Russell knelt down next to the piece of bloody flesh and meat that was once the woman he now loved and began to touch it, then pulled back his hand, took a deep breath, and began his work.

Don't use any of the skin that isn't still attached to my body, Saffron had told him. *Cut away a section of my cheek, then cut that section in half lengthwise, top to bottom, got it?*

Feeling as if he were murdering a child, Russell wiped away the blood and viscera on her face until he found an unharmed section of cheek flesh, and did what he had to do. Once the section of flesh was split in half (Dominique was right, his dagger was *amazingly* sharp, making the delicate work simple, if no less sickening), Russell took a clear plastic evidence bag from his jacket pocket (another occupational hazard—he *always* had an evidence bag on his person), carefully slipped the two sections inside, then sealed it tight.

He looked at Father Dagobert. "You all right, Father?"

The priest shook his head. "That poor girl. The horrors she must have endured..." His gaze met Russell's. "She'll find peace with us...as will you, Detective."

"Blew my brains out, Father. From what I was taught, I bought myself a one-way ticket to Hell."

Dagobert put a hand on Russell's shoulder. "It doesn't quite work that way, Peter. Yes, it was a sin, but God is not so angry that He would turn away a soul for having been in *that much* pain. You've nothing to worry about, I promise."

"Do you know how to get to—"

"Yes. Come."

They exited the *ex-voto* room and entered the next rippled doorway—

—and emerged in the Burn Unit lab of the Department of Dermatology in the basement of the Tulane University Medical Center.

"Where's the goddamn refrigerator?" snapped Russell.

Dagobert pointed to the large silver doors in the wall opposite them. Russell ran over and grabbed the handle, pulled—

—and the doors wouldn't open.

He looked down and saw the short chain and secured padlock.

"*Fuck!*" He pulled out his gun and said to Dagobert: "Go over to the doors, Father, and watch for anyone. I'm gonna make a bit of noise."

The priest did as Russell told him. "There's no one about."

Russell took two steps back, aimed, and fired three shots in rapid succession at the lock—which blew open and clattered to the floor. Russell quickly yanked the chain from around the door handles and opened the refrigeration unit.

You'll be looking for Petrie dishes with collagen-based growth mediums in them—just find one that looks like it's got yellow Jell-O in the bottom. Take the lid off, then put the two sections of my skin on top of the yellow stuff, all right? But make sure that the halves that face down are identical: the outer layer of skin on both halves should be facing you.

Done.

He froze. "Jesus...now what?"

Think, think, c'mon, you don't have time for this—

—he remembered the smell of her breath when she stood close to him in the hotel room, how close their lips were at that moment, how tempted he'd been to kiss her just to see what it felt like to share a moment of tenderness after you were dead—

—and he had it:

As soon as that's done, look around for some lactated Ringer's solution—okay, I've confused you. Look for a spray bottle—there should be several of them nearby, if not right on top of the refrigerator. Spray it all over my skin samples, then put the cover back on the Petrie dish.

He found the solution, sprayed, and covered the dish.

"Now the incubator," he said to himself.

"Someone's coming," said Dagobert.

Russell found the incubator and began to open the lid—

Put the dish on top of the incubator, not inside. If you put it inside it could be a while before anyone finds it and realizes it's not an authorized sample. The top of the incubator will be slightly warm. That little bit of warmth plus the growth medium in the dish should be enough to keep the cells alive for a few more hours. That's all you've got left, and I want to leave with you.

He put the dish on the incubator, then noticed that someone had set a pair of houseplants on top of the thing, as well. He moved the plants closer together in order to hide the dish.

"All done, Father."

The security guard shone his flashlight through the windows of the lab door as Dagobert and Russell slipped through the ripple—

—and stepped back onto the soil of the cemetery.

The ghosts all stared at Russell, silent.

Oh, pleaseGod, no, he thought.

A few seconds later, de Marigny laughed loudly. "Wha' ya waitin' for? Give dat little gal a kiss 'fore I do it fo' ya!"

Russell spun around and there was Saffron, kneeling on the ground and shuddering. He fell to his knees and pulled her to him.

"I g-guess th-this is the part where I thank you," she whispered.

"I thought I was going to lose you."

"...just like a cop...won't let you get away no matter what."

He smiled and kissed her.

"Y-you done g-good, Pete."

"Smart girl, you're a very smart girl."

"Dean's list every quarter." She placed one of her hands against his cheek.

"I saw your body...Christ, I'm so, so, so sorry."

"You and me both." Then: "So I guess this means we're stuck with each other, huh?"

That's when the echo of the child's terrified scream reached them. Russell was on his feet immediately, his weapon in his hand. "Not within reach of my arm," he snarled through clenched teeth, then shouted: *"Not within reach of my arm!"*

Without thinking about it, he ran toward the scream, and the ghosts followed him.

Lighted torches illuminated the path through the cemetery as the ghosts passed ribbons and ravels of tissue and sparkle-tape that clung to the ancient headstones and the hand-carved, love-polished crucifixes hanging from the outer walls of the above-ground tombs that shone in the moon- and torchlight liked marble jewelry cases, stone angels whose eyes bespoke approval spilling down the sides of the entryways. Russell jumped over dead flowers and overturned statues, skidded around corners where the moss hanging from the monolithic oak trees turned the way into a jungle, and stomped through the thick vegetation that might have ensnared him had he still been a part of this world; at last he rounded the final corner and there, less than fifty feet away from him, stood the beasts with the child, who was laid out on an overturned headstone like a slab of meat on a butcher's block.

The man was taunting the Down's Syndrome boy with something thin, shiny, and sharp, while the woman ran her hands over the child's face and chest, eventually working her way down to his belt buckle, which she began to loosen. The child's eyes looked downward at his sailor's cap on the ground, and when he tried to reach for it the woman made a fist and struck him hard in the stomach. The child's face turned red and he threw back his head to scream but the pain was too intense for any sound to escape him.

Ignoring the layers of blue-gray ripples that he passed through, Russell sprinted toward them screaming, *"Hands in the air and move away from the kid RIGHT THE FUCK NOW! Right now or I'll kill you where you stand!"* He slammed to a halt ten feet from them, the 9mm pointed directly at the man's head.

"Suc au'lait!" cried de Marigny. Several dozen ghost slaves echoed his surprise.

"What?" shouted Russell.

"Dat be Madame and Dr. LaLaurie! Dey kill many, many of dere slaves, some of them in very nasty ways."

The murmur of the ghost slaves became more and more angry.

"Some evil never dies when it should," whispered Father Dagobert. "Those two should have joined the devil in Hell over a hundred-and-fifty years ago."

It didn't matter a damn to Russell that the tour guide had been right, that the ghosts of New Orleans could affect the world of the living between midnight and sunrise—he just wanted them away from the child.

"Move!" he shouted at them.

Dr. LaLaurie smiled a hideous grin. "My, my, my—a white man avenging nigger slaves. Why bother yourself? They were little more than animals."

Russell gripped the wrist of the hand holding the gun to steady his shot. "You've got till three, then I shoot."

"Or is this about the *girl*? Ah, of course. You looked like a smart man to me, one who would not bother himself with the likes of those worthless, black-skinned dogs." He gestured with obvious distaste toward the ghost slaves.

Russell gritted his teeth: "One..."

Dr. LaLaurie parted his hands before him; in one he held a scalpel, in the other, a bone saw. "But I see that you're one of them, after all, aren't you? Merely a ghost, no threat to me or my wife."

"...Two..."

"And this child! What use could a mongoloid moron like this be to the world? Best to use him for experimentation and wet, private pleasure, don't you—"

Madame LaLaurie made a sudden move, and in the second before she could bring the dagger down into the child's throat Russell squeezed off three rounds in quick succession that should have struck her in the chest, throat, and right eye and crumpled her dead to the ground.

But they passed right through her, winging off the stone pillars of a nearby crypt.

She pulled back the knife, looked at her husband, and laughed.

The child, unharmed, very still, very frightened, pulled in ragged, wheezing breaths.

"Why the hell didn't it work?" shouted Russell.

"Because your gun, like yourself, is still not fully a part of the World of the Dead."

Dr. and Madame LaLaurie, now realizing Russell was no threat to them, leaned back against the headstones and smiled hideously.

Russell threw down his gun and reached for the dagger Dominique You had given to him. "Then I guess we do it the messy way."

Dagobert grabbed hold of his arm. "I thought you wanted justice."

"I'll make do." He couldn't take his gaze from the LaLauries' arrogant expressions.

Delphine LaLaurie, her hand placed firmly on the child's chest, laughed.

It was then that Russell saw the first shadow move on the roof of the crypt behind the LaLauries; slowly at first, perhaps a nightbird fixing its nest, but then the moon- and torchlight revealed, albeit briefly, the taut sinewy muscles of a dark arm, and soon the ghost-slave on the roof was joined by another, then another, and then several more, all of them lined up and squatting, ready to pounce.

"They're waiting for you to give the word," whispered Dagobert.

Russell squeezed the handle of the dagger.

Neither of the fiends made a move to harm the child.

But for how long? wondered Russell.

Then: *Distract them.*

He walked toward them very, very slowly, arms parted before him so both of them could see the dagger in his hand.

"You can only kill us one at a time with that," said Delphine LaLaurie. "It matters not which of us you strike first—the other will make quick work of this—" she looked down at the boy, "—this piece of human shit."

"May I ask a question of you, Dr. LaLaurie?"

Happy that the balance of power had now shifted his way, LaLaurie nodded.

"Why did you do it? Any of it, *all* of it?"

"There's a tribe in Africa, Detective, called the Masai, and every so often they chose one of their elders, or a cripple, or some other useless member of the village like this child here, and they give them a huge party, then take them out into the jungle and leave them there for the hyenas to eat alive. It's their way of not only controlling the population but of thinning out those elements that might taint the purity of their tribal seed.

"Why do we do it? Because the world, from pole to pole, is a jungle, no different from the one where the Masai feed the hyenas. Its inhabited by various species of beasts, some of which rut in caves and devour their young, others that wear tailored suits and dine on their rivals' broken businesses. All of these beasts have only one honest-to-God function, and that is to survive. There is no morality, no law, no imposed man-made dogma that will stand in the path of that survival. That humankind survives is the only morality there is. And for the White Race to survive, we must be superior, we must dominate all lesser creatures, and in order to ensure that, it is not only vital but necessary to destroy, to eliminate, to thin out and expunge any undesirable element that threatens to stop the march of progress. Now, you're a smart man, Detective, so let me ask a question of you: What possible use to the world—aside from medical experimentation—is this child or those ignorant slaves behind you?"

Russell shrugged. "I guess maybe you ought to ask them yourselves." He drew back his arm and tossed the dagger through the air; the first ghost slave reached out from the roof of the crypt and caught it in his hand as he simultaneously dropped to the ground directly behind Dr. LaLaurie; an instant later the others were on the ground and tackling the LaLauries, tearing away at their clothing and using the dagger to cut apart Delphine's whip, using the strips of leather and clothing to tie the LaLauries' hands and feet.

The ghost slaves pulled the murderers to their feet and then waited. The child had leaped from the headstone, grabbed his sailor's cap, and now huddled in the doorway of the crypt that was to have been his murder site.

Russell looked at Dagobert. "Now what?" Was it just him, or had the atmosphere in the cemetery suddenly gotten much warmer?

"After they disappeared, the late Judge William Radcliffe issued an order that, if ever the LaLauries were to return to this city, they were to be arrested and executed at once." The priest then turned toward the crowd and called, "Captain Pierre Gustav Toutant!"

Still dignified in the Civil War uniform he wore at the moment of his death, Toutant came forward. "Yes, Father?"

"Your men still have their weapons?"

"Yes, sir."

"Then I believe you have an execution to carry out, sir."

Toutant snapped his hand up in a sharp salute, clicked the heels of his boots together, then turned and called for his men to assemble front and center.

The dead of Shiloh came forward, each man readying his rifle for one final duty.

The LaLauries were marched over in front of one of the largest marble crypts in the cemetery and stood against its wall. The ghost slaves then stood along each side of the crypt, well out of firing range.

There was no place for the doctor and his socialite wife to run.

The dead of Shiloh lined up in two rows.

Toutant barked: "Company—ready!"

The first row of soldiers knelt down and aimed their rifles while the row behind them remained standing, then readied their own weapons.

Russell looked at Saffron. She was wiping sweat from her forehead.

"It isn't just me, is it?" he said.

"No—it's getting hot."

Toutant made a quick inspection of his men, then stood off to the left and pulled out his sword, holding it high above his head. "Company—take aim!"

The air itself seemed to be boiling over with heat.

Russell looked over at the LaLauries and saw that the air around them was glowing a deep red. Their clothes seemed to be smoldering.

The air was suddenly filled with the stink of sulfur and putrescence.

The first flame spiked up next to Delphine LaLaurie's feet, spread across the ground to her husband's, then began to encircle them as they rose ever higher.

Toutant, nerves of steel, raised his sword a little higher and shouted "Fire!"

The guns went off at the same time the flames around the LaLauries rose as high as their heads, and in the midst of the conflagration Russell saw a third figure rise up, a man three times the size of anyone he'd ever seen before, with coal-dark skin and eyes red as flowing blood. The figure released a deep and bone-chilling laugh. Its breath stank of slime and brimstone and the fungus from a cesspool. It pushed out its massive arms and lay a clawed hand atop the head of each LaLaurie, then lifted their charred but still moving forms above the flames.

Then it—and they—began to sink down as if caught in quicksand.

Russell could not take his eyes off the gigantic ram's horns that jutted forth from the figure's temples.

In a flash, it was over. A cool breeze wafted through the cemetery and the LaLauries were gone.

All was shocked silence for a moment; then, at last, Father Dagobert turned to Russell and said, "I never would have believed there would come a day I would be happy to lay eyes on the devil." The priest shrugged. "Looks like I was wrong."

The child finally found its scream then, and other voices from elsewhere in the cemetery yelled back in panicked, urgent tones. The beams of several flashlights cut a new path through the darkness, and Russell stepped back, through one of the ripples, where the living could not see him.

Saffron put her arms around his waist.

All of the ghosts stood and watched as the tourists with their flashlights came around the corner with the police officer on horseback they'd gone after when first hearing the child's screams.

A little while later, amidst the dizzying, whirling Visibar lights of police cars, the child's parents, in tears, fell to their knees and embraced their most precious little boy.

Russell allowed himself a tight-lipped grin.

"Think you'll be okay now, son?" asked Harold Crider. "Think you can move on in peace?"

Russell looked down at his fading flesh, then at Saffron. "I think maybe, yes."

A hand slapped him on the back, and de Marigny proclaimed loudly, "Dat's good. Dis heh war you been fightin', it over fo' ya now. Time to come 'long with us and pass a good time in a beddah place dan dis!"

"In a second," said Russell, taking hold of Saffron's hand. "The rest of you go on, we'll be right behind you."

The ghosts—those of New Orleans and those that had been within Russell's mind for most of his adult life—passed through a final ripple and disappeared.

"That *was* what I think it was, wasn't it?" Saffron whispered.

"That," replied Russell, "was justice. *Justice.*"

"Thank you," Saffron whispered.

He watched the police and paramedics swarm around the little boy and his mother and father, he studied the joy and relief on their faces, and then he thought about pain in its most mystifying expressions—but only for a moment. "My pleasure, miss; my very, very great pleasure."

She squeezed his hand. "C'mon, lover, dey be waitin' fo' us obber dere!"

"The cajun thing doesn't really work for me."

"You need to get a sense of humor."

"Yeah, I get a lot of complaints about that."

They turned, hand in hand, and walked toward the bluish-gray ripple.

"Never thought I'd end up with a cop," Saffron laughed. "Though you are kind of yummy."

"Think I planned on spending eternity with a Goth chick?"

"Aw," she said in mock pity, "you don't need to worry. I won't bite."

They passed through the ripple and vanished from the world of the living; all that lingered—and it lingered only for a moment before being drowned out by the noise of emergency vehicle sirens—was the soft echo of Saffron's voice as she whispered: "That is, unless you *want* me to."

And the ghosts of New Orleans rested easy.

About the Author

Gary A. Braunbeck's work has garnered 7 Bram Stoker Awards, an International Horror Guild Award, and a World Fantasy Award nomination. He's published over 200 short stories, 7 novels, and (now) 8 short-story collections. He is the creator of the critically-acclaimed Cedar Hill series of novels, which includes *Prodigal Blues*, *In Silent Graves*, *Keepers*, *Coffin County* and the forthcoming *A Cracked and Broken Path*. His short-story collections include *Things Left Behind*, *Rose of Sharon*, and *Halfway Down the Stairs*. He lives in Worthington, Ohio. He doesn't get out much and is desperately lonely. You would pity him should you meet him in person. He probably needs a hobby. You can visit him on Facebook or at garybraunbeck.com.

CPSIA information can be obtained
at www.ICGtesting.com
Printed in the USA
LVHW031119010321
680247LV00002B/332